"You really are crazy, you know that?"

"I prefer to think of it as resourceful."

She rolled her eyes and shook her head again. "What do you want us to do?"

He held up one of the sticks of powder. "I'm going to throw one of these out in front of that pile of crates," Bowie explained. "Your job is to make sure that I don't get shot in the process. As soon as I light this thing, you start shooting. Are you ready?"

"I reckon," she answered skeptically, taking a firm grip on her rifle. Bowie scratched a match alight and held it to the first fuse. Sparks immediately began cascading to the ground.

"GO!" Following Hanna's lead, Frannie and Daniel opened up, firing faster than before; Bowie rolled to his knees, cocked back his arm and threw the stick of powder as hard as he could, then ducked back behind the pile of dirt. He reached up, grabbed a big handful of Hanna's sleeve and yanked her down beside him to wrap his arm around her shoulders. "FIRE IN THE HOLE!"

Valentine's Revenge

A Bowie Tyler novel

*Chuck
Buchanan*

Sisley Creek Press
Durkee, Oregon

Sisley CreekPress
33369 Sisley Creek Road
Durkee, Oregon 97905

This is a work of fiction. Any resemblance between the characters and any person, living or dead, is purely coincidence.

ISBN 978-0-9824580-3-7

Foreword

Let me say up front that the story before you is a work of fiction. It is not meant to relate actual history, though the majority of it unfolds in a historical setting, what is today Baker County, Oregon; in addition, I've tried to include some historical fact about travel to the Oregon gold fields.

Many readers will recognize the names of rivers, creeks and streets. While I have made an attempt at representing the landscape and geography as I know it today, at the same time, I've exercised my right of "poetic license" and taken a few liberties with my timelines, my settings and my characters. None of these people ever existed in Baker County, though some of them maybe should have.

Baker County has a rich history of commerce in gold, both mineral and agricultural. Many thanks to Charles Chandler, whose stories of the annual migration of his family's broodmare band from their winter home on the ranch between present-day Haines and Baker City to the Deer Creek drainage and back inspired Marcus Tarrington's words about the toughness of the Chandler horses.

Thanks once again to my editor, Beverly Coomer, who asked me at one point in the process, "Are you going to use actual names, or make up your own? Don't I recognize some of these places?"

It's my sincere hope that you, the reader, gets as much enjoyment from reading this tale as I got from writing it.

Chuck Buchanan
Durkee, OR
October, 2011

August 14, 1850

"Where *were you?!" The pain-wracked voice rang from the wainscoted walls of the high-ceilinged room. Lying in the stark hospital bed wrapped in multiple layers of bandages, Cyrus Valentine resembled nothing so much as an Egyptian mummy, raging eyes flaming behind the blood-spotted linen wrappings. Severe burns covered his body and anguish flooded his soul as he battled the horrible memory of the tragic fire that had destroyed his house and killed his family only the day before. While attempting to enter the fully-engulfed wreckage of his home to save his wife and infant son from the conflagration, a falling beam had struck him on the head, slamming him to the flagstone floor of the portico before he could force his way inside.*

Standing stoically in the face of his closest friend's anguished accusation, Randolph Martin could find no words to express either his utter dismay at the scene of his friend's tragic loss, or the sense of overwhelming inadequacy at his own inability to stop the inferno's horrible destruction. An attorney who had graduated near the top of his class from Yale Law School - along with his lifelong friend Cyrus Valentine - Martin was also the captain of the local fire brigade. He had been far across town at a dinner party when the alarm had sounded; without his leadership at the firehouse, the relatively untrained men of the recently established brigade had been late in reaching the blaze. Once they had finally arrived at Valen-

1

tine's house, their unorganized and disjointed efforts had been in vain. By the time Randolph had arrived to bring order to the chaos, the house was a total loss. Valentine's family was dead, and Valentine himself was in an ambulance racing to the hospital.

"I'm so sorry, Cyrus; I was across town," Randolph tried to console his distraught friend. "I got there as quickly as I could."

"You should have been..." Cyrus began, anger cracking his pain-wracked voice.

"I'm not clairvoyant, Cyrus," Randolph interrupted firmly. "How was anyone to know a fire would start in your house, or any other house for that matter? It's summertime, and you know that we rarely have such fires this time of the year!"

"So, because you didn't think there was any danger, I have lost all that was most precious to me! Or if you had trained your men appropriately, my family might still be alive!"" Cyrus' voice, bitter with loss and grief, overflowed with hateful accusation.

"The fire brigade is new, Cyrus, and the men are working hard to be prepared for any circumstance. What more would you have me do?" Randolph answered, his voice filled with remorse. "If I had it within my power, I would gladly undo what happened, but I cannot! I am truly sorry!"

"Your apologies will not restore my body, or the lives of my wife and son!" Cyrus hissed, his weak, smoke-roughened voice filled with quiet menace. "But I will have a reckoning, Randolph. Mark my words! I will have a reckoning!"

~1~

July on the Wyoming plains can be hot, relatively speaking. Most days are actually not too terribly uncomfortable temperature-wise, but today, the little town of Hardin -- named for Hardin Gillespie, the first rancher to settle in the valley back in the 1850's -- held its breath under the unrelenting weight of a three o'clock sun that was hotter than anything even the oldest of local residents could remember. The rough, desiccated lumber siding the false-fronted businesses facing each other across the dusty thoroughfare that did duty as Main Street, shone silvery under the molten rays pouring down from the cloudless blue overhead. Few of the fronts of the buildings had ever seen paint, and many of those that had were in dire need of a fresh coat. The faded lettering proclaiming the nature of each of the buildings was made more indecipherable by the glare. In a vain attempt to escape the heat, or even to just forget about it for a minute or two, Bucky Gault and his associates had taken refuge under the shade of the split-shake roof sheltering the boardwalk that fronted the Bull Run Saloon, passing a bottle of rye back and forth between their tipped-back chairs.

The general opinion of the residents of Hardin

County was that Bucky Gault needed to be run out of town; who should do the deed was what had everyone stumped. Bucky was greased lightning with a pistol and it was generally agreed that he could shoot the wings off a gnat at fifty feet without scuffing the gnat. On the other hand, the general populace of Hardin County were farmers and ranch hands, not gunfighters. Gault and the two gun-slicks he ran with spent their days swaggering along the boardwalks of the town, crowding the honest folk off the splintered pine and into the street, as if daring one and all to take exception to their shenanigans. They got away with it because Gault had already shot one man, beat the hell out of a few more and run the sheriff out of town. Admittedly, some of the citizens he'd whipped were of the less savory variety, and the man he'd shot *had* been carrying a gun. What had the townsfolk up in arms now, though, was the fact that the gunman had also whipped a couple of the local farmers, who were decidedly not up to the task of taking on a hard case like him. The townsfolk were afraid that if Bucky didn't kill whoever tried to take him to jail, he would at the very least hurt them badly. To make matters worse, Bucky, who stood six foot two in his sock feet -- when he had socks -- had begun partaking of the wares of the town's business establishments without proper monetary compensation to the owners of said wares. In short, he was stealing, and there was no one to stop him.

For his own part, Bucky Gault was pretty sure that he was bad to the bone, and he was the sort who just plain couldn't seem to leave well enough alone. Any newcomer to the town was considered fair game to be roughed up and run out of town -- preferably with empty pockets -- just for the hell of it. So far he'd been overwhelmingly successful in that endeavor. But sooner or later, every tough man comes across someone who's either tougher or smarter...

"Howdy, gents." The words broke through the three men's heat-and-whiskey-induced lethargy; startled out of their reverie, they all turned to look at the speaker -- a short, chubby fellow dressed in dirty, trail-worn clothes -- who had just reined a sweat-darkened sorrel up to the hitchrail. A Greener coach gun rode in a vertical scabbard just ahead of his right knee, and a short-barreled Colt revolver was holstered butt-forward in front of his right hip. The Colt had recently replaced the double action Starr that had been his weapon of choice in the past. Engrossed in their bottle, the ne'er-do-wells hadn't heard him approach. The rider kept his hat brim tugged low to shield his eyes from the sun.

"Hot day, ain't it?" Without waiting for an answer, he clambered down from his Texas-rigged slick fork saddle to wrap his reins around the rail. He stepped into the meager shade of the overhead, then used his battered black hat in an attempt to beat some of the accumulated dust from the wrinkles of his blue calico shirt and stained whipcord britches. Spurs with blunt-tipped star rowels hung on the heels of his tall, mule-ear boots. The walnut handle of a razor-sharp "Arkansas toothpick" protruded from the sheath sewn into the top of his right boot. His green eyes were bloodshot from heat and dust; his blonde hair was in need of cutting, and several days' worth of stubble covered his jaws.

The lanky, bearded Gault looked the newcomer up and down for a moment, then snickered and nudged one of his traveling partners in the ribs with a red-clad elbow. "Looky what we got here, Jack," Bucky said loudly, his words echoing from the buildings of the suddenly vacant street; he obviously didn't care one way or the other whether the stranger heard him. "I do believe we got ourselves a pilgrim!" Jack Bellows, who sat slumped against the clapboard wall to his immediate left, tipped his chair forward and his hat back, squinting as he gave a once-over to the cause of the jab to his midsection.

The heavyset rider appeared to ignore Bucky's words as he returned his hat to its perch atop his head and started for the batwing doors of the saloon, seemingly intent on nothing more than a cold beer -- if such was to be had. Nate Walters, the scruffy redhead seated on the far side of Bellows, replied in a rough, scratchy drawl, "Looks like he's got dirt in his ears too, Bucky." Walters grinned, showing decayed and tobacco-stained teeth beneath a ragged mustache. "He don't seem to hear too good."

The newcomer paused to look at Bucky and his cohorts. "Were you men speaking to me?" he asked quietly, one eyebrow lifting quizzically.

"Do ya' see anybody else around here close?" Gault sneered.

The dusty rider's bloodshot gaze swung the length of the street, which had emptied almost magically when Bucky's first words echoed off the front of Miss Mabel's Millinery across the street and came back to rest on Bucky. "Actually, the entire street seems to be deserted," the rider replied in a reasonable tone. "Now if that's all you wanted to know, I'll be going about my business. I've ridden a lot of miles today and I'd like a drink and something to eat." He turned lazily back toward the saloon's weathered doors and the promising blackness inside.

"Now ain't you the gent!" Bucky declared roughly. He hated to be put off. He reached out and grabbed a handful of blue calico sleeve. "You'll go when I say you can go!"

Without a word the "pilgrim" jerked his sleeve from his assailant's grasp and swiftly bent and grasped the leg of the precariously tilted chair, upending Bucky. The sudden disappearance of his seat served to crack the gunhand's head against the wall of the saloon, stunning him. Semi-conscious, with stars dancing through his brain, Gault came down hard on his back on the planks of the boardwalk in a tangled heap of grubby clothes and broken chair. A pair of heartbeats later his two friends, caught totally unaware by the swiftness of the rider's actions, slammed their chairs forward to the boardwalk and were reaching for their guns when they found themselves staring into the unwavering eye of the short-barreled Colt revolver that had appeared in the rider's left hand. Wherever pistol packers gathered, Jack Bellows and Nate Walters were reckoned to be fast men, but neither one had seen the fat man pull that pistol; the Colt had just materialized as if by magic. "Now, do you boys really want to do that?" the heavy-set blond asked mildly. He wagged the barrel of the pistol at them and the two men carefully raised their hands to shoulder level. "No, I don't believe you do. Apparently you boys're smarter than you look."

At the stranger's feet, Bucky was beginning to stir. The rap on his head had briefly scrambled his thought processes; his brain was clearing now and he was madder than a stepped-on baby. Even though he was still lying on his back on the scarred planks of the boardwalk, he snarled, "I'll kill you for that!" as he fumbled for his gun. Keeping his pistol pointed at Bellows and Walters, the stranger leaned down and batted Gault's hand aside as he plucked the Colt from the small-town badman's holster and tucked it behind his own belt.

"Not today, you won't," he declared matter-of-factly. Bucky sat up and was trying to get his legs underneath him when the heavyset rider's left boot came down hard on his splayed right hand, grinding it into the splintered wood of the boardwalk and pinning him in place. Gault howled in pain, cursing loudly. The fat man told him, "You just stay planted for a minute. I need to talk to your playmates here." As he turned back to Bellows and Walters, his boot twisted on the back of Bucky's hand; Bucky let out another howl.

"Yer breakin' my damn hand!"

The stranger ignored Gault's complaints while he spoke to the other two, whose eyes were twitching back and forth between the unwavering pistol muzzle staring into their faces and their cursing friend. "How about you boys reach down with two fingers and shuck those pistols out into the street, then we'll all go for a little walk down to the sheriff's office?"

Over the noise of Bucky's squalling and cursing, Bellows growled, "There ain't no sheriff here," as if that should make some kind of difference to the man in front of them.

"I know that," their captor replied. "I understand you boys ran him off."

"We sure did!" Walters declared proudly. "So it ain't gonna do you no good to take us down there!"

The stranger calmly reached into his shirt pocket with his left hand, took out a silver star and pinned it to the front of his dusty blue calico. "I beg to differ with you, my friend." Walters' face fell as Deputy Bowie Tyler's own lit up in a big smile. "It'll give me a place to lock you three up. Now, shuck those guns!" he ordered. He wagged the Colt again as he lifted his boot from Bucky's hand. Gault immediately cradled the offended member in his lap, glaring down at the scratches and scrapes made by Bowie's boot.

Walters reached very carefully down to his right hip with his right hand and just as carefully lifted his pistol from the holster with two fingers. He tossed the gun into the dust of the street, then brought his hand back to shoulder level. Bowie looked directly at Bellows. "Your turn."

The longer Bellows sat looking down the barrel of Bowie's gun the madder he got. *Nobody treats Jack Bellows like that and gets away with it*, he thought angrily. "You go to hell!" he snapped.

"JACK! NO!" As Walters shouted, Bellows' hand dropped swiftly to the scuffed walnut grips of his converted Navy Colt. The barrel was clear of the holster and swinging toward the object of his ire when an explosive blow to his chest slammed him against the wall of the building. As he stared in disbelief at the star-packer, Bellows coughed and felt a warm liquid trickle down his chin. He tried to lift his pistol; to his dismay he found that his arm wouldn't obey his brain's commands, and his sight was dimming rapidly. His hand opened; the pistol dropped to the boardwalk as he slid down the wall, leaving a crimson streak on the whitewashed planks. He fell alongside the Navy Colt and rolled over, staring sightlessly at the shingled roof overhead.

Bucky sat nursing his aching hand and head,

stunned into silence by what had just happened. He couldn't believe that Jack had been stupid enough to draw against a man with the drop on him.

In the echoing silence following the gunshot, the townsfolk began to emerge from the doorways along Main Street like prairie dogs from their burrows. "You can get up now," Bowie told Bucky gruffly. "Your friend's gonna' need some help getting your partner here to the undertaker."

With a grimace of pain, Gault bent to take Bellows' feet while Walters wrapped his arms around the dead man's chest from behind. When they had their deceased friend in a secure grip, Bowie asked, "Which way's the undertaker?" Walters pointed south down the street with his chin.

"Down yonder."

"Let's go, then," Bowie ordered. "The sooner we get there, the better."

~2~

The parade down Main Street to the under-taker's place of business - a small, white-washed clap-board house with green trim around the windows, sitting all alone at the end of the row of buildings on the east side of the street - was short and humiliating for the gunhands-turned-corpse-bearers. Bucky Gault had a pounding headache, and Nate Walters still had some of his former partner's blood spattered on his face and clothes, with more soaking into the front of his shirt as he walked.

Bowie regretted killing Jack Bellows; he was tired and he'd been caught off guard when Bellows went for his gun. Still, that was no excuse; he wasn't some rookie who hadn't been in such a situation before. He'd been too focused on Bucky, figuring him for the most dangerous of the trio. Even so, it never should have happened. Going on nothing but gut feeling, he'd jumped to the erroneous conclusion that the other two wouldn't be ambitious or touchy enough to do anything stupid with a gun pointed at them: he'd been wrong. He would have some explaining to do when he saw Judge Martin again; Bowie knew that his boss would not be impressed with any explanation that he might offer.

Several of the local citizens were standing silently along the sides of the street, watching Bowie and his prisoners pass by. The majority of them had never seen a man killed, and the looks on their faces had Bowie thinking sourly, *I should have taken the time to just club the idiot unconscious.*

The undertaker's house stood back from the street behind a weathered picket fence that leaned comfortably against the leafless trunks of a pair of small cottonwoods which had been planted to either side of the gate in the vain hope that they might, some time in the future, provide shade for the house. Bowie pushed open the gate, then stood aside as his prisoners carried their burden through the opening and followed the pretentious slate walk to the door of the house beyond. A hand-painted board sign hanging from a loop of wire hooked over a horseshoe nail driven into the wall beside the door read "UNDRTKR" in black paint. "You boys hold up," Bowie ordered. "I'll get the undertaker." Gault and Walters came to a sullen stop and stood glaring down at their dead partner as Bowie stepped up onto the porch. As he lifted his hand to knock on the brightly-painted green door, the panel swung soundlessly open before he could touch it.

A broadly smiling fellow of just over Bowie's five-foot, four-inch height and of indeterminate age stood in the doorway looking at Bowie and his companions expectantly. He was nattily dressed in a cutaway coat and four-in-hand tie, pinstriped trousers and spats. "I suspect from the appearance of yonder gents' burden that you have a job for me," he said cheerfully. "It has been a bit quiet lately. Last business I had was Missus Swanson last month." He stuck a slender, pale white hand out toward Bowie. "Jebediah Berlyle at your service!" he exclaimed.

Bowie shook the proffered hand dubiously. "You are the undertaker, right?" he asked. "These boys," he hooked a thumb over his shoulder, "seemed to think so. So does this classy sign here on your wall."

"Absolutely!" Berlyle assured him. "Embalmer, carpenter, rock chiseler, and whatever else I need to be to get the job done." He grinned at Bowie. "I'm thinking of having a fancy, painted shingle made up, maybe some gilt lettering, you know, something with a little more style. Might bring in more business, eh?"

"O-o-okay," Bowie answered slowly, drawing the word out, unsure what to make of the man's enthusiastic demeanor. He reached into his pocket and brought out five dollars, holding the bills out to Berlyle. "Will that cover the burial?"

"Absolutely!" Berlyle seemed to like that word a great deal. He snatched the money from Bowie's hand. "And for an additional five dollars I'll provide mourners, courtesy of the local saloon. I'll even guarantee that they'll be fully and appropriately clothed!"

"Nope, I don't think so," Bowie answered. "This unfortunate gent will just have to go to his reward unlamented. Where do you want him?"

When Berlyle was sure that he wasn't going to get any more money out of Bowie, he became all business. He turned succinctly back into the house, took a stained white knee-length cotton jacket from a hook on the wall just inside the door and slipped it on. "Follow me," he called flatly over his shoulder.

Bowie stepped aside and waved the two men and their grisly burden forward. "You heard the man, gents. Look alive...so to speak." He waited until they went through the door, then followed them into the house.

Berlyle led the way to a small interior room floored with oilcloth-covered planks. The shades were drawn, making the room quite cool and shadowy in spite of the heat outdoors. The two men deposited Jack Bellows' body on a wooden table standing in the center of the room, then stood looking everywhere but at the corpse as Berlyle made one more attempt to get a few more dollars from Bowie. "You're sure you don't want me to..."

"I'm sure," Bowie answered firmly. He turned to his prisoners. "To the jail, boys." As he left the house with the two gunhands, he called carelessly over his shoulder, "Take care, Mister Berlyle. I'll be back as soon as I know what you need to put on the marker."

Outside the gate they turned north and Bowie followed them to the jail - a squat stone and log structure that seemed out of place on a street of false-fronted wood-plank buildings. The building consisted of a single large room containing a battered roll-top desk, a pot-bellied stove and blue enamelware coffeepot, and two ladder-back chairs. An empty gun rack was nailed to the logs at the end of the room opposite the desk. Dust covered every horizontal surface.

Across the back of the room and spiked to the logs of the wall, a narrow iron-slat cage accessed by a single iron-slat door stood lockup duty. The door hung open and a large brass lock dangled from the hasp. A pair of narrow cots, devoid of blankets or other creature comforts, stood end-to-end opposite the door. Of their own accord, Gault and Walters walked into the cell and sat down on the cots. Bowie swung the door closed, snapped the lock shut, then told his prisoners, "Don't go away, boys, I'll be right back." The only answer was a snarl from Gault. Bowie shrugged and left

14

the jail in search of the telegraph office, which he found next to Tolliver's Saddle Shop.

The telegrapher, who also acted as postmaster, turned out to be a woman, younger than Bowie -- *and a whole lot prettier*, he thought to himself. She was perched behind a solid oak counter which held a pad of paper, a pencil tied with a piece of string to a nail driven into the counter top, and a nameplate reading 'Miss Gertrude Wheeler' in brass letters on some sort of dark wood. She looked up from her copy of *The Hardin Gazette* when Bowie stepped inside. "May I help you, sir?" the slim brunette asked flatly, her tone all business.

"You most certainly can, Ma'am" Bowie answered with a smile. "I need to send a telegram." Gertrude Wheeler pushed the pad of paper to him, pointed at the pencil and went back to her newspaper.

"I thought they only let old men be telegraphers," Bowie commented wryly. "You're far from that." He bent to the pad and wrote out a short message to his boss saying only that he had completed the job he had been sent to do. It was a given that he'd fill in the details when he got back to Laramie; consequently, he saw no sense in spending money on sending a lengthy explanation.

"Mister, if you're trying to get on my good side, I don't have one, so don't bother," the telegrapher responded icily without looking up. "At least not as far as traveling gunhands are concerned."

Bowie chuckled. "Thought so." He passed the paper across to Miss Wheeler. "Could you send this as soon as possible, please?" When the telegrapher saw the name Bowie had signed to the telegram form, she reached under the counter.

"If you're Deputy Tyler, I got a message here for

15

you," she told him. "It just came through a little bit ago. It sounded important when it came over the wire." She came up with an envelope and handed it to Bowie.

He thanked the young woman, dropped four bits on the counter and turned toward the door. Bowie ripped open the envelope and started to read, then stopped dead in the middle of the floor as a word that his mother wouldn't have approved of - had she lived through the cholera epidemic that took both her and Bowie's father when he was a small boy - slipped from his lips. He dropped the envelope and its contents on the floor and hurried out the door. The telegrapher slid off her stool, strode through the door at the end of the counter and disgustedly knelt to pick up the crumpled paper. *Durned cowboys can't even pick up after themselves*, was written on her frowning features. She didn't bother to look at the note; she'd read it off the wire just that morning, and Miss Wheeler already knew what the message said.

~ ~ ~

Bowie hurried back to the jail, the words of Judge Martin's telegram churning in his brain.

Son and wife taken Stop BT only available deputy Stop Bring prisoners if possible Stop
R Martin

His horse, tied in the shade alongside the jail, looked askance over its shoulder as Bowie rummaged

16

through his saddlebags and drew out two pairs of manacles. He blew through the door and into the small building, snagging the keys to the steel-barred cell from a hook on the wall as he trotted by. His two prisoners were sitting dejectedly on their cots; they jumped to their feet when the jail door slammed open.

"Let's go, boys!" Bowie ordered. "We're heading to Laramie!"

"What's the big roarin' hurry?" Bucky whined. "You just got done lockin' us up, for Pete's sake!" All he wanted to do was sit and nurse his aching head and throbbing hand.

"Suffice it to say we're leaving," Bowie answered curtly. He unlocked the cage door, swung it open and tossed the manacles inside, then closed the door again. "Put those on. And hurry it up."

"You want us to chain ourselves up?" Walters asked incredulously.

"Nope, I want you to put 'em on each other, and make 'em tight," Bowie answered. "And like I said, hurry it up!"

When the manacles were in place he asked, "You boys do have horses, right?"

"Down at the livery," Walters responded sullenly.

"Good. You lead off." Bowie pointed toward the door. A half hour later, the deputy and his two prisoners were on the road to Laramie.

~3~

Deep darkness and pain greeted Daniel Martin as he opened his eyes as wide as he was able: flashes of phantom color streaked across his vision as his optic nerves fired in a fruitless effort to find something for his eyes to focus on. His battered body was jostling from side to side; now that he was conscious, each jolt made his head throb harder until every beat of his heart sent a stab of pain through his temples. Dazed and confused, Daniel tried to bring his hand up to his face in an effort to determine the reason for the darkness he was trapped in, only to find that his hands were bound beneath him. He fought the bonds single-mindedly until his wrists were slippery with blood; his numb fingers felt the size of sausages. Unable to free his hands, he stopped fighting and began making a concerted effort to clear his head and figure out where he was.

Beneath Daniel, splintered lumber gouged his skin through the thin shirt covering his back. For a pair of minutes that crawled interminably by, he listened through the pounding in his head to the clattering of steel-shod wheels over rock, and realized that he had been thrown like so much baggage into the rough-timbered bed of a freight wagon.

Through the stiff and stinking tarpaulin covering him, Daniel could feel the warmth of soft flesh rolling slackly against him with the motion of the wagon. Permeating the thick material covering his face, a hint of fragrance brought him at last to full awareness, shocked into consciousness by the familiar scent of his wife's perfume.

"Marta!"

Daniel tried to scream her name: the coarse cloth of the gag between his teeth nearly made him vomit. He immediately clamped his jaws closed, afraid that if such a thing happened, he would choke to death before anyone knew he was in trouble. Someone had to be driving the wagon they were imprisoned in, but the black hood shrouding Daniel's head kept him from knowing anything else about his surroundings.

As he lay helplessly trapped with his wife beside him, Daniel frantically searched his mind for some recollection of the events leading up to their current situation. Bits of memory flickered like magic lantern pictures through the foggy shadows that seemed to fill his aching head ...

Daniel and Marta were just sitting down to their evening meal in the kitchen of their modest home when heavy footsteps resounded on the back porch, and an insistent pounding echoed on the pine-paneled kitchen door. Cautiously Daniel rose and crossed the room. As he turned the knob and slowly opened the door, he was met with a shove that sent him staggering back into the kitchen. A husky man dressed in coarse miner's clothing and carrying half a pick handle in his knotted right fist followed him through the door; behind the miner, several other similarly dressed ruf-

19

fians crowded the small porch. Before Daniel could begin to mount a defense, the pick handle slammed against his skull and he felt himself falling. He crashed to the smooth-sanded wood flooring where he lay stunned, half-conscious and unable to move. A single crumb of bread on the floor was grasping at the vestiges of his fading attention when suddenly, over the ringing in his skull, he heard Marta scream, then the tinkle of breaking glass; cursing filled the air. Marta fell across Daniel in a loose-limbed sprawl. Vainly willing his muscles to move, Daniel struggled to push himself up from the floor. In the midst of his attempt the pick handle descended again, and his world went black.

~ ~ ~

Two days after he booted his horse past the last saloon in Hardin, Bowie and his prisoners rode into Laramie, where he turned his charges over to the jailer, Harry Koller, in the basement of the courthouse. Once relieved of Gault and Walters, Bowie stabled all three horses at a nearby livery, then immediately headed for Judge Martin's office.

Eunice Carstairs, the Judge's fashionably dressed, middle-aged secretary, was comfortably seated behind her desk when Bowie opened the door to the outer office. Missus Carstairs was the arbiter of the Judge's schedule; one of her many duties was to see that her boss was not needlessly disturbed. "Good afternoon, ma'am," Bowie said politely as he removed his hat. Missus Carstairs sniffed derisively.

"I believe you could use a bath, Mister Tyler!" she declared in a lofty tone, her gimlet-eyed stare boring into Bowie, who managed not to faint under the pressure of her displeasure. He was used to that; Missus Carstairs was generally displeased with him, or at least appeared to be so. Instead, he gave her his most innocent smile.

"I believe you might be right, but I understand that the boss is in a hurry," Bowie answered genially. "Is he in?"

Missus Carstairs imperiously pointed her plump, freckled finger toward the open door to Judge Martin's office. Bowie thanked her politely, then knocked on the door frame. Behind him, Missus Carstairs shook her head in resignation as she went back to her work.

"Come in and close the door!" Judge Randolph Martin ordered in answer to Bowie's knock. As Bowie stepped into the office and swung the door shut, the Judge took off his spectacles and laid them on the blotter in front of him, reaching up to rub his eyes tiredly. Bowie had never seen the man look so fatigued and careworn. Still, his boss had the energy to say, "It's a good thing Missus Carstairs isn't a vengeful sort. Otherwise, she could do a great deal of harm to all you deputies. You all pick on her." Before Bowie could frame an answer, his boss continued, "Never mind, just sit."

Bowie immediately dropped into the leather-upholstered chair that stood across the wide oak desk. He wanted to ask about the telegram he had received, and about the Judge's family, but he instinctively knew that he should keep quiet. The Boss would tell him what he needed to know when he was ready.

The tired-looking jurist sat silently, staring

down at his folded hands. The ticking of the Regulator clock above the windows behind his desk echoed loudly from the oak-paneled walls of the high-ceilinged room. He sagged wearily in his high-backed leather chair, dark shadows under his eyes and new wrinkles around his mouth. The deep creases across his forehead hadn't been there on Bowie's last visit to this office, and when he raised his eyes to meet those of his deputy, they were red-rimmed.

"My son and daughter-in-law have been kidnapped from their home by a man named Cyrus Valentine," Judge Martin stated without preamble.

"What?" Bowie asked, incredulous.

Silently Judge Martin pushed a folded newspaper across the desk. In bold black type across the top of the page the headline screamed, '**LOCAL PREACHER DISAPPEARS**'. "This is the local newspaper from a gold camp up in Oregon called Baker City. My son and his wife were living there."

"How do you know that this Valentine gent is the one..." Bowie began.

A folded letter joined the newspaper on the desktop blotter. "This is Valentine's way of letting me know that he has taken my son and his wife." Judge Martin drew in a deep, ragged breath. "I would like you to bring them back. How you accomplish this task is up to you."

He reached into the top middle drawer of his desk to retrieve a metallic object, which he then tossed onto the desktop. The object flickered in the light of the single hurricane lamp standing next to the thick, leather-bound blotter centered on the wide expanse of polished oak, before coming to rest face-up in the center of the ink-stained pad of paper. The highly polished star of a United States Deputy Marshal's badge met Bowie's startled gaze.

"What's this?" Bowie asked quietly, though he was sure that he knew full well what was coming next.

"That is your authority to travel wherever, whenever, and however you need to in order to fulfill your mission," Judge Martin answered firmly as he sat back in his chair and scrubbed his hand across his face. He turned his weary gaze on Bowie again. "Just bring back my family." His voice broke as he turned his chair to stare sightlessly out the window behind his desk.

His words drifted back to Bowie over the rich leather of the high-backed chair. "Missus Carstairs has all of the information that I have been able to gather regarding the Baker City area and Valentine's activities."

Bowie waited for further instructions; the only sounds in the cavernous room were the ticking of the clock and the tinkle of spur rowel and jingle-bob as he shifted his feet. After a minute had passed with nothing more from Judge Martin, Bowie picked up the badge and lifted himself from the chair. He tucked the badge into the pocket of his vest, picked up the letter and the newspaper, then said softly, "I'll take it, but I won't use this badge as a hunting license; I believe you know that, sir." He waited for several more seconds to allow his superior to comment before he went on, "If that's what you want, then you'd better find somebody else to give it to."

"I know that you won't do anything you don't have to do," the Judge answered quietly. "Please just bring my family back. Daniel and Marta are all I have." He didn't turn around. Bowie left the office to stand in front of Missus Carstairs' desk.

"The boss said..." Without a word, the

secretary handed Bowie a large envelope. He took it from her hand, ticked the brim of his hat with his finger in thanks and left the office, leaving the door ajar behind him, his thoughts busy with his assignment. Missus Carstairs sat looking after him for a few moments before she lifted her considerable bulk from her chair and walked lightly to the Judge's door. Without knocking, she entered the office and moved to his desk.

"Bowie Tyler is one of your best deputies," she told her boss firmly. "I don't necessarily agree with his methods, but if anyone can bring Daniel and Marta back safely it will be him!"

The distraught magistrate abruptly swiveled his chair to face her. "Bowie's methods are often indeed unorthodox, Eunice. But you don't know Cyrus Valentine the way I do," he answered tiredly. He steepled his hands in front of his face, tapping the ends of his index fingers against his upper lip several times before continuing in a soft tone, "According to my research, the man has become utterly ruthless and he will stop at nothing to get what he feels is his just desserts. It is quite obvious that he believes that he has been wronged." He paused, reflecting on the past for a moment. "He wasn't always that way, you know; we were once very good friends. Actually, I'd lost track of him and I wasn't sure he was even still alive until the letter came."

Missus Carstairs waited, but he said nothing more; he just stared off into the distance, north toward Oregon. The secretary finally turned and headed back toward her desk. At the door she paused and turned toward her boss. "I'll be praying for Daniel and Marta."

"And I'll be praying for Bowie Tyler," the Judge replied.

24

~4~

With the heavy envelope in his hand, Bowie left the courthouse and headed for his boarding house. Missus Carstairs was right; he did need a bath. He wouldn't turn down a good meal, either. He stepped inside the Widow Bleeker's door and was met by the lady herself. "You stink, Mister Tyler!" she declared. "To the bath with you!" She pointed to the door down the hall. "The water's hot, and there's soap and a towel next to the tub. Toss out your clothes and I'll see that they're washed."

"Yes, ma'am," Bowie answered meekly.

An hour later, bathed, freshly shaved and dressed in clean clothes, Bowie strolled casually toward the kitchen in hopes of cadging a snack from Missus Bleeker before dinner and found that, as was usually the case, she was already taking care of him. On a plate on the end of the long dining room table sat a slab of pie. Alongside the plate were a blue enamelware cup of steaming coffee and a fork. "You're much too nice to me," Bowie told his landlady, who had just come into the room from the kitchen.

"I am indeed, Mister Tyler," Missus Bleeker replied sternly, but her features softened as she regarded her favorite boarder. "Dinner in an hour, Bowie." She returned to the kitchen and her meal preparations.

After dinner Bowie sat up late going over the information his boss had given him regarding Cyrus Valentine and Baker City. The majority of the information pertaining to the gold camp came from a few tattered copies of a newspaper with the grandiose name of *The Bedrock Democrat*. If the newspaper's writers were to be believed, Baker City and the surrounding area were booming and everyone was getting rich. There were also several pages of information in the Judge's elegant handwriting, as well as the letter from Valentine himself, which was brief and to the point:

> *My Dearest Randolph:*
> *Your son and his lovely bride are in my custody. I have not yet decided their fate, but believe me when I say that my revenge will indeed be sweet. You have cost me much, and the time has come for you to suffer as I have. I will be contacting you again one day soon.*
> *Sincerely,*
> *Cyrus Valentine*

The papers Judge Martin had provided gave a fairly complete picture of Valentine as a wealthy entrepreneur whose business practices appeared to skirt the line between right and wrong, quite possibly stepping over that line on occasion. He was well educated, and in fact had been a contemporary of Judge Martin at Yale Law School. The manuscript did not say it in so many words but Bowie got the impression that the two men had once been friends. If so, there was no mention of what had caused the rift between them.

Another, smaller envelope contained a ticket on the Union Pacific Railroad, a bundle of banknotes and a handwritten message containing the only instructions Bowie needed:

Bowie: This train ticket will take you to Kelton, Utah. From there, you will take a Northwest Stage Company coach to Baker City. Good Luck.

Judge Randolph Martin

~ ~ ~

The rocking of the wagon brought Daniel back to the present. He had no way of knowing how long he had been unconscious; morning and evening, day and night were jumbled and confused inside the agony sloshing through his head; lying in a state of pain-washed semi-consciousness, he could only wait for the seemingly interminable journey to end. The wagon clattered over one final rock and came to a rattling halt. A baritone voice barked, "Whoa, mules!" In a matter of moments the tarpaulin was pulled from the wagon bed where the two captives lay.

"See if they are awake," a cultured voice ordered. "But do not remove the hoods. If they have not regained consciousness, awaken them."

A rough hand grabbed Daniel's jaw and shook it. He struggled against the hold as the voice of the wagon driver rumbled, "Y'er awake alright." The hand released him and he felt Marta being shaken. "So're you," the voice said.

Daniel was jerked to a sitting position and roughly dragged to the back of the wagon. With his numb hands bound behind him, he was helpless to do anything to steady himself; as his shoulder scraped roughly along the sideboards, he felt another sliver dig into his bruised flesh. His feet dropped over the tailgate of the wagon. "You sit right there whilst I untie yer feet, boy!" the deep voice ordered. "If you try to kick, I'll knock you into next week!" Daniel felt a tugging at his ankles and found his feet swinging free. "Jump on down here so's you can walk," his captor commanded. "I ain't gonna' carry you." Daniel slipped down from the tailgate to land staggering on wobbly legs. He nearly pitched forward as the blood rushed into his numb feet, and he swayed dizzily against the wagon.

A rough hand gripped the young man's arm tightly and guided him into a stumbling walk, along what felt like a well-packed trail underfoot. As the hand yanked him to a stop, he heard the rasp of a key turning in a lock obviously in need of some oil. The rattling of a heavy chain followed by the squeal of rusty hinges preceded the breath of cool air that pressed the dank muslin of the bag against his cheek. A heavy-handed shove to the small of his back sent him stumbling into whatever room or building had just been opened. "You stand right there, and don't turn around 'til I say ya' can," the wagon driver ordered. "I'm gonna' cut yer hands loose." For a moment he felt the pressure of a knife blade on the rawhide binding his wrists, then his hands came free.

The sudden agonizing rush of blood to his numb fingers forced a gag-muffled groan past his lips as he began to rub his swollen hands together. The door behind him slammed, the key turned in the lock, and

Daniel suddenly suspected that he was in more trouble than he'd ever been in his life: not even the war had put him in such danger. The damnable agony of his situation was that while he didn't have the slightest idea why he was here, he was helpless to know where Marta was. The worry over his wife was the greatest torment of all.

Daniel kept his back to the door as he cautiously lifted his hands clumsily to the hood covering his head. He listened for the voice of his captor, but the only sound was the sudden, cheerful trill of a meadowlark singing to the world somewhere outside his prison. With his swollen and tingling fingers he fumbled at the drawstring knotted under his chin. The knot at last gave way, and he pulled open the puckered mouth of the black muslin bag. The sudden rush of cool air over his sweaty face was a welcome relief after the stifling heat inside the sack. Daniel pushed the cloth up onto his forehead, then reached behind his neck for the knot in the gag wedged between his teeth. With a quick yank the knot came free, and he was able to spit the sodden fabric onto the floor. He stood for a moment working his jaw, but when he heard the lock on the door rattle behind him, he quickly pulled the bag back down over his face.

The door swung open and Daniel heard the tap of hurried footsteps on the stone floor, as if the person had been shoved into the room. The door swung shut and the lock rattled again. The only sounds to greet Daniel's ears were silence and the hurried breathing of the new occupant of his dark and unknown quarters. Daniel yanked the bag off his head once more, tossed it toward a nearby table he could barely see in the gloom and turned hurriedly toward the new arrival.

"Marta!"

Daniel strode quickly to his wife's side. He took her in his arms and held her for a moment, then began untying the string holding the bag closed over her head. He hurriedly lifted the hood from her head and untied the gag. "Are you alright?" he questioned as he held her at arm's length to ascertain her condition.

"Except for my hands," she said in a matter-of-fact tone which belied the angry fire glittering in her eyes. She turned her back to Daniel and lifted her hands; he hurriedly yanked loose the knots in the leather thongs binding her slim wrists behind her back and spun her around to face him again. Her bonds had been much looser than the rawhide strips the wagon driver had cut from Daniel's wrists; consequently, her fingers were barely swollen. They held each other tightly. "Do you know where we are?" Marta queried after a minute.

"No, I don't," he answered honestly. "In fact, I'm not even sure what day it is, and I can't figure out why anyone would do this to us. All I know for sure is that there's a creek nearby -- I could hear it when they dragged us out of the wagon."

A rope-sprung bunk, pegged together from rough-hewn timbers and complete with corn shuck tick, was bolted to the wall diagonally across the floor from the entrance to the room. A pair of coarse, remarkably clean woolen blankets were the only bedding in sight. Daniel moved to the bed and sat down; Marta took his hand as she sat down beside him.

"Someone will notice we're gone and come for us," she declared confidently, her brown eyes surveying their surroundings as she spoke. There was little enough to see; their prison appeared to be a natural cave, the entrance of which had been walled in with heavy timbers. The room was oval, with smooth walls arching up to a domed ceiling only a few feet higher than Daniel's head. The floor was well-worn, hard-packed dirt. A bucket of water stood in the middle of a table that was placed almost exactly in the center of the room and flanked by a pair of ladder-back chairs which looked oddly out of place in their current meager surroundings. The door into the cave was stoutly built of thick planks bolted together with iron straps. Dust motes danced in the muted rays of light angling into the room from a small barred window near the top of the door. Perched on a shelf chipped into the wall, a single unlit lamp, a box of matches and two fat tallow candles - their wicks unblackened - offered the only other potential sources of light in the room.

"I want to believe you're right, my love," Daniel answered quietly, "but I fear that you hope against hope. How could anyone find us, when even we don't know where to look?" His shoulders slumped as the import of his words echoed in his own tired and aching brain. He had never been one to shelter his wife from life's realities; she would have thought less of him if he had tried.

"Someone will come!" Marta repeated firmly. Daniel had always admired her sure, simple faith, but he couldn't help feeling that in this instance it was misplaced. No one knew where they were.

"And if not, we will just have to make our own way out of this, this...!"

"And I suppose you have a plan?" he asked her with a smile.

"Not yet, but I've no doubt one will come to us, Lord willing," she answered confidently. "He will provide."

Daniel's fingers went to the white collar at the neck of his black shirt. "Indeed," he said musingly. "Indeed."

~5~

The sudden rattling of the rusty lock in the heavy plank door turned the couple's attention to the entrance of their prison. Foolish though such behavior might be, Daniel rose to his feet, unwilling to face his captors from a position that would allow them to look down on him. Marta stood stiffly erect beside him, clinging to his hand with both of hers. The man who had clubbed Daniel in the kitchen of their home stepped into the room, then moved to one side to stand with his back to the wall beside the door. The double-barreled Greener shotgun dangling in his right hand had been cropped off to pistol-size; the muzzles were pointed at the floor, but Daniel could see that the hammers were both cocked. The unkempt man stared fiercely at the couple as he waited for his companion to enter. When the second assailant limped into the room, Daniel felt Marta's fingers tighten on his as she stared at the two defiantly.

The Martins' captors could not have been more different in appearance. The fellow carrying the shotgun was stoutly built and heavily muscled and was dressed in worn, rough miner's clothing: laced rough-out brogans and heavy canvas britches. Both man and clothing were in need of a good scrubbing; even the bone buttons securing his dirty muslin shirt had seen better days, and his coarse jaw was unshaven. His bulging blue eyes accentuated his broken teeth, yellowed from the tobacco he rolled in his jaws as he stood silently waiting for the newcomer to speak.

In stark contrast, the new arrival was foppish in appearance. He stood over six feet in height, which was exaggerated further by the black stovepipe hat he wore. The silk lapels of his dark green velveteen jacket framed the ruffles of a snow-white gambler's shirt and a neatly tied scarlet silk puff tie. He wore tailored dove-gray wool trousers tucked into the tops of highly polished knee-high riding boots. Leaning heavily on an ebony cane topped with a gold dragon's head, he stared malevolently at Daniel and Marta. Clean-shaven aside from a neatly trimmed mustache, his features were regular, and he might have been considered handsome except for the livid, puckered scar that pulled down the corner of his mouth, then turned up across his cheek to disappear beneath the snug silk patch covering his left eye, serving only to accentuate his rakish demeanor. The scar reappeared above the patch, tracing a ragged path diagonally across his pale forehead to disappear beneath his hat. After several long moments he at last began to speak.

"Ah, my dear Mister and Missus Martin." He spoke in the cultured tones Daniel had heard outside when he was first taken from the wagon. "I do hope that you are finding your new quarters satisfactory." His predatory smile was made even more menacing by the brutish scar on his face. "I believe you may plan to be here for some time to come."

"What do you want with us?" Daniel demanded. "We've done nothing to deserve this kind of treatment!"

The man's smile faded. "You were born, Reverend Martin! That is what you have done! And that is sufficient!" Disdainfully, he turned his back on his prisoners and limped toward the door. Before exiting, he faced them once more. His tone was icy. "Do not attempt to escape, sir; if you do you will be shot." He limped outside, followed by his shotgun-toting henchman. The door slammed and the lock rattled once again.

The couple stared defiantly after their unknown captor until the door closed and the key grated in the lock. When they were sure they were alone, Daniel's shoulders slumped; he trod heavily back to their bunk and collapsed on the blankets. Marta silently joined him; they sat together for several minutes in a comforting embrace. With a sigh, Marta put her head on Daniel's shoulder. "It sounds as if we are going to be here for a while," she whispered.

Daniel slipped his arm from Marta's shoulders, got to his feet and began to walk the perimeter of their prison, looking for an exit of some sort in the rock walls, knowing all the while that his search would be fruitless. His only discovery of note was at the narrow end of the oval of packed-earth floor. There he found a rough-hewn pole door, spiked together from split juniper logs -- the bark still in place -- and suspended on leather hinges. In spite of himself, Daniel's pulse quickened with hope that he might have found a means of escape from their predicament.

The rough surface of the door showed no sign of a latch; instead, a loop of rope nailed to one of the poles near the edge served as a handle. With some effort, Daniel pulled the door open. Rather than a passage or tunnel, in the darkness behind the portal there appeared to be a crude wooden structure with a hole in the center. It took him a moment to realize that he was looking at a seat. He stepped forward and looked down into black nothingness below the opening; at that moment it dawned on him that he had discovered an indoor outhouse which used an apparently bottomless void as a depository. A golden glow approached from behind him, and a moment later Marta appeared at his side carrying the now-lighted lamp. She looked down with a snort of sour amusement.

"Obviously our host, whoever he may be, has thought of everything." The curent of air flowing down into the opening ruffled the pages of the tattered Montgomery Ward catalog hanging from a leather thong stapled to the inside of the door. "It appears that he intends for us to stay indoors at all times," she commented wryly. She turned away with a quiet sigh, her free hand going to the small of her back. Seeing her retreat, Daniel immediately released the door, which, unnoticed by either of them, closed of its own accord.

"Are you all right?" he asked worriedly.

"Yes, I'm fine," she assured him with a quick smile. "My back just aches a little. Ever since the baby began to move around, I've had backaches. It's nothing to worry about, but I believe I'll lie down for a while. The ride out here - wherever here is - on the floor of that filthy wagon was rather tiring." She went to the bunk and inspected it for any unwanted occupants; the blankets appeared to have been recently washed, so she lay back on the cot and closed her eyes. Soon her breathing deepened as she eased into sleep, the lines of exhaustion on her face slowly relaxing.

While she slept, Daniel paced the floor of their prison; he had always been able to think better when in motion. As he walked back and forth, he applied himself to the problem of who their captor might be, and the meaning of the cryptic words he had spoken. "Because I was born?" Daniel spoke the words in quiet puzzlement. "How could my birth have any affect on a man I've never even seen before?" Like a beagle hot on the trail of a rabbit, the questions chased one another endlessly through the tangle and fog enveloping his tired and throbbing brain as he persistently searched for a way to convince the man in the silk hat to set them free.

-6-

The Baldwin locomotive's whistle screamed its warning to another darkened little town standing silently in the moonless expanse of the night. Near the middle of the single passenger coach attached to the express car, Bowie lifted a hand to pull his hat down a little further over his eyes. He'd been hearing the same strident shriek for the last twenty hours and he was almighty tired of hearing that whistle and feeling the continuous clunking of the train's wheels over the rail joints rattling up through the floor and the seat into his backside. The seat cushions had long since lost any softness they might have had when he first boarded the train.

The whistle sounded again as couplers clattered and the train began to slow. Bowie sat up tiredly, stretched, and pulled his watch from his vest pocket. In the dim light from the turned-down kerosene lamp at the rear of the car he could see that it was just after one o'clock in the morning – meaning yet another water and fuel stop.

Bowie yawned widely and pulled himself to his feet. Around him the other passengers were stirring, some only shifting position in their seats, while others stood as he had done, trying to work out some of the kinks from the long hours of travel. A baby near the rear of the car began to whimper; its pretty blonde mother rocked and sang softly to the child until the fussing subsided.

After a half hour or so, the whistle tooted, the train started with a jerk and everyone settled back into their seats. By the time daylight broke through the coach windows they would be traveling alongside the Great Salt Lake.

Bowie had just gotten himself situated in the most comfortable position he could find and tipped his hat down over his eyes again, when he felt a tug on his sleeve. He did his best to ignore whoever it was, but the next tug was even harder. With an exasperated sigh, he lifted his hat brim to look at whoever was interrupting what little rest he might be able to get on the hard seat. "What do you..." he began curtly.

His assailant interrupted him, a high-pitched voice ringing out with surprising volume for the size of the source, and clearly audible over the clattering of the car's wheels over the rail joints. "Hey mister, are you a cowboy?" The voice belonged to a small boy, some-where in the vicinity of four years old, neatly dressed in bib overalls, a cloth cap, and clodhopper shoes. Be-fore Bowie could draw breath to answer, the little fel-low went on, running the words together into one long sentence. "You sorta' look like a cowboy to me but yer kinda' fat I wanna' be a cowboy someday can you teach me to be a cowboy my pa's a farmer we're goin' to Or-egon where you goin'..."

The torrent of words was suddenly interrupted when a calloused hand picked the boy up by his overall straps. "I'm sorry Michael bothered you," the owner of the hand said in a deep voice. Bowie looked up at a man who had to be the boy's father. Tall and slender, the stranger was dressed in wash-faded canvas britches that showed signs of wear, and a neatly patched muslin shirt with the sleeves rolled halfway up his muscular forearms. Bowie remembered seeing him earlier, sitting with his family at the front of the car. The lanky fellow stuck out his free hand and said, "I'm Joshua Beckman. And you've already met Michael. As you can see, he's fascinated with cowboys."

Bowie chuckled as he shook the proffered hand. "I don't reckon I'm much of a cowboy, Mister Beckman. I'm Bowie Tyler, and your boy really wasn't a bother. He kind of took me by surprise, is all."

The sharp-featured, fashionably dressed brunette in the seat behind Bowie sniffed audibly. "No bother to some, possibly!" she snapped, snorting in a decidedly un-ladylike manner.

Bowie winked at the squirming Michael and his father before turning in his seat to speak to the lady. "If you'll pardon my saying so, ma'am," he said with as sincerely a solemn look as he could muster, "young master Michael's not nearly as bothersome as some folks' snoring is." He touched the brim of his hat with a finger. "Ma'am," he said, then turned back to face the front of the car.

"Well, I never!" the lady huffed as she lurched up out of her seat and went unsteadily toward an empty seat at the rear of the coach. The movement of the car as the train swung around a curve nearly upended her into the lap of the gambler in the seat ahead of her destination, but she managed to arrive at the empty seat unscathed, and flounced onto the cushions with a sour look on her face.

"I believe you may have accused her of conduct

unbecoming to a lady," Joshua Beckman said with a chuckle. Bowie just smiled as the Beckmans returned to their seats near the front of the coach. Once more he tipped his hat down over his eyes and went back to trying to sleep.

~ ~ ~

The great clock that punctually declared the time of day to the city of Laramie from the courthouse tower now struck the midnight hour. The chimes echoed through the empty building, startling Judge Randolph Martin from a reverie that was half sleep, half subconscious thought. The great edifice was empty, all the workers and government functionaries having long since gone home; as the echoes of the chimes died away, the only sounds in the rambling structure were the normal creaks and groans of settling timbers that one hears in such a big building at night. Mrs. Carstairs had urged him to go home, but after the death of his beloved wife Clarissa that seemingly long ago September his house was not just empty; it was lonely.

He had loved Clarissa deeply and still felt her loss. Consequently, in this time of crisis he felt a subconscious need to stay here, in the seat of his authority. In his role as judge, he held the destiny of many in his hands, although he wasn't vain enough to think that he was infallible. Judge Martin had never knowingly sentenced an innocent man to prison, and he had in fact pardoned several who he'd learned after-the-fact were innocent. Here he held power in his hands; at home, in the comfortless confines of his house, he was just a

41

widowed man.

Tiredly he rubbed a hand across his haggard face and chuckled grimly, quietly. "Yes, you're a powerful fellow, alright," he said sarcastically, his voice loud as it echoed in the empty room. "And about as much in control of your own destiny as the fish in the ocean." He sighed ruefully, but he believed that after hours of thinking back over the happenings of the past, he had finally found the answer to the question of why Cyrus Valentine, a man he'd once been proud to call his friend, had kidnapped Daniel and Marta.

Daniel's latest letter lay on the blotter in front of him. It had arrived a day before the package had come containing the newspaper from Baker City and the letter from Valentine.

Dear Father, the letter began in his son's neat handwriting.

I hope this missive finds you well. Marta and I have settled into our new home and things are going well. I have begun teaching the Lord's word in the little church whose deacons I wrote you about, and to date my messages have been well received by even the more unruly members of the local populace, some of whom occasionally put in an appearance in the pews. Perhaps the fact that I make no secret of having been a soldier has helped in that regard, in that I believe that I am perceived as something more than a "city dude". My having had occasion to take one of said rowdies to task physically behind the church on a bright Sunday afternoon a few weeks ago may also have helped that perception along.

Further, I have good news! Marta is in the family way, and expects to deliver our first child in the relatively near future. To date her condition has not caused her any undue discomfort, at least to my knowledge, beyond her being slightly nauseous in the morning for a few weeks. When I commented on this, I was informed in no uncertain terms by my lovely wife that such sickness is normal for a woman in her state. We hope that you will be able to travel here to Oregon after the baby arrives. It would mean so much to us both to have you here for the christening.

Your loving son,
Daniel

Judge Martin had reread the letter for perhaps the tenth time. At the mention of the baby, the random thoughts that had floated through his tired brain as he slumped against the cushions of his leather-covered chair had suddenly come into sharp focus, and he now understood without a doubt Valentine's motive for the kidnapping. Somehow, Valentine had discovered that Marta was with child. That was the only possible answer. He didn't waste time pondering how the man had made the discovery; such speculation would contribute nothing to his problem. Instead, he decided to send Bowie a telegram; with the building vacated for the night, however, sending a message would have to wait until morning. In addition, it was entirely possible that at this hour of the night the receiving station in Baker City would be deserted.

He was relatively certain that nothing would happen to Daniel and Marta right away. Deep down, he knew that Valentine would want him to first suffer the same volume of anguish and helplessness that Cyrus had felt when his family perished in the tragic fire so many long years ago. He had hoped that his former friend and classmate would be able to put the past behind him, but it seemed that the passing of the years had merely made Valentine more bitter and vindictive. Judge Martin stared down at the letter from Daniel. "And now I know what the reckoning will be, don't I, Cyrus? You have decided to destroy my family, just as the fire destroyed yours, haven't you?" he asked his distant adversary bitterly. He got to his feet. "Hang on, Daniel," he said into the darkness outside his window. "Help is coming."

~7~

The train rolled into Kelton, Utah, at the northern tip of the Great Salt Lake, in the morning of a gray, gloomy and overcast day. The hot, dry wind whipped dust devils from the unpaved street, causing pedestrians to go about their business with one hand holding their hats in place. Several barking dogs, accompanied by an equal number of small, dirty-faced boys, ran beside the slow-moving locomotive as it approached the depot, only to scatter like frightened quail when the engineer blew a long blast on the whistle. With a loud hissing of steam and the squeal of wheels on steel rails the train came to a stop next to the plank platform outside the station.

As the clanging of the couplers receded, the passengers climbed tiredly to their feet and stood, trying to stretch out the kinks from too many hours spent sitting on seats with not enough padding, before turning to gather their belongings. Bowie reached beneath his seat to retrieve his saddle. He laid it on the cushions, then reached to the overhead for his saddlebags. "I knew you was a cowboy," young Michael Beckman said from the aisle. "Didn't I say you was..." His words were cut off when he was hoisted aloft once again by his father, who had followed him down the aisle.

Joshua Beckman stuck out his hand. "Take care, Bowie," he said. "Maybe we'll see you again sometime."

"If you're headed for Oregon, that might happen sooner than you think," Bowie said with a smile. "I'll be taking the stage from here to Baker City."

"We won't be traveling in such high style, 'though we will be heading toward the same general locale: we've a place east of there," Beckman replied. "My brother Jed is meeting us here at the station and then we'll be traveling on by wagon. You'll get there way before we do, but we still might run into you. Take care." Beckman turned away, and Michael waved merrily at Bowie over his father's shoulder.

Bowie waved back at the boy, then picked up his elkhide-cased Greener shotgun from where it leaned against the seat cushions under the window. He hoisted his saddle up onto his shoulder, took Greener and saddlebags in his other hand and headed for the door at the end of the car. When he stepped down onto the platform and looked around, it was obvious that Kelton was, if not an important place, at least a busy one. Everywhere he looked, freight wagons and people were moving purposefully up and down the wide main street. He knew from the papers Judge Martin had given him that Kelton was the jumping-off place for the gold fields in Idaho and Oregon, and it seemed that business was booming. The miners might not be getting rich, but the freighters who supplied the mines appeared to be making money hand-over-fist.

Across the busy street from the railroad depot Bowie spotted the Northwest Stage Company office; in his eagerness to complete the next phase of his journey, he stepped off the platform without looking both ways. The jingle of harness and a lusty curse regarding Bowie's ancestry drove him back onto the platform as a buckboard driven by a burly man in a silk hat raced past Bowie without slowing. The heavy-set deputy shook his head ruefully at his own carelessness, then peered carefully in both directions before stepping down from the platform again. This time he made it across the street unscathed.

At the stage depot, Bowie discovered that he'd missed that day's coach by "'bout an hour or so". The next one leaves tomorrow morning," the agent informed him. "If you're here by seven or so, you can't miss it."

Bowie paid for his ticket, then asked, "Do you have some place I can leave my gear?"

"Yessir, I do," the agent answered. "Right back yonder through that door" - he pointed back over his shoulder - "is the strong room. And I've got the only keys."

"That works for me," Bowie replied with an innocent smile. "That is, if you're gonna' be here at stage time. I'd hate to have to leave my gear here because of a lazy agent."

The agent stared at him for a few seconds, ready to get mad, before he realized that Bowie was joking. "I suppose next you'll be asking for the best hotel in town!" the gray-haired fellow exclaimed testily with icy humor of his own.

"Nope," Bowie answered. "Just someplace with a little privacy and no bugs; I'm a light sleeper. I've found that most hotels aren't particular about either."

"I do believe your best bet'd be Missus Johnson's boardinghouse. Last I heard this morning, she still had one room left."

"Can she cook?" Bowie wanted to know.

"It ain't the best food west of the Mississippi, but it'll fill you up," the agent answered. "And the beds are clean," he added with a smile.

"That sounds good to me," Bowie replied. "Now if you'll just point the way, I'll tuck my gear and get on down there to see if that room's still available." The agent obliged; Bowie deposited his saddle and Greener in the depot's strong room, then headed for the boardinghouse, where he did indeed get the last available room. Its furnishings consisted of a narrow, feather-tick bed, both headboard and footboard butting against the narrow room's walls, that was neatly made up with a hand-tied quilt and two thick goose-down pillows, and a small, mirror-backed table, which held a gaily-patterned washbasin and matching water pitcher and stood beside the west-facing window. In place of a closet, a half-dozen pegs had been driven into a short length of split log that was spiked to the wall over the foot of the bed. Bowie pulled the roller shade down over the window to darken the room slightly, pulled off his boots, hung his gun belt on the back of the rickety chair next to the bed and dropped onto the thick quilt with a heartfelt sigh.

The piercing clang of a cookhouse triangle echoing through the building some hours later jolted Bowie from his nap. As he opened his eyes and stared at the ceiling, he was stirred to consciousness by a woman's commanding voice summoning, "Come and get it 'fore I throw it out!" He swung his feet over the side of the bed, reached for his boots and shoved his feet into them. He stood and scrubbed a hand across his face. As he reached for the doorknob, a hand-lettered sign on the back of the room's narrow, whitewashed door caught his attention. "*HOUSE RULES*" was printed in large letters aslant the top of the page, followed by a relatively short list of do's and don'ts. Near the top of the list, right after "*Keep your spurs off the furniture*", the list's author had written, "*No visible firearms at the dinner table*". Bowie chuckled as he reached into one of his saddlebags and took out a small canvas-wrapped bundle that smelled of gun oil. Unfolding the cloth revealed a stubby-barreled, double-action Forehand & Wadsworth pocket pistol.

If a firearm could be called cute, this one was exactly that. Its short barrel, nickel finish and slender carved-and-checkered walnut grips were in pristine condition. It had been residing in the gun case of a store in Colorado just begging to be bought when Bowie found it. His first thought had been that the little gun might come in handy some time, so he'd handed the storekeeper two silver dollars and left the store with the pistol and a box of cartridges. When he had returned to Laramie, he'd had a seamstress sew an extra-large, reinforced pocket inside his vest for the small pistol. A local gunsmith had bobbed off the hammer spur and smoothed all the gun's edges to keep it from snagging if Bowie had to get it out in a hurry. The short barrel and .32 S&W cartridge wouldn't win any long-range target matches, but would certainly suffice for defending oneself across the width of a dining room table. Bowie opened the break-top action, made sure that the pistol was loaded, then slipped it into in his vest and headed for the door; he meant to find out for himself how good or bad Missus Johnson's cooking might be, but not without a little reassurance in his pocket.

To somebody whose last meal had been a pretty sorry boxed lunch in the passenger car of the Union Pacific train, the smells drifting up the stairs were mighty appealing, and Bowie's stomach growled in response. When he entered the dining room, the Beckman family was seated along one side of a long table covered with red-checked linen. With them was a man wearing overalls and a gingham shirt whose resemblance to Joshua Beckman marked him as the brother of whom the tall farmer had spoken on the train. Young Michael Beckman looked up from his plate of fried chicken, mashed potatoes and gravy long enough to wave at Bowie before diving back into his food.

"I thought you were leaving for Oregon," Bowie remarked as he dropped into the empty chair across from the older Beckman brother.

"We needed to get some supplies and make a few last minute repairs, and it was getting too late in the day to leave, so we decided to wait for morning," Joshua replied. "Missus Johnson was good enough to let us put our stock in her corral, and we're camping out yonder." He hooked a thumb over his shoulder.

The food, as the stage line agent had told Bowie, wasn't the best food west of the Mississippi, but to a hungry man it was pretty good; there was plenty of it, and Bowie was a man who liked to eat. The coffee was just the way Bowie liked it: strong and black.

With his hunger pangs in abeyance for the moment, Bowie excused himself from the table and took his last cup of coffee out to the house's front porch. With the setting of the sun, the breezes wafting across the surface of the great lake glowing golden in the fading sunlight had cooled quickly, as often happens in desert country where there is little of substance to hold the heat. As Bowie sat with his stubby legs stretched out in front of him, Joshua stepped through the doorway and lowered himself onto the wicker seat of the ladder-back chair next to Bowie's and began to pack tobacco into a small clay pipe. The tall farmer struck a match on the porch railing, and his head was soon haloed with fragrant blue smoke. When the pipe was drawing to his satisfaction, he looked off into the distance; his quiet voice drifted alongside the fragrant vapors that meandered on the light wind.

"My brother and me have filed on some ground in a canyon with good water out east of Baker City," he commented. "We've got a couple of snug cabins and a good barn built, and we've got the beginnings of an orchard started. We're well enough along that I decided to bring the family out. Lizzie and Michael have been back east with her folks since last fall." He chuckled when he saw the look of surprise on Bowie's face. "That orchard thing sounds kinda funny, don't it?" he asked. Bowie nodded.

"Well, where we're at there's more ground standing on edge than there is laying out flat, 'though we do have some good bottom ground next t'the crick," Beckman went on. "Trees don't mind standing on a hillside, and there's always a market for good fruit. We brought some seed stock from back east t'plant, and we should have our first marketable crop next year, if we're lucky. We planted mostly apples, apricots and cherries, and my brother's a mean hand at making applejack. Meanwhile, we've got a big garden in and there's lots of deer, elk, and bear to be had. Since we've been there, we've made enough selling meat to the miners over toward Baker City to keep us in whatever grub we can't grow ourselves. We're doing alright." He lapsed into silence, contentedly puffing on his pipe.

The two men sat quietly enjoying the evening,

as off in the distance the last of the day's sunlight reflected from the surface of the Great Salt Lake.

~8~

The Northwest Stage Company coach rattled to a creaking stop in front of Lawson's Station. The brightly painted coach swayed on its leather thorough-braces as the weary passengers clambered to the ground to stand in the dust of the station yard yawning and stretching. A few tried to slap the dust of two days travel on the Concord's hard leather cushions from their clothes, finally giving up the effort as a waste of energy when the driver called, "We're leavin' in twenty minutes, folks! You'd best get on in and eat, and freshen up if you're of a mind to. Washbasin's around the corner, and I reckon you know where to find the outhouse if ya' need it."

Following his fellow travelers, Bowie strolled to the door of the long, low stone building that housed the stage station and trading post, slipping through the door and stepping to the side to let his eyes adjust to the dimness after the bright sunlight of the yard. A single smoky kerosene lamp, its wick badly in need of trimming, and a half dozen homemade tallow candles did their best to push the shadows into the corners of the room.

"Come and get it, folks!" a matronly woman, her gray hair neatly tied up in a bright red kerchief, cheerfully greeted the newcomers as she placed a fragrant platter of steaks alongside a large, blue enamelware coffeepot on a long trestle table. "All we got's elk meat today, but it was a young-un, so it's good eatin'."

The passengers lowered themselves to benches alongside the table and hurriedly forked chunks of fragrant meat onto a motley collection of chipped enamelware and china plates. A pan of fluffy biscuits was chased around the table by a pot of sand plum jam. Bowie sat up to the table with the rest and was pleasantly surprised at how good the food was. It had been his experience that stage station food was many times marginal at best; this meal was not one of those. It was obvious from the way the food was disappearing that the other passengers felt the same way. The cook stood to one side, beaming with pleasure. "I do like to see folks eat!" she declared happily. "Don't be shy; there's plenty!"

The driver, a white-haired paunchy fellow, wearing a beaded buckskin vest and a beat-up, high-crowned derby sporting a tattered eagle feather in the band, stomped into the room. "Five more minutes, folks!" he barked. "Anybody who ain't seated by then gets left here!"

"Oh, quit your snarlin' and set down and eat, Wiley!" the cook exclaimed. "You'll do no such thing, and you darn well know it. Your boss would have your hide if you left anybody here."

"I ain't got time, Nora!" Wiley protested. "I gotta' be in Baker City by tomorra!"

"You aren't gonna' make it," Nora retorted. "Hap Connors was in yesterday, and he said that three of the crossings are washed bad. He fixed things the best he could, but he was in a hurry, so you'll just have to take it easy. You'd best sit down and eat; you're gonna' need the energy," she commanded.

Wiley heaved a sigh. "I reckon you're prob'ly right," he answered ruefully. He dropped onto the end of a bench and began filling his plate with steak and biscuits.

The sudden clatter of steel-shod hooves on the packed dirt of the station yard silenced all conversation in the room. The diners heard the hostler's voice raised in protest outside the open door before the thud of a blow silenced him in mid-word. While everyone else stared apprehensively at the station door, Bowie was moving. He slipped from his seat, crept silently to the door at the back of the room and eased it open. The young woman he had been chatting with across the table saw him and started to speak, but Bowie pressed his finger to his lips in a request for silence as he slipped out the door and closed it quietly behind him.

Two armed figures swathed in linen dusters and wearing cloth masks over their faces swaggered through the open front door, waving guns and cursing. The stage passengers, temporarily perplexed and confused at this sudden disruption of their otherwise uneventful day, stared in confusion at the apparition confronting them. A pudgy mens' clothing drummer dressed in a wrinkled linen suit suddenly pushed himself foolishly to his feet, pulling a small pistol from his jacket pocket as he rose. Before the salesman's thumb could draw back the hammer, the leader of the masked invaders took a swift step past the end of the table and backhanded the unfortunate gentleman across the forehead with the butt of his pistol. The merchant went down in a heap with blood streaming across his face.

"Anybody else wanna' be a hero?" the leader

growled in an incongruously high-pitched voice. When there was no response, the slender, quick-moving gunman tossed a cloth sack into the middle of the table where it came to rest on top of the platter of fried elk meat. "I didn't think so!" the robber barked. "Now all of you stuff your valuables in that bag, and be quick about it! Money, watches, whatever!" The passengers remained frozen in place until the intruder suddenly fired a shot into the roof overhead. Through the haze of powder smoke, he snarled, "Move, dammit!" The passengers began a frantic scramble to reach into their pockets and reticules for whatever they had that might be valuable.

Bowie stood with his back to the stone wall beside the door, listening to the voices from within. He started when the shot blasted inside the station, but he quickly decided that rejoining his fellow passengers without knowing the situation could possibly get him killed. He ran lightly along the wall to the corner of the building, where he stopped and took off his hat. He set it on the ground behind him, then peered around the corner, careful to expose only enough of his face to allow him to see who or what might be nearby. Beyond the far corner of the station, he could see the stage team's lead animals stirring nervously in the traces. He could also see the worn soles of a pair of boots, their toes pointed at the sky. Whoever the boots belonged to was sprawled on the ground, unmoving. After a moment's consideration Bowie concluded that the boots belonged to the hostler, who he was sure had been struck down when the robbery first began.

"Hurry and get done up there!" someone suddenly ordered from some place out of sight beyond the coach team. "These damn horses are gettin' antsy!"

56

Bowie drew back out of sight as another voice answered roughly, "Don't get your knickers in a knot -- I'm almost done." He waited a moment, then peered around the corner again; seeing no one, he hurried silently along the wall toward the front of the station. He could hear horses stamping about and hoped that the hostler hadn't been trampled, but until he knew more of the situation out front, there was nothing Bowie could do for that unfortunate soul.

"I'm gonna' take these jugheads out back and water 'em," the first voice declared. "You can holler when y'all are ready to go."

"Yeah, yeah," the other voice replied waspishly.

Bowie turned and hustled his bulk to the rear of the building and around the corner. Once out of sight, he flattened his back against the wall and waited. At the sight of an old ax handle leaning against the wall at his feet a sudden idea for thinning out the opposition blossomed in his brain. He picked up the weathered piece of hickory and got a good grip on it just as the robber who was tending the mounts rounded the corner leading four horses, both of his hands full of bridle reins. The masked figure looked at Bowie in surprise for a heartbeat before dropping two sets of the reins and reaching for the birds-head grip of the Colt belted high on the outside of his linen duster. Bowie's hand flicked out; the ax handle tunked into the robber's skull just below his right ear. The gunman crumpled to the ground as Bowie scrambled to get the horses under control before they could stampede back around the building.

When the horses were gathered up and tied to the corral fence behind the station, Bowie borrowed a rope strapped to one of the saddles and returned to the unconscious bandit. He reached down, pulled the outlaw's pistol from the holster, shucked the shells from the cylinder and tossed it next to the building, then grabbed the man's wrist and rolled him over onto his belly. There seemed to Bowie that something about that wrist felt decidedly different than he'd expected.

Cutting a length from the coil of rope, Bowie tied the outlaw's hands behind his back, then reached up and pulled off the flour sack mask; what he saw rocked him back on his heels. Long auburn hair wrapped in a tight braid disappeared under the collar of the linen duster. Long lashes of the same color lay on the one lightly tanned cheek that Bowie could see. He grasped the "man's" chin, turned it up, and beheld the face of a good-looking young woman. "Damn," Bowie muttered under his breath. A dark bruise was rapidly forming under the girl's ear and at the corner of her jaw from the ax handle's blow. Bowie quickly tied his prisoner's feet together, then stood and dragged her over next to the building. He trotted along the back of the building with the ax handle and the rest of the coil of rope in his hand.

When he snuck a look around the corner of the building, the first thing Bowie saw was someone's backside clad in tight-fitting wool trousers and the worn soles of a pair of boots, perched on the top of the coach. The owner was bent forward, rummaging through the luggage piled there. A carpetbag with ladies' underthings protruding from the open top flew down from the roof of the coach and joined several other open satchels in a heap on the ground.

Bowie stepped up onto the hub of the coach's front wheel, reached up with the ax handle, and tapped one of the boots with the wood. "What the hell do you want now?" the duster-clad figure demanded, whirling to look down. Bowie reached up, grasped the lapels of the duster in one work-hardened fist and yanked the bandit headfirst off the top of the Concord. The outlaw let out a squawk as he thumped to the ground. Bowie whacked him with the ax handle. Quickly trussing the masked bandit and pulling off the mask, Bowie discovered once again that he was a she. *There seems to be a decided trend forming here*, Bowie thought wryly. He picked the girl up, stuffed her unceremoniously onto the floor of the coach, then headed for the station.

Bowie hurried to the door, carrying the ax handle in his left hand. He flattened his back against the wall to the left of the door and drew his pistol, holding it barrel-up beside his shoulder while he waited for the remaining bandits to come out of the station; there were only four horses, and he'd already captured two of the robbers, so he figured that there could only be two left inside, unless someone had been riding double.

He didn't have long to wait. The door slammed open and the first robber trotted out with a bulging flour sack in one hand and a pistol in the other. Bowie stuck the ax handle between the runner's feet; the sudden tangle of hickory, boots and linen duster tore the wood from his hand and sent the outlaw stumbling across the packed dirt of the yard to crash headlong into the side of the coach. The bandit's hat came off and her long, brown hair tumbled down around her shoulders. This one hadn't been hooded, just masked with a scarf. Bowie had just enough time to register the fact that this one was female like the rest, when the last robber backed out of the door. "Nobody comes out this door 'til you hear us ride off," the robber shouted.

"Connie, get the horses up here!" the masked

intruder hollered, looking to the left. With no sign of either Connie or the horses, the outlaw looked back to the right, and directly into the muzzle of Bowie's gun.

"Connie won't be bringing the horses," Bowie said with a smile, but the pistol never wavered. "She's, uh, shall we say, indisposed?" The smile left his face as he held out his left hand. "Now let the hammer down on that shooter and hand it here, and nobody will get hurt." A flash of anger, or possibly desperation, went through the eyes behind the mask. "Don't be stupid!" Bowie barked. He cocked the Colt. "Just hand over the gun!" Slumping shoulders admitted defeat as the robber lowered the hammer and offered the pistol to Bowie, butt-first.

"You might as well take off the hood, too," Bowie ordered. "I already know your partners in crime are women, so I would imagine you are, too." The lanky, red-haired teenager pulled the flour sack from her head, revealing a pug nose liberally sprinkled with freckles and angry, snapping blue eyes. Bowie let the Colt's hammer down, but kept the pistol in his hand.

"What'd you do with Connie and Marlene, you bastard?" the redhead snarled. "I know you didn't shoot 'em, 'cause I'd've heard the shots!" She glared at Bowie as she started cussing him. She knew a lot of the right kind of words, and she knew how to put them together in chunks.

When the rush of expletives wound down Bowie politely asked, "Does your momma know you talk like that?" When she appeared to be about to resume her tirade, the chunky deputy told the girl forcefully, "Lady, the next thing out of your mouth had better be just your name and nothing else, or I'll stuff that flour sack in it! Now shuck the duster, and let's see if you're still armed and dangerous!"

"You can kiss my ..." the redhead began heatedly.

In a flash, Bowie holstered his pistol, grabbed the young lady's wrist, spun her around and yanked the duster down around her upper arms. He spun her the other way, grabbed the flour sack hood from her hand, pried her jaws open and shoved the tail of the sack between her teeth before tying the heavy cloth in place with a bandana from his pocket. He kicked her feet out from under her, dropped her on her belly and sat on her legs while he tied her feet. He turned around and tied her hands, then rolled her over and propped her in a sitting position against the station wall.

"I told you," he declared, "but you just wouldn't listen!" He raised his voice and called through the station door, "You folks can come out now! The robbery's over!" One of the passengers, a middle-aged fellow sporting scraggly chin-whiskers and a cheap suit, peered tentatively out the door, his eyes widening at the sight of the two young women, one in a heap by the coach and the other trussed up, gagged and glaring at him over the scarf.

"Damn, mister, where'd them two girls come from?"

"Beats me," Bowie answered. "But I know where they're going. To jail, if there's one somewhere remotely close to here."

"No, I mean what're they doin' here?" the confused passenger queried. "And where'd the robbers go? We didn't hear no horses."

"They *are* the robbers!" Bowie snorted disgustedly. It was obvious to him that this gent was either drunk, blind, or stupid, or possibly all three. He turned his back and walked over to where the girl who had crashed into the side of the coach sat in the dust with her back against a wheel, groaning and holding her head. She squinted up at Bowie from between her hands as a thin rivulet of blood coursed down her face from a cut at the edge of her scalp.

"What'd you do with Janelle?" she asked painfully. It was obvious that she had a splitting headache. "And who in hell are you?"

"If that's Janelle," Bowie hooked a thumb over his shoulder, "I just tied and gagged her; nothing too serious. As for who in hell I am, I'm a federal marshal." The girl's face paled, and she swallowed loudly as he continued, "I do believe you ladies have gotten yourselves in a hole here that you'll have a bit of trouble digging yourselves out of."

"We ain't in jail yet, mister," she replied, her voice shaking as she made a try at bravado. "Why do you think we picked this station to pull this job?"

The stage driver stepped outside in time to hear what the comely young bandit said. "She's right, mister," the driver confirmed. "The nearest law's a long day's ride back the way we came!"

"Damn!" Bowie exclaimed, to no one in particular.

~ ~ ~

While Bowie trussed up the robber who had been inside the station and dropped her next to the one who had crashed into the side of the coach when he tripped her, the stage passengers filed out of the station and sorted through the sacks of loot for their belongings. A couple of the men helped the hostler to his feet and into the station. Bowie hauled Marlene out of the coach and set her next to the others with a curt "Watch those three" to the stage driver. "Yessir," the driver answered. The deputy retrieved his first captive from the back of the station, dragging the tightly bound young woman through the dirt by the collar of her duster. He dumped her unceremoniously with her companions, who were all grumbling under their collective breaths.

"Does anybody know any of these "ladies"?" Bowie asked. The station cook strode around and faced the four disheveled girls, looking intently at them.

"Drusilla Parsons, your folks would sure be proud if they could see you right now, wouldn't they?!" she demanded of the girl who had helped to gather the passengers' valuables inside the station. The teenager tried to stare back defiantly, but couldn't hold the woman's icy gaze.

"You ain't gonna tell 'em, are you Aunt Nora?" Drusilla queried tremulously, suddenly ashen-faced. "My pa'd tan my hide for sure!"

"Not tell them?" Aunt Nora asked incredulously. "You just tried to rob a stage coach!"

"I take it you know this young lady then, ma'am?" Bowie wanted to know.

"I should: I changed her diapers!" the station keeper retorted. "She's my niece!" She bent and brushed the hair away from the faces of the others, who were trying to keep their identities hidden. "This one," she lifted Connie's chin, "is Connie Barkley. Her folks ranch over south of here." She turned Marlene's face up. "Marlene Rawlins. She lives up the river a piece. So that means the last one has to be Janelle Curtis. They're all cousins." She stepped back and addressed the four girls, for on closer inspection 'ladies' was an overstatement; the oldest one looked to Bowie to be about seventeen. "You girls are in a heap of trouble. The deputy here is gonna haul you in, and prison is no place for a young lady. You'll be old before you come out."

She winked back over her shoulder at Bowie. "If you make it out."

Bowie moved toward the corner of the station. "Ma'am, can I speak to you in private for a moment?" As the cook approached him, Bowie turned his back to his prisoners and the stage passengers. "I don't really have time to take these girls for a day's ride back to that jail," he began, frustration beginning to surface in his voice. "How far is the closest one's house?"

"My sister's place is about five miles south of here. Have you got in mind what I think you have?"

"Well, the stage passengers have got their fixin's back," Bowie answered. "I think maybe turning these girls over to their own folks to take care of would be a whole lot easier than the alternative -- providing their parents will do something with them."

"I think I can pretty much guarantee you that my niece won't sit comfortable for a month once my sister and her husband get a' hold of her," Aunt Nora replied. "And I'm sure I can arrange for something similar for the others. But you'll have to get 'em back to their folks. I can't leave the station."

"If you have a horse you can loan me, I'll take care of it," Bowie assured her. "You just point me in the right direction."

"That I can do, Deputy."

"Please, call me Bowie. It's easier."

"And I'm Nora Lawson. Most folks around here call me Aunt Nora." She held out her hand and Bowie shook it amiably.

"I'm most pleased to meet you, ma'am, especially seeing as how you just saved me a day's ride each way to put your niece and her friends in the hands of the 'proper' authorities!"

Bowie returned to the passengers, who were milling around the coach repacking valises and bags. "Folks, whenever Mister Tucker here," - he motioned to the driver - "is ready to go, you'd best get on your way. I'll take care of our 'friends' and catch tomorrow's stage. There is another stage coming tomorrow, right?" He looked at Tucker, who nodded curtly. "Excellent. Now if you'd throw my saddle and my gear on down here, you can get moving."

Wiley Tucker climbed up on top of the coach and swung Bowie's gear to the ground. "You heard the man, folks," he told the passengers. "Gather up yer goods and let's get this here show on the road."

~9~

The stage had been gone for roughly half an hour. Bowie led his borrowed mount, followed by the four horses belonging to his charges, to the front of the station; the animals were tied nose to tail with rope halters. Bowie spoke brusquely to the surly group. "Ladies, here's the plan: I'm going to untie your feet and put you on your horses, one at a time. Once you are on your horse, you will not move unless I tell you to. Is that understood?" The girls, torn between anger at being tied up and fear of what the consequences of their recent actions would be, glared icily at him, but all nodded.

"Fine." He went to Drusilla and untied her feet, then helped her hoist herself unceremoniously onto the horse she claimed was hers. He did the same on down the line and soon had all four of the 'stage robbers' seated on their horses.

"I won't tie your feet together unless you give me cause," Bowie told the girls. "I'd hate to have it said that one of you fell under your horse and got trampled because you couldn't set your saddle and couldn't get your feet loose."

"We can set a saddle just fine," Connie grumbled. "Where are you takin' us?"

"You'll find out in due course," Bowie answered with a sly grin. He touched his forefinger to the brim of his hat in salute to Aunt Nora, who stood with her hands on her hips in the station doorway. She was trying with little success to hide a smile of her own. "Thank you for your help, ma'am," he called. "I hope to see you again in a few hours." He heeled his mount into a walk, and with a jerk the string of horses started off.

An hour later Bowie stopped his entourage in the yard of a log ranch house set at the foot of a high ridge, dotted here and there with small groups of black or red cattle resting in the shade of scattered juniper clumps. A black and white dog ran out to bark at the newcomers, and the ruckus brought the rancher - a slender, muscular man dressed in washed-soft homespun - out of the log barn which stood to one side of the house. When he saw the stranger and his charges, the fellow's stride increased rapidly until he was practically trotting when he reached the deputy and his prisoners. A slight woman whose dark hair was liberally frosted with gray appeared in the doorway of the cabin, drying her hands on a flour sack towel.

"Mister, you better have a good explanation for why my daughter and these other girls are tied up and their horses are bein' led!" the one whom Bowie assumed was Nora Lawson's brother-in-law exclaimed forcefully.

Bowie pinned the deputy marshal's badge to his vest. "I believe I do," he answered unceremoniously. "Your daughter and her partners in crime here tried to rob the stage station north of here a little while ago. I

67

just happened to be a passenger on the coach involved and managed to convince them that it was a bad idea."

The slender man walked up to Drusilla's horse and looked up at her. "Is this true, Dru?" he asked sharply. With a contrite look on her face, Drusilla nodded. He turned to Bowie and held out his hand. "I'm Carl Parsons, Drusilla's father. What exactly are your intentions regarding these girls?"

"Mister Parsons, my original intention," Bowie answered, "was to take your daughter and her friends to jail. But considering the distance involved, and the fact that they didn't get away with the robbery, I thought I might turn them over to their folks. I think you can probably find some way to convince them of the error of their ways, can't you?"

"Mister, you can bet your last dollar on that," Parsons assured him. "And I believe I can vouch for the Barkleys, the Rawlinses and the Curtises."

"Good. Is there someplace you can keep the other three here, or do I have to ride all over the country tracking down the rest of their parents?"

Parsons chuckled. "I've got a storage room down yonder in the barn that they'll all fit in, 'though it might be a bit cozy." Bowie started to speak, but Parsons interrupted. "Don't worry; my daughter will be in there with 'em, and she won't be able to let 'em out. They'll have to fight a few mice for seating space, but that shouldn't worry a bunch of big tough desperadoes like them. I'll send word to their folks, and they'll be secure until the 'posse' arrives!"

The girls looked stricken at the mention of the mice in the storeroom. "In that case, lead on," Bowie replied wryly. A few minutes later, the detainees were locked in the barn and Bowie was drinking coffee at the kitchen table with Parsons and his wife, Marie. "I really hate to see four young girls go to prison," Bowie admitted to Drusilla's folks. "And since they really didn't get away with it, maybe a good dose of parental discipline will change their minds about taking up a life of crime."

"Don't worry, Deputy," Mrs. Parsons told him firmly. "We'll see to it that they never do anything even remotely like this again!"

Bowie drained his cup, rose to his feet and picked up his hat. "I'm much obliged for the coffee, ma'am."

"We're obliged to you for not sending our daughter to jail," Marie replied humbly.

"I reckon that if you can find her a more respectable line of work than robbing stagecoaches we'll be even. Take care, now." Bowie strode outside, stepped into the saddle and turned his borrowed horse back toward the stage station. The sun was just touching the western hills and the early evening was peaceful, except for the occasional squeal of outrage echoing from the barn. Bowie grinned to himself as he heeled his mount into a trot.

~10~

A letter from Valentine arrived in the morning mail. Judge Martin slit open the envelope, and two simple lines in Valentine's familiar handwriting greeted his gaze.

Make your way to Baker City and await instructions.
You will be contacted.

Though his expression was blank as he stared at the parchment before him, Martin's mind was working furiously. He had sent Bowie to Oregon just a week before; the deputy should have arrived at his destination. If so, then there was obviously nothing to report, or there would have been some news. It was not Martin's custom to second-guess one of his men; rather, Valentine's letter, brief though it was, told the Judge in no uncertain terms that if he wanted to see his family again, he would have to go to Oregon himself. Deep down he had known that all along, but he'd tried to convince himself it wouldn't be necessary; Valentine's letter proved otherwise.

He got to his feet and strode to the door leading

to the outer office. "Eunice, please check my calendar and make a list of the most pressing appointments, and another list of what can be postponed indefinitely. And please do so as soon as possible."

Startled, Missus Carstairs could only stare at the Judge's back as he spun on his heel and returned to his desk. Sensing the urgency in his request, she immediately began to review the Judge's schedule for the next few weeks' court cases, winnowing the list down to those that were most in need of immediate attention. The slate was getting shorter, but it was still daunting. Ruthlessly, she pared it further until at last she had two documents which were as concise as she could make them.

At first, the secretary was too busy to wonder why she had gotten such an unusual request. However, once her assignment was complete and she had time to think, her initial confusion turned to concern. Surely Judge Martin wasn't thinking of going to Oregon? The more she thought about the Judge's orders, the more Missus Carstairs was convinced that going to Oregon was exactly what he had in mind. She quickly finished the task Judge Martin had requested and sighed quietly as she approached his door. Tapping lightly on the door frame, she looked into the judge's darkened office. "I have the lists you wanted, sir."

Judge Martin spun his chair around from where he'd been staring out the window, plans for his trip to Oregon spinning through his tired brain, to face her. She strode across the room to his desk and handed him the two sheets of paper. He glanced at them briefly, then looked up at her gratefully. "Thank you, Eunice. It appears that as soon as I am finished with the Bartleby trial, my docket can be left open for several weeks."

Eunice looked down at him with an uneasy feeling in her heart. "Are you going to tell me why?" she asked simply.

His expression was solemn as he responded quietly. "I think you already know why. Specifically, Cyrus Valentine has made it plain that taking Daniel and Marta captive isn't enough; he wants me to come to him. I believe he wants to see my face when he exacts his revenge."

"But you're..."

"Needed here?" he said. "Hardly. Anyone conversant with the law could do as well."

"What I meant to say is that you are not a gunman. How will you protect yourself?"

"I will not be in any danger until Valentine is able to confront me," Judge Martin assured his loyal secretary. "And you never know -- I might just surprise you." He smiled wearily and turned his chair back toward the window. "The Bartleby trial will be over tomorrow afternoon. Please see that I have passage on the train to Utah on Friday morning. I'll purchase a seat on the stagecoach from there to Baker City once I arrive at the end of the rail line in Kelton."

~ ~ ~

Cyrus Valentine restlessly paced the one-room cabin's packed-earth floor, six steps each way. The thump of the crippled attorney's ebony cane and his limping footsteps were muted by the surface underfoot. The flickering light from the Victor lamp carelessly placed on the pine plank table against one wall competed with the sullen glow from the stone fireplace in throwing menacing shadows around the twenty-by-twenty-foot room. Muted daylight oozing into the room from the oilcloth-covered window fell across stacked supplies and did little to brighten the area.

He had made his plans with care; his only desire was to bring the man who had wronged him all those years ago to this place so that he could witness Randolph Martin's comeuppance in person. At the same time, Valentine realized that as a territorial judge, Randolph had resources beyond his control. Although his strategy would take time to yield the expected result, he was willing to wait. He had been waiting for over a quarter of a century for this; a few more weeks weren't too much to ask, were they? Nevertheless he paced, nervously burning off some of the anger that forever smoldered inside him and had driven him relentlessly for so long as he had watched Randolph rise to power, and waited patiently for his chance at vengeance.

The injuries Valentine had sustained in the fire so many years before pained him constantly, but the cane helped, as did the bottles of laudanum he kept close at all times. The doctors had told him that in time the pain should subside, but Valentine had chosen instead to nurse his agony, and he clung to it in order to keep his thirst for vengeance alive. He depended on the laudanum as a means to avoid being overwhelmed by his inner demons, never realizing that the very elixir that kept him functional was slowly but surely diminishing his capacity for rational thought. He wasn't slipping into insanity per se, as some of his past business adversaries claimed; rather, the constant ravages of pain and opium were dulling Valentine's once brilliant mind.

The timid tap on his door startled Valentine

from his reverie. "Come in," he snapped, as he interrupted his incessant pacing and leaned heavily on his cane. Digger Hartley stepped into the small cabin and removed his cloth cap. Digger was a man of few scruples, and those he did have could generally be bought for the right price. Cyrus Valentine had deep pockets and a chip on his shoulder, making the two of them a perfect pair; consequently, they had been employer and employee for years. It was often convenient for even an apparently proper businessman such as Valentine to have access to a thug like Digger.

At first, kidnapping Daniel and Marta Martin hadn't bothered Digger or the men he'd hired to help him abduct the couple from their home. Between the hoods the couple had worn, and hurrying to get the dirty deed done without alerting the Martin's neighbors that something was amiss, Digger had managed to ignore the visible evidence of what Daniel did for a living. It wasn't until their hoods had been removed and he'd seen the white collar around Daniel's neck and heard the boss call Daniel "Reverend" that Digger began to have second thoughts.

Hartley had been raised in a strict churchgoing family, and had sat through many a tortuous sermon as a boy. While that had been a number of years, mining camps, and nefarious enterprises ago, some vestige of his early religious teaching still remained, and now what passed for Digger's conscience was pricking him. Somehow, it just felt wrong to be laying a pick handle, or even hands, on a 'man of the cloth', no matter how well it paid. He stared down at his boots for a moment while he gathered the courage to speak to Mr. Valentine. It had been his experience that his mercurial employer could console or condemn with a look and a word; he'd been on both ends of the spectrum and never knew which it would be. Digger looked up at Valentine with his gaze centered somewhere in the vicinity of the boss man's silk cravat. "Uh, boss," he began, "I hate to bother you, but...are you sure this was a good idea?"

"What are you talking about?" Valentine asked gently.

"Kidappin' a preacher!" Digger declared in a rush. "And that woman's in the family way! I heard 'em talkin'! Sets me to wonderin' why we done it!"

"Let me do the worrying," Valentine replied after a brief pause. "Nothing will happen to them as long as they do as they are told. Trust me."

"I ain't worried about what'll happen to them, boss...I'm worried about what'll happen to *us*."

"Nothing is going to happen to *us*," Valentine sneered. "I seriously doubt you'll be struck by lightning, or anything of the sort." The attorney chuckled evilly. "Just keep in mind that your job is not to worry about whom you kidnapped or why; your job is to do as I order. Suffice it to say that I *do* think this was a good idea." He paused to light a cigar. "But remember this," he snarled through an aromatic blue cloud, his temper suddenly flaring. "If those two escape, what the Almighty might someday do to you is nothing compared to what I will do to you in the here-and-now! I suggest you go and earn the money I pay you! I have a great deal of time and money invested in the Martins, and it is up to you to see that they remain in our hands!" Veins stood out on Valentine's forehead, and his face was flushed a deep mottled red. He turned his back on Digger as he reached into his pocket for the bottle of laudanum that nestled there.

~ ~ ~

Judge Martin ascended the stairs to the attic of his house as the stars began to appear in the evening sky. In the far corner of the dusty space, a travel-worn dome-lidded trunk rested beneath a veil of dusty cobwebs. Martin set his kerosene hand lamp on a nearby table and used the broom in his other hand to sweep the trunk free of the dusty covering, then reached down and pulled it over closer to the light. The trunk was locked and had been for many years, but since he had kept the lock oiled, the tumblers turned easily when he inserted the key. He took a deep breath; the hinges creaked as he lifted the lid on a chapter of his life he had thought was closed forever.

The contents of the trunk were covered with what appeared to be a wagon sheet, but was actually a full-length linen duster, creased and permanently soiled from years of hard use in all sorts of weather. Bone buttons gleamed dully in the yellow lamplight. Memories of past trails ridden brought a soft, nostalgic smile to the judge's lips as he lifted the garment from its resting place and laid it aside. Beneath the coat a sweat-stained gray felt hat -- its brim notched from a past meeting with the razor-sharp blade clasped in a drunken drover's hand -- laid crown-up on a pile of folded and wash-faded clothing. Randolph set the hat atop the duster and lifted a pair of canvas trousers from the trunk. He shook the creases out and held them to his waist. He prided himself on keeping fit, and in the fact that his waistline was the same as it had been since

76

his days as a fire captain; he was sure that the pants would still fit him now.

The faded red-striped cotton shield-front shirt which he brought from the trunk next showed its age but was still serviceable; it would fit as well. The remaining item residing in the trunk was a lumpy muslin bag. His hands rested on the coarse cloth for a full minute before he took the bag from the trunk, set it on the dusty table near the lamp and untied the drawstring.

The smell of gun oil and leather drifted on the dusty air, triggering a cascade of memory and emotion that washed over him as he stood staring down into the dark puckered opening for several long minutes. The contents of the bag represented a side of Randolph Martin that few in Laramie, even his deputies, knew. His wife had known, of course, but she was gone -- taken from him by cancer four years before.

Randolph reached into the bag and drew out a holstered pistol. The worn cartridge belt was wrapped neatly around the gun and holster and buckled back to itself to make a compact bundle. He lifted the hammer thong and pulled the converted '51 Navy Colt revolver from the snug leather holster, then expertly thumbed the hammer to half cock, flipped open the loading gate and rotated the cylinder, listening to the crisp clicking of the action as it turned. The chambers were empty, just as he had left it, but he was always careful to check the state of any weapon he picked up. He weighed the gun in his hand as his past drifted forward into the shadows of the dusty attic, a past far removed from his present, but one that remained an indelible part of him nonetheless...

The judge shook himself from his reverie. *Back to the present, Randolph.* Lifting a box of cartridges from the trunk, Martin closed the lid, then bundled up the clothing and gun. He carried his gear down the stairs and into his bedroom, where he deposited everything on the seat of the ladder-back chair next to his bed before taking a seldom-used carpetbag from the nearby closet. *If Valentine thinks that he's getting a dog to kick, he'll soon discover that this old dog still has plenty of wolf where it counts.* He looked at his reflection in the gilt-edged oval mirror which hung on the back of the closet door. "I hope you haven't lost your touch, old man." The determined, piercing gray eyes returned his steady gaze. "We can't afford any mistakes."

~ ~ ~

The clean-shaven gentleman arrayed in immaculately pressed tweeds who confidently strode the center aisle of the Union Pacific passenger coach to select his seat early on that cool, sunny Friday morning was a far cry from the traveler who boarded the Northwest Stage Company coach in Kelton, Utah three days later. That reclusive individual's worn range clothing, wear-creased linen duster and aged but well-maintained pistol riding comfortably in a cross-draw holster in front of his left hip belied their owner's identity as the territorial judge who intended to arrive at his destination unrecognized and unannounced. The wide, sweat-stained brim of the weathered Stetson was pulled well down over Randolph Martin's face as he settled into the Concord coach's window seat for the long ride to Oregon.

~11~

As the coach creaked to a stop, the driver called, "Ten minutes, folks. Ten minutes. The stock need water." After striking the Snake River north of the City of Rocks station thirteen hours rough and dusty travel from Kelton, the coach road followed the river for some two hundred thirty miles, passing through Fort Boise and the Boise Basin gold country. Although there were stations every ten to fifteen miles along the route, it was sometimes necessary to make unscheduled stops to refresh the horses.

Randolph knew from his research that the coach road would soon be turning away from the Snake at Farewell Bend -- so named by the hardy pioneers as they bid goodbye to the larger river to follow a smaller stream known as the Riviere Brule, or Burnt River. Early travelers on the Oregon Trail had named it for the fire-blackened hillsides they had encountered when they first came through the area. The first pioneers had to cut roads through the stream-side brush, and were often forced to climb part way up the canyon walls in order to make their way. Later, the coach road had been carved out and travel was easier, but the trail still crossed the river -- which was more of a creek at this time of year -- a number of times. The crossings were often washed out, and passengers were some-times required to either get down from the coach and push, or help their driver to rebuild the crossings. Such hindrances to frontier travel were considered to be part of the deal, so to speak, and were taken in stride by most travelers.

Randolph stepped down from the coach, then turned to offer his hand to the shapely redhead who had sat across from him since leaving Fort Boise. She was dressed in utilitarian traveling clothes and ap-peared to be an accomplished traveler. While they had chatted a bit with each other and the other passengers -- a woman and her two children -- as the miles had passed, they had only exchanged pleasantries regard-ing impersonal subjects such as the weather, which had been good so far. Neither had learned much about the other, including names. That was soon to change.

The woman thanked him in her lilting soprano and Randolph smiled his welcome. He thought he could detect just the faintest hint of Virginia or the Carolinas in her words, but he wasn't quite sure. Though he felt that she might be within ten years of his own age, there was an ageless quality about her beauty that made it impossible to tell for certain. For the first time since his wife had passed, he was beginning to feel the stir-rings of interest in a woman. The feelings were not of a carnal nature, as might be expected, but emotional. Her bemused expression and the way she seemed to view the world around her with humor and skepticism appealed to him; he was much the same himself. He made up his mind to learn her name, and any other details he could discover, at the earliest opportunity.

The coach horses drank their fill and the driver hollered, "Let's get back aboard, folks. We got a long ways to go." The passengers were climbing aboard the coach when the driver touched Randolph's sleeve; as he turned, the driver motioned him away from the door. "You keep that pistol handy, mister," the driver whispered quietly. "I've been hearin' rumors that the Mulcahey clan is operatin' in this part of the world."

"The Mulcahey's? Who are they?" Randolph asked just as quietly.

"They're a bunch of no-good stock rustlers who decided to start stickin' up coaches. I hear tell they held up a coach a couple of weeks ago up north of here on a different route, and there's some almighty narrow stretches comin' up in yonder canyon. So you'd best be watchin'." The driver chuckled. "You might give Miss Frannie the high sign too, if you've a mind to." He turned toward the coach.

"Miss Frannie?"

"That purty redhead you been sittin' across from all the way from Fort Boise," the driver grinned. He started his climb to the seat.

Randolph face and voice showed his puzzlement. "Why would I want to do that?"

"'Cause she's right handy to have around if something happens. You'll see. Now you'd best get inside." Settling himself on the box, the teamster picked up his long blacksnake whip and gathered the reins as Randolph, mulling over the teamster's words, returned to his seat and closed the door. With a lurch the coach began to roll.

"What was that all about?" the redhead wanted to know.

"Our pilot up there," he pointed at the ceiling, "seems to think we could possibly be held up by someone he called 'the Mulcahey clan'. Since I'm armed, he wanted me to know; he asked me to tell you as well, 'though I'm sure I can't imagine why, if you'll pardon my saying so."

"Thank you for the warning," she answered calmly. "You watch behind us and I'll keep an eye to the front." She laughed quietly as she shook her head. "The Mulcaheys...who'd have thought...?" She smiled at Randolph. "It has been a somewhat boring trip so far," she commented drily. "Maybe Allen Mulcahey and his kin will liven things up." Randolph looked at her skeptically for a moment, taken aback by her easy acceptance of the possibility that the coach might be robbed. *Is this lovely lady armed?* he wondered silently as he turned to the task assigned to him by his traveling companion. *And if so, why?*

The first part of the trip up the Burnt River went uneventfully; so much so, in fact, that Randolph found himself dozing off in spite of the roughness of the ride. They passed into the mouth of the canyon: the sheer rock walls stood up on either side, closing them in and blocking the morning sunlight, except where an occasional draw fed into the canyon from one side or the other. Their route wound through the canyon, frequently crossing the river, for several miles until they came to a narrow defile. Here the road had been widened with dynamite, but there was still relatively little room between the overhanging wall of brooding rock on the left and the sheer drop into the river on the right.

As the coach entered the widest spot in that particular part of the track, a shot suddenly blasted the midday stillness and echoed through the rocks. Even the chuckling of the water over its stony bed below the road seemed to still for a moment. The passengers jounced roughly against each other as the driver reefed

82

on the lines and stamped on the brake. "Whoa up, you brutes!" he yelled. The coach shuddered to a halt and a harsh Irish brogue cut through the dying echoes of the shotgun's roar.

"It's pleased I'd be if ye' would all step down from the coach and present yer pretties," the voice declared loudly, "and be quick about it, 'er me laddies'll blow ye' loose from yer boots!"

Randolph looked in amazement at the redhead. She had dragged a small carpetbag from beneath her seat and was calmly rummaging through it. After a moment, she withdrew a Smith & Wesson revolver from the bag, opened the action far enough to insert a .45 caliber shell in the one empty chamber in the cylinder, then closed the action. She held a finger against her lips for a moment as she tucked the short-barreled pistol into her reticule, then said loudly, "We'd better do as the man says. I would hate to see anyone get hurt." She gave Randolph an innocent smile as she motioned for him to open the door.

The other woman and her children wasted no time in exiting the coach through the door nearest the river, while Randolph and the redhead exited through the opposite side. Randolph stepped down, then reached up to help the lady to the ground.

"Now ain't you the gent?" a rough voice sneered. Randolph turned and placed himself between his traveling companion and a roughly dressed man wearing a bandana mask and holding a pistol.

"It wouldn't hurt you to be a bit more mannerly yourself, my good man," Randolph said calmly.

"I ain't your good nothin', mister!" the holdup man snapped. "Now you and her git your butts around t'other side of the coach." He waved with his gun barrel. "And keep your hands where I can see 'em." He paid no attention to the redheaded traveler -- assuming that she was harmless -- and was intent instead on keeping Randolph under his gun.

The trio walked around the front of the coach team to where the driver and the woman and her children stood. The adults held their hands in the air; the children, a boy and a girl, were crying as they clung to their mother's skirts. Two masked riders, one armed with a shotgun, the other holding a long-barreled revolver, had their guns pointed in the general direction of the captives while another of their number climbed up the side of the coach.

The man behind Randolph pushed him roughly forward; he stumbled, and as his hands came down the right one slid inside his duster and drew the pistol concealed underneath. When the bandit shoved him again, Randolph threw himself to the ground. As he rolled onto his back he thumbed back the hammer of the pistol and shot his attacker twice in the chest, then in one smooth motion came up onto his knees in the dirt. He blasted a shot at the masked desperado hanging on the side of the coach; as he watched his target fall from the side of the Concord, a flurry of shots rang out from behind him followed immediately by the clatter of steel-shod hooves on rock as the mounted outlaws spurred their horses away from the gunfire.

He glanced quickly at the teamster, who now stood with the fallen outlaw's pistol clasped in both hands, blazing away at the two men galloping madly down the road away from the coach, a pair of riderless mounts trailing in their wake. The redhead was standing beside the driver in a picture-book target stance, calmly thumbing back the hammer of her Smith and

84

Wesson and firing methodically at the retreating out-laws.

One of the riders had a spreading stain of crim-son on his back and was clinging desperately to the sad-dle horn with both hands while his horse ran free. Just before horses and riders disappeared around a turn in the canyon, the wounded man fell from his saddle and rolled into the river. The remaining outlaw and all of the riderless horses raced on, out of sight.

Randolph pushed to his feet, pistol in hand. The first bandit he had shot lay on the ground staring sight-lessly at the sky. The second highwayman, who had been climbing up the side of the coach when Randolph shot him, was rolling back and forth on the ground cursing bitterly in pain and holding his shattered right elbow.

The redhead snapped the Smith open and re-loaded, then walked over and looked down disdain-fully as she nudged him in the ribs with her toe. "I'll thank you not to use that sort of language in front of ladies." When her victim snarled another impropriety, she bent down and placed the still-warm muzzle of her gun against his forehead, directly between his eyes. She snicked the hammer back as she observed confidently, "Perhaps the shooting has damaged your hearing. I told you to be quiet." The wounded man's eyes widened as he instantly froze the string of epithets trailing off into a gasp as he felt the steel of the gun on his skin; he didn't seem too eager even to breathe.

"That's more like it. Now lay still while we de-cide what to do with you." She turned her back on the wounded outlaw and winked conspiratorially at Ran-dolph. "Sir, would you be so kind as to check on our fellow passengers?"

"Of course," he answered reluctantly. He couldn't fathom her reasoning, but was fairly certain that she planned to allow the wounded outlaw to escape. Such behavior went against his principles as an officer of the court; however, he was many miles from his courtroom, it was her play, and as a stranger to the area, he decided not to interfere. He strode over to the large granite boulder where the mother and her children were crouched, the children apparently petrified with fright. The children stared wide-eyed at him as he approached. "Are you all right? Are any of you injured?" he asked the woman, concern evident in his tone.

"None of us have been shot, if that's what you mean," the mother snapped sourly, "but I'm not sure my children will ever be 'all right'!" She glared at him as she got to her feet. "Those men only wanted money!" she went on stridently, her voice rising. "I see no reason why you had to shoot them! Had we given them what they wanted, none of this... this... bloodshed would have happened! And my children would not have been forced to witness such needless violence!"

Randolph heaved a resigned sigh. "Madam, it has been my experience that their sort of 'man' never wants 'only money'," he responded dryly. "Trust me, I know of what I speak." He heard rocks rattle behind him and spun around in time to see the wounded man disappear behind the coach. He started to follow, but the redhead intercepted him with a hand on his arm.

"Let him go," she said matter-of-factly. "It will simplify our lives considerably. The way he's bleeding he probably won't make it far. I know for a fact that the nearest house is at least six or seven miles from here, and he doesn't have a horse. I doubt he can walk even a mile in his condition."

"That's a somewhat callous attitude, isn't it, Miss…" Randolph began.

"It's Missus," she interrupted. "Missus Francine Kinsella. My friends call me Frannie." She held out her hand. Surprised at her forwardness, Randolph took it; her grip was unexpectedly strong. "And I consider my attitude pragmatic. I personally have better things to worry about than taking a two-bit outlaw through fifteen miles of rough canyon just so the law can hang him."

Randolph couldn't help but chuckle at her words and her tone. He doffed his hat and said, "And I am Randolph Martin." He looked down at the pistol in her hand and cocked his eyebrow. "I don't believe I've ever met a lady who carried such a large caliber weapon."

Frannie slipped the pistol back into her reticule. "I'm a gunsmith," she remarked simply as she closed her bag . "Shall we go on with our trip? I'd like to get home."

The other woman listened to the conversation between Randolph and Frannie with a look of horror spreading across her plain visage. "How could you be so, so… insensitive?" she demanded, outraged. "Come, children!" She gathered her two equally plain-faced offspring and practically shoved them into the coach. "I suppose you're going to let that man you murdered lay there in the road while you go on your merry way, aren't you?" she snapped at Randolph.

"Madam, the taking of a human life is never grounds for merriment," he answered calmly, "but in answer to your question, what would you have me do with him? I hardly think you want him riding in the coach with us, do you?"

"The least you could do is bury him!" the woman

retorted indignantly without a hint of uncertainty in her tone.

Randolph stared at her incredulously. "Look around you, madam!" he snapped. "Everything is solid rock, or very nearly so!"

Before the woman could frame her reply Frannie stepped between them. "You're from the East, aren't you?" she asked brightly. There was no need to wait for an answer; the expression on the matron's face was answer enough. "Out here, there isn't always time for the hoity-toity niceties you're used to back there. So I would be most pleased if you would close your mouth and get yourself in the coach so we can go on. I'm tired and dusty, I want to get home to a hot bath, and thanks to Mulcahey and his crew, we're now well behind schedule."

The woman's mouth came open, but before she could speak, Frannie cut her off. "MOVE!" the redhead barked. The startled matron spun and threw herself into the coach, nearly trampling her daughter in the process. "Thank you," Frannie said pleasantly. She turned to Randolph. "Shall we go?"

While the foregoing conversation was taking place, the stage driver dragged the dead outlaw out of the road and dumped him unceremoniously behind a large boulder. He brought back the outlaw's wallet and held it out to Frannie. "Miz Frannie, I'd appreciate it if you'd keep aholt of this until we get to town. The sheriff might want t'know who he's comin' out here after." Frannie took the wallet with a nod, and the driver climbed up to the box and gathered his reins while she and Randolph climbed inside. Randolph was still swinging the coach door closed as his trousers hit the seat, the driver's whip cracked and the coach lurched into motion.

The woman and her children were seated together on the rear seat, so Rand was "forced" to sit next to Frannie on the front, rear-facing seat, a hardship he managed to endure stoically, though hardship was probably not the right word to describe his current circumstances. He found himself intrigued by this woman who not only could shoot but was a gunsmith to boot. In the past he had always been attracted to women who were on the delicate side, much like his beloved wife; he now found himself surprisingly interested in someone who was the complete opposite. He glanced down at her left hand, checking for a wedding ring, but none was in evidence.

"What does your husband do, Missus Kinsella?" Randolph asked carefully.

"I asked you to call me Frannie," she replied with a smile.

"You said that your friends call you Frannie," Randolph answered with a small smile of his own. "I hardly think our acquaintance has been lengthy enough for us to be considered such."

"Anybody who handles a gun, and himself, the way you do, I consider a friend," Frannie answered with a saucy smile. "Just to be clear, my husband is dead. A horse rolled on him four years ago last April." Randolph's heart leapt, and Frannie must have seen something in his eyes. "Don't you be getting any ideas," she warned, her own emerald green eyes twinkling. "A lot of men have come around making calf eyes at me, and so far I've run them all off. They all seemed to be more interested in my shop than they were in me."

"Believe me, Frannie," Randolph assured her, "if I come around making 'calf eyes' at you, it won't be because of your shop." He immediately realized what he had said, and blushed while Fannie laughed.

"My smithy's on Church Street in Baker City," Frannie said simply, then turned her gaze out the window, allowing her embarrassed traveling companion a little time to regain his composure. The other woman and her children pointedly ignored the entire conversation. A few miles down the road, Randolph finally got himself reorganized enough to bring up one of the questions that had been in his mind since the attempted holdup. "Does that sort of thing happen often?" he asked Frannie.

"What, the holdup? Actually, that's the first time in quite a long time that the coach has been stopped on this trail that I can remember," she said. "The other attempted robbery was at one of the stations back down the line. A bunch of the local farm girls..."

"Farm girls?" Randolph interrupted in amazement.

"That's right, farm girls," Frannie chuckled. "But that one was supposedly broken up by a fellow traveling on that stage who said he was a federal marshal. He took an ax handle to the 'young ladies' and hauled them cussing and hollering back to their parents. Nobody got shot, but some of the girls had knots on their heads; so did the station's hostler. Or so the gossip goes."

"The gossip didn't happen to say what this federal marshal looked like, did it?" he asked innocently.

"Just that he was short and somewhat on the chubby side," Frannie answered. She misinterpreted the look on his face. "You're not..."

"Not what?" Randolph asked distractedly. Though he thought it odd that his deputy would 'take an ax handle' to a group of young girls, he would with-

90

hold judgment on the matter until he had a chance to talk to Bowie Tyler. "Pardon me for interrupting you once again, but I get the feeling that I may know that young man." He was not quite ready to let anyone know about the connection between Bowie and himself.

Frannie had a puzzled look on her face. "How could you possibly know him?" she asked quietly, gazing at Randolph with suspicion. "Who are you, anyway?" She sat back to wait for an answer; she got a question instead.

"You say I'm now a friend, and friends trust each other," he replied, looking intently into her piercing emerald eyes. "Can you trust me when I say that I can't tell you now, but that you have my word that you'll know everything soon?" He hoped, even prayed a little, that she would let the matter slide for the moment.

"I guess I can live with that," Frannie answered softly. "But I'm holding you to your word." The last part of their conversation had been in low tones, their words indistinguishable over the rattle of hardware and the creak of the leather thorough-braces. From the incensed look on the face of the woman seated across the coach, it was obvious that she didn't particularly care if she ever exchanged a spoken word with her fellow passengers again. Frannie's voice suddenly grew louder. "So, who did the work on your pistol?"

~*12*~

Late in the afternoon of his third day in Baker City, Bowie Tyler finally hit what he felt was, considering his lack of progress so far, pay dirt. After presenting his credentials to all and sundry in the Baker City police department and sheriff's office, Bowie had spent the first days of his time in Oregon rooting out information about the Martins from Daniel and Marta's neighbors. The night that Daniel and Marta had been abducted, an old woman who lived down the street from the Martins had heard her chickens raising a ruckus. A pack of stray dogs had been plaguing the birds recently; when she went out to run them off for the umpteenth time, she had seen a freight wagon just pulling away from the rear of the small frame house where the Martins lived. Several riders had accompanied the wagon.

"Are you some sort of lawman or something, young man?" she asked suspiciously as if suddenly realizing that she might be talking out of turn.

"Yes, ma'am, I am," Bowie answered with a disarming smile. "I work for Daniel Martin's father, who's a judge."

"I guess that's okay then. What else would you like to know?"

"Were there any kind of freight company markings on the wagon?" Bowie asked as the woman tried to recall the events of that evening.

"It really was getting too dark to tell," the matronly woman replied. After a moment she added, "It looked like it was tarped down tight, though, like they had something in there they didn't want getting away... or didn't want anybody to see."

"What about the men? Did you recognize any of them? How were they dressed?" Bowie shot questions at her in rapid-fire fashion, unable to believe his luck.

"I didn't recognize any of them," the woman replied patiently. "The driver was a burly fellow with chin whiskers, dressed like a miner. They were all pretty much dressed the same."

"Which way did they go?"

"The wagon turned and headed toward Main Street." The woman paused. "You know, that's a funny thing - when the wagon turned, those riders scattered. They didn't follow the wagon at all. Does this in any way help you with whatever you're doing, young man? I certainly hope so. The Martins are such nice people."

"It gives me a bit more to work with," Bowie answered thoughtfully. "And I thank you very much for the information, ma'am."

"You're very welcome, young man."

He ticked a finger to his hat brim, thanked her again and turned to go, striding rapidly toward Main Street. It was too late in the day now to try to follow the wagon's path even if he knew where it went, but at least now he had a little more to go on, including a description of one of the men. He would try canvassing some of the downtown businesses in the morning to see if anyone had seen a bearded miner driving a freight wagon. The woman had said that it was nearly dark when she

had seen the wagon, which would more than likely pre-
clude anyone from noticing it. It was a long shot, he
knew, but he might get lucky. He was relatively certain
someone had seen the wagon; he was just as certain
that there'd also be more than one wagon in town with
a bearded driver.

Early the next morning when he talked to the
owner of the business closest to the Martin's home, it
turned out that he had been clairvoyant.

"You can't be serious, young man!" Oliver Olson
exclaimed from his position behind the counter of Olson's Dry Goods. "Do you know how many freight wagons go by my windows on any given day, most of them
with tarped loads?" The merchant chuckled and said,
"I wish I could help you, but I just don't know. I may
have seen that wagon you're looking for, but it's just as
likely that I haven't, and you did say that the wagon left
in the dark."

"That's the kind of answer I expected," Bowie
sighed, frowning. "But I had to ask." He thanked the
proprietor and headed out the door to continue his
investigation along Main Street. When he finally returned to his hotel after dark, Bowie lay awake well into
the night trying to devise a plan; he finally settled on
renting a horse somewhere and riding out, circling the
town and inquiring about lone freight wagons driven
by bearded miners. He'd keep circling further and further out until he whittled the number of freight wagons
down to one -- if he ever did. He knew that such an endeavor was basically pointless, but it would allow him
to learn the layout of the surrounding area. He would
also use the time to discreetly gather more information
about Valentine's activities since arriving in Baker City.

~ ~ ~

Daniel was worried. While he and Marta were comfortable enough physically, the stress of not knowing why they had been imprisoned was taking its toll on even the ever-practical Marta. They had seen their captor only once, and that was on the day they had arrived at their current accommodations. Daniel had been wracking his brain ever since, trying to remember if he'd ever seen that imposing figure before. At the same time, he struggled with discerning why his own birth could possibly endanger him and his wife. Every time he tried to arrive at a logical explanation for their situation he drew a blank. Little did he know that deep, bitter emotion, rather than logic, had the most to do with their present state of affairs.

It was on the day that Bowie started his quest for the proverbial needle in a haystack that Daniel noticed something different about their accommodations. As he came from the facility behind the wooden door, his hand slipped off of the latch. Normally, the door swung shut slowly; this time, after a gradual start, it suddenly slammed into the frame with a surprisingly loud bang. Daniel and Marta were both startled and looked at each other in astonishment. "What in the world...?" Marta began. Daniel opened the door again. Releasing it resulted in the same loud boom.

"Something must have changed in the shaft below here," Daniel said. "Bring me the lamp, would you please?" Ever since the pair had been in residence here neither one had felt the slightest inclination to look below the wooden seat behind the door, other than to make sure that it was secure the first time one of them used it. Now it appeared that some further investigation was called for.

"Hold the door, would you, dear?" Daniel took the lamp from Marta as she grasped the door firmly. Daniel stepped inside and lowered the lamp as best he could through the opening in the wooden platform. He took in a deep breath and held it, then gingerly stuck his head into the hole as well. When he stood back up his face held a look of curious speculation.

"Well, what did you see?" Marta demanded.

"There's a horizontal shaft down there," he indicated with his empty hand. "I can't tell how big it is because it's too far down. It looks fairly big, though, and it seems to be the source of the breeze that is pulling the door shut." As he spoke, a muted rumble echoed from the shaft followed by a puff of dust that blew up and was quickly sucked back down.

"Apparently there is some sort of mining activity going on nearby," Marta said. "And if a breeze can make it through that tunnel you saw..."

"Maybe we can, too," Daniel finished. "The next question is, how do we get to the tunnel?"

Marta pondered the situation for a moment, then replied matter-of-factly, "We'll need to make a rope of some sort. Perhaps we can use the bedclothes. And we'll need some means of lighting the way once we get there. I really can't see us carrying this lamp, so we'll need some candles. We already have matches."

The sudden rattle of the lock on the outer door startled the couple out of their musings. Daniel hurriedly stepped away from the privy and set the lamp on the table as Marta slipped innocently into the chair next to him. Daniel picked up the pen he had been writing with before they made their discovery just as the door opened and Digger Hartley appeared with a cloth-covered pot in one hand and two bowls in the other, followed by another man carrying a pot of coffee and two heavy china mugs. A shotgun-armed guard stood in the doorway.

"Good Lord, not stew again!" Marta exclaimed in a disgusted tone. "Is that all you men know how to cook?"

"This ain't Delmonico's, lady," Digger growled as he unceremoniously slapped the food and the bowls on the table. "You'll just have to make do."

Marta glanced sideways at Daniel; instinctively he knew to let her run with whatever plan her agile mind had come up with, and he nodded almost imperceptibly. She pushed herself to her feet. "I wouldn't have to 'make do' if you men would let me do the cooking," Marta responded with icy acid in her voice. "I'm certain I could produce something much more appetizing than this swill you've been feeding us, unless, of course, your employer told you to torture us!"

Digger would gladly take on any man in a fight, fair or unfair, but he was at a loss as to how to handle the feisty woman glaring up into his face with her hands planted on her hips. As he had told Valentine, he wasn't entirely comfortable with the idea of holding a woman prisoner, and he for sure wasn't comfortable with the thought that she might be hurt in some way and that he'd be held responsible. Kidnapping would probably only get him thrown into prison, which was no big deal -- he could handle that. But hurting a woman of Marta's obvious quality would get his neck stretched, and Digger figured he was already tall enough. He folded without making the slightest attempt to dissuade her.

"No, we ain't supposed to torture you. We're just s'posed to keep you here." As he paused to consider his options Marta could almost see the frantic spinning of his brain reflected in his eyes. "I gotta' talk to the boss in a couple of days. I'll ask him. Now are you gonna' eat this or not?" He pointed at the pot.

"Yes, we'll eat it," Daniel said hurriedly. He'd been on the receiving end of Marta's sharp tongue before and he could see a possible opening they might be able to exploit, but he didn't want her words to slam shut the door of opportunity that looked to be swinging their way. He should have known Marta better. She simply nodded demurely, then sat down at the table as Digger and his companion made a hurried exit.

When the door was again locked and the sound of hurried footsteps had faded away, Daniel turned to Marta. She had a victorious smile on her face. "How did I do?" she asked.

"You were magnificent!" he declared. He leaned over and kissed her soundly.

~*13*~

Bowie had spent two long days from daylight 'til dark in the saddle of a livery horse that was nowhere near as good an animal as the sorrel horse he'd left at home. In fact, he ended each day with his legs as tired as if he'd been doing the walking himself, just from trying to kick the animal into some semblance of motion that would get him from one place to another in a reasonable amount of time. At the time that Bowie had rented the horse, the stableman had claimed that it was the best he or anyone else in town had. Since the stable was close to Bowie's hotel, the convenience at first seemed to make the lack of quality of the mount somewhat palatable. But no more; when he returned the horse to the livery at the end of the second day, he'd had enough. "I think it's time I either move along to a different stable, or you dig me up something with a little more gumption than this pile of soup bones," he informed the stable operator bluntly when he dismounted in front of the man's barn.

The liveryman began to protest, but Bowie ignored him. He'd seen a sign out at the edge of town advertising horses for rent, and what he'd seen in the corral there as he passed by looked a lot better than what he'd been riding. The stable was tucked out of the way along the creek that ran into Baker City from the southeast; he'd ridden out to the west the first day and had seen the sign only when he'd come back into town this evening. While this newly discovered establishment was further from his hotel than the current one, if he could get a better horse, it would be worth the extra walk. Besides, there might even be room in the hotel stable for another horse if he got one rented; he was darn sure going to check.

Bowie led the sorry excuse for a horse into a stall and stripped his gear while the stableman flapped along behind him, cackling querulously like a hen laying eggs. Tired of the racket, Bowie turned on his noisy assailant. "Did you ever read Shakespeare?" he asked conversationally, his calm demeanor belying the fact that his fondest wish was to punch the livery operator square in his long, pointed nose.

"What's that got to do with you talking down about my horses?"

"Because, in the words of that immortal Englishman, 'Me thinks thou dost protest too much'. Something along that line, anyway. In other words, after spending two days astride that rack of bones you rented me, I'm completely convinced that everything you've told me since I've been here is pure bunkum and I'm taking my business elsewhere." Bowie gathered his gear, pitched the man two dollars and stomped from the barn.

Once out on the street Bowie had a decision to make. If he went to the right he'd end up at his hotel. Left would take him to the stable along the creek. If he packed his saddle and things to the hotel, he'd just have to carry the whole works back in the morning when he went looking for a horse. If he went to the left he would

100

have to take his saddle with him, but if he could rent a horse he might be able to keep it at the hotel. At the worst he would have to leave his gear at the stable. So, left it would be.

By the time Bowie hiked the quarter mile to the sign next to the creek, it was full dark. He had a kink in his neck and an ache in his right elbow from hauling the saddle on his shoulder, and a knot on his head where the stock of the scabbarded Greener had belted him across the back of the skull when he hoisted the saddle across his back. There were no streetlights in this part of town, but the moon was nearly full and shed enough light for him to see the turnoff to the stable. He crossed the bridge over the creek, boot heels thumping a hollow cadence on the boards, and walked into the stable yard, where he was met by a ferocious-sounding shepherd dog whose tail was wagging furiously the whole time it was raising the alarm. Bowie set his saddle on the ground, knelt down and held out his hand for the dog to sniff. "Come here, fella," he said in a soothing tone. "I'm not here to steal your horses." The animal obviously didn't believe him because it didn't come any closer; neither did it cease raising a fuss. By the time Bowie got his feet back under him a man Bowie assumed was the dog's owner had come from the house nearby with a lantern in one hand and a shotgun in the other.

"Can I help you, mister?" A stocky individual whose whipcord britches were tucked into the tops of tall, highly polished Texas-heeled riding boots raised his voice to make himself heard over the incessant barking of the dog. The shotgun was pointed in Bowie's general direction, but not directly at him. "Shut up, Shep," the newcomer ordered sternly. Apparently sat-

101

isfied that it had done its duty, the pooch ceased barking and lay down alongside its owner's boots where it continued to regard the deputy suspiciously.

"Your sign out yonder says you rent horses," Bowie answered quickly. "Sorry I'm so late, but I just got done returning something that was supposed to be a horse to the livery down the road and thought maybe I could do better here."

The fellow snorted. "Damn straight you can do better here!" he declared confidently. "Old Man Tinker wouldn't know a good horse if it trotted up and nipped the end off that pointed snout of his." He chuckled. "Might make him sit up and take notice, though." He set the lantern on the ground and held out his hand for Bowie to shake. "I'm Marcus Tarrington. All my horses are Chandler stock, or at least the mares are. That's a name that's well known in these parts for good stock. Them mares and their colts run out yonder on the ridges along Deer Creek all summer, so they know rocks, timber, and mountains. That's some steep country, and you won't find a better mount anywhere."

"Bowie Tyler," the deputy replied as they shook hands. "And I know a man back home who says the same thing about his horses."

Tarrington chuckled again. "I reckon any man with good horses says the same. Not that it's any of my business, but where's home, if you don't mind my asking, that is?"

"Not at all. Currently I'm residing at the Antlers Hotel in beautiful downtown Baker City," Bowie answered. "But Wyoming, most days."

"You're a little ways from your bailiwick, ain't you?" Tarrington commented. Before Bowie could answer, the horseman went on. "But that ain't my business, I reckon. Let's go on out here and see if anything I've got strikes your fancy." He picked up his lantern and led the way to the nearby corral. "How much ground are you planning on covering, Mister Tyler?"

"Please, call me Bowie," the deputy returned. "Mister Tyler passed away some years ago. I'm really not sure how far I'm going to have to go, but if you've got something that travels good, I'd appreciate it."

They walked to the corral fence, where Tarrington lifted the lantern above his head so that the golden light glowed on the backs of the sleepily stirring horses; heads turned to regard this interruption of their evening's rest. "No offense intended, but just how good a rider are you, Bowie?" Tarrington questioned. "The reason I'm asking is, that sorrel there, hiding behind the rest of these nags, is a traveling fool, but he occasionally needs the kinks worked outta' him of a morning. Once he's going, he's got a jog that he can keep up all day long, and it's kind of like sitting in your mama's rocking chair." He stopped and regarded Bowie.

"Sounds like my kind of horse," Bowie replied. "I think I'll go in and say hello, if you don't mind."

"Be my guest," Tarrington said. The deputy bent down, took his rope from his saddle and shook out a loop. "You won't need that," the stable owner assured him. "All my horses are trained to stand and let a man walk up to them."

"Then it'll make a good halter," Bowie answered over his shoulder. He stepped into the corral and walked toward the sorrel. It was hard to tell for sure in the dim light, but the horse looked cleanly built, and its steps as it moved deeper into the herd were light and graceful. The gelding had a long, slim neck and delicate head, muscular hindquarters and legs built for power and speed. The closer he got to the animal the more Bowie liked the look of it. "I think you'll do just fine," Bowie crooned to the horse as he walked up and held out his hand for the horse to sniff. He stepped forward and ran his hand up its neck, then slipped the loop of rope over horse's head and twisted a small loop around its nose. The sorrel stood as if rooted to the ground, but when Bowie turned and walked toward the gate the lead never tightened. When Bowie moved, the horse moved, and when Bowie stopped the horse stopped.

Bowie took the rope off and walked back toward Tarrington. "I'll take him," he said. "How much?" After five minutes worth of good-natured dickering, they agreed on a price. Bowie shook Tarrington's hand to seal the deal.

"Have you got some place I can leave my tack? I don't want to pack it all the way to the hotel if I don't have to."

"Sure do. You can leave it in my saddle shed." Tarrington led the way to the log barn that made up one end of the long rectangular corral, where Bowie deposited his saddle and blankets on an empty rack and hung up his bridle. "You might want to leave the Greener, too," Tarrington suggested. "Folks in town are starting to think that they're civilized, and they might get excited if they see you carrying it down the street. It'll be safe enough in here. Shep'll make sure nobody steals it." He reached down and affectionately ruffled the shepherd's ears.

Reluctantly Bowie slid the shotgun back into the scabbard on the saddle and left the shed. He'd had that Greener a long time, and he'd hate to have anything happen to it, but the livery owner more than likely had the right of it. Tarrington swung the door shut and

104

slipped the pin into the hasp.

"I'll be here at daylight or shortly after," Bowie said as the two men shook hands. "Unless something comes up between now and then, that is." As he walked, Bowie found himself anticipating the morning and the possibility that the red horse might buck to start the day. It had been a while since a horse had challenged him, and he was actually looking forward to the possibility.

~14~

Stepping into the lobby of the Antlers Hotel after his long walk back to town, Bowie noticed the travel-weary gentleman standing at the front desk. Talking to the clerk with his back to the front door, the fellow seemed to be a stranger, but for reasons he couldn't identify, Bowie was sure he knew the man. He didn't recognize the clothing, but there was something about the way the newcomer carried himself that looked familiar. As Bowie stepped closer and heard the new arrival's voice, he stopped in his tracks, a shocked expression on his unshaven face. Judge Randolph Martin, dusty boots and sweat-stained gray hat belying his identity, appeared to be checking into the Antlers, and Bowie hadn't even known he was coming to Baker City.

Bowie eased back into the shadows beside a potted tree standing near the doorway, and waited for the fellow at the counter to turn away, in hopes of seeing his face and confirming the man's identity. But the down-turned brim of the gray hat kept the stranger's face shadowed, except for a brief glimpse of a stubbled chin when he bent to pick up the carpetbag sitting at his feet. The traveler turned away toward the stairs with the bag and a room key on a leather tag hanging from his left hand. His right hand unconsciously flicked the tail of his linen duster back and away from the old Colt holstered comfortably in front of his left hip.

Bowie waited for the figure to disappear up the stairs before he stepped out into the light. His sudden appearance startled the clerk. "Where'd you come from?!" he blurted out suddenly.

Bowie grinned at him. "It's a secret," he said brightly before dropping a serious expression over the humor. "I could tell you, but then..." He let the sentence trail off, then winked at the clerk and reached for the register. Before he could touch the book the clerk jerked it out from under his hand.

"That's private property!" the scrawny fellow declared tartly. "And we hold the privacy of our guests in the highest esteem!"

"Yeah, right. High enough esteem to leave the book out on the counter all day," Bowie answered derisively. "Just give it here." He held out his hand but the clerk drew back, taking the book with him, eying Bowie with hostility.

"Why do you want it?" the clerk asked in the tone of petty bureaucrats the world over.

Bowie glanced carefully over his shoulder, tipped his hat back off his head and leaned over the counter, crooking a finger and stage-whispering at the clerk, who leaned suspiciously forward. "Because I think the gent who just checked into your hotel may be a notorious killer who's wanted in at least seven states, that's why! And if he's who I think he is, I need to find out for sure so I can go get the Sheriff."

The clerk glared at Bowie for an interminable moment while he mulled over what he'd just heard; the tick of gears turning in the man's head was almost audible in the room. Finally he handed the book across the counter, then stood frowning at the deputy with his arms crossed on his chest.

Bowie flipped through the pages to the last line, saw that the latest signature was indeed that of his boss and closed the book with a snap that made the clerk jump. Bowie dropped the register on the counter with a thump, rattling the pen and inkwell in their holders, and turned away. "Nope, ain't him," he said back over his shoulder. He started for the stairs, grinning to himself. He heard a derisive snort from behind him and he chuckled under his breath.

At the top of the stairs Bowie turned left and headed down the hall to Room Twelve, the number that had been written in the book. As he knocked on the thin panel, the sound of movement inside ceased and a familiar-sounding voice asked cautiously, "Who is it?"

"Bowie Tyler."

Chair legs scraped, the latch rattled, then the door opened a crack and an eye peered cautiously around the edge of the opening. When Judge Martin recognized Bowie, he stepped back and swung the door wide. "Come in, come in," he invited his deputy into his room warmly. "I was going to attempt to find you tomorrow, but you appear to have saved me a search." He slid the Colt in his right hand into the holster on the dresser, then stuck the hand out to Bowie. As they greeted each other Bowie started to speak, but Randolph stopped him. He'd seen the deputy looking at his gun.

"This must come as a bit of a surprise to you, I imagine."

"You could say that," Bowie commented wryly. The Judge went on to relate the details of the last letter

108

he'd received from Cyrus Valentine, and how he had been ordered to travel to Baker City where he was to wait for further instructions.

"I don't know how or when I'll be contacted," Judge Martin finished. "Valentine didn't say which hotel to select, but this one was recommended to me by Frannie..." He saw Bowie's eyebrows lift in surprise; clearing his throat sheepishly, he continued quickly. "The lady in question is a gunsmith here in Baker City. She has a shop on Church Street. I met her on the stage from Kelton and only learned of her profession during the holdup."

"Okay, now I'm really confused!" Bowie exclaimed. "What holdup?"

Martin hurriedly gave him a sketchy account of the holdup, finishing abruptly. "I would have made it to the hotel much sooner, but we were at the Sheriff's office for quite a while." He gazed steadily at Bowie with a knowing look. "What do you have to report? I believe I heard something about another holdup, this one involving several young women..."

Bowie's face turned red and he shuffled his feet. "Uh, well, yeah, there was an attempted holdup, but, well, they didn't get away with it, so..."

Judge Martin burst out laughing. "Don't worry about it, Bowie. I'm sure that you did what you thought was best under the circumstances. Just make sure that you turn in a report when you get back to Laramie."

Relief spread across Bowie's face. "I haven't found out a whole lot about your son's disappearance so far," he said after a moment. "I did finally run across one witness who claims to have seen a tightly-covered wagon with a bunch of outriders in the area of your son's house the evening that he was supposed to have disappeared, but the riders scattered and the wagon blended into the usual traffic. I've been riding circles around the town asking questions for the last couple of days, and I'm pretty sure that the wagon went southeast or east, but that covers a lot of ground. I've also found out a fair amount about Valentine's activities in the area, a little at a time. He doesn't seem to leave town much. I really need to find somebody I can talk to about him in detail." He looked up from where he'd been studying the holstered pistol on the dresser top.

"That's something," Martin responded quietly. "I don't really expect Valentine to contact me any time soon, because he wants me to suffer from not knowing where Daniel and Marta are, or if they're even still alive, though I feel sure that they are. He probably has spies everywhere, but I'm hoping he doesn't know about you yet. You're my ace in the hole, so to speak."

"How will I know when he contacts you?" Bowie asked. "I'm assuming that you're planning on me following you to whatever meeting place Valentine comes up with, right?"

The Judge thought for a minute before he said, "We'll use Frannie's shop for a message drop."

"That should work," Bowie answered. "You said her shop's on Church Street, right?" Martin nodded. "In that case it shouldn't be too hard to find. After all, how many lady gunsmiths can there be in a town this size?"

With business mostly taken care of, Bowie finally had to ask. "What's with the range clothes and the pistol, Judge? And can you really use that hogleg?"

"I'm a little rusty, but I can use it," the Judge replied coolly. He had neglected to tell Bowie about the man he'd shot during the holdup, only saying that the holdup had been unsuccessful; he didn't go into detail now. "And Bowie, please call me Rand..."

"But sir..."

Rand lifted his right hand, requesting silence from his deputy. "Please hear me out. I know that I have not encouraged familiarity in our relationship in the past, and when we are in my courtroom I will require the same formality as before. But here, and now, you are the only one of us who holds any kind of jurisdiction; I am nothing more than a worried father who hopes to get his family back unharmed."

Bowie mulled over Rand's words for a few seconds before smiling and sticking out his hand. "Since you put it that way..." The two men shook hands for probably the first time in their relationship.

Rand glanced wistfully down at his worn but comfortable shirt and britches. "I wore these clothes, or others just like them, for several years. As amazing as you may find it to be, before I became a judge I carried a badge just like the one you have in your pocket."

Bowie digested this unexpected bit of information for a few moments. "Sir, I mean Rand, I believe that you could do pretty much whatever you set your mind to." He gestured toward Rand's gun belt. "May I?"

"Be my guest."

Bowie slipped the Colt from the holster, swiftly unloaded it and laid the cartridges near the holster. He flipped the loading gate shut, worked the action a few times, reloaded the pistol and slid it back into the leather. "Whoever worked on that gun knew what he was about!" Bowie declared appreciatively.

"It was a factory job," Rand replied. "I sent it back to Connecticut to the manufacturer to have the work done on it. I've thought about replacing it a time or two with a larger caliber, but it fits my hand so well that I really hate to do it. Unless..." His voice trailed off as an idea came to him. "Maybe I need to go see Frannie tomorrow," he mused.

The tall, mahogany-cased Blaisdell clock in the lobby below struck the hour of nine, the chimes echoing faintly up to the two men. "I reckon I'd best get to my own room and get some sleep," Bowie said, yawning. "It's been a long day. I'll find that shop tomorrow, and I'll check with your lady every day until you hear something."

Rand stood up from his seat on the bed and put out his hand, pointedly ignoring Bowie's "your lady" comment. He was thoughtful as they shook hands. "Thanks again for your help, Bowie."

"You're welcome, sir."

"I told you..." Rand began.

"I know, I know, but it's taking a little bit to get used to calling you something besides 'boss'. You'll just have to bear with me until I get it right, if I ever do. It's kinda' hard to teach old hound dogs new tricks, ya' know, and right at the moment I'm dog-tired."

Bowie listened at the door for a moment before he slipped out into the silent hallway and turned toward his room. Rand watched him walk away, then closed the door behind him, sank down on the bed and scrubbed his hands over his haggard face. Stiff bristles rasped across his palms. *Better find a barber tomorrow*, he thought fleetingly. With his hands still covering his face he closed his eyes and bowed his head.

"Lord, please help me get my family back," he prayed silently, earnestly. "And please watch over them and protect them while you do. Amen."

~15~

After her confrontation with Digger Hartley, Marta took over cooking for the few men who were at what Daniel had come to think of as "the prison camp". As a result, the quality and variety of the food improved considerably. She even managed to convince Digger to bring in some eggs so she could make a cake. Just before the end of the war, Daniel had seen Elmira Prison in New York up close, and knew that their present quarters were a great deal more comfortable than any offered to the Confederate prisoners of war there; still, the captivity was galling. It was especially so because there was seemingly nothing Daniel could do to remedy the situation. He had forsworn violence when he became a man of the cloth; he had seen enough of "man's inhumanity to man" during the war to last him a lifetime. And because he was at a loss as to how he and Marta could escape without violence, he was forced to sit and do nothing.

Daniel had always been a man of the outdoors. He had grown up in the towns of the burgeoning Wyoming territory, but loved the mountains and wild country. In his early teens he had befriended an old man who lived in a cabin on the outskirts of South Pass City and who claimed to have trapped beaver alongside

Jim Bridger and Kit Carson. Whether or not his stories were true, the old man's brain contained a fountain of knowledge about the ways of the wild creatures and how to survive away from civilization, and Daniel had drunk deep from that fountain. He felt sure that if he could only get Marta and himself free from the trap they were in, he could lead them safely home, no matter where they were: he just needed the chance. And so Daniel paced the confines of his prison, doing whatever he could think of to keep himself physically as well as mentally prepared to take advantage of whatever opportunity might come his way.

The key rattled in the rusty lock and the door swung open, lifting Daniel from his frustrating meditations. Marta strode into the room, as regal in her bearing as any queen, and Daniel was struck once again by the radiance her pregnancy lent to her face. Hers was not the classic beauty of poem and song; her nose was the tiniest bit crooked, the result of a fall from an apple tree as a child, and her chin was perhaps too square. Instead, in Daniel's mind, the glow on her face carried her beyond such earthbound terms. One of the guards followed her dutifully into the room, carefully balancing a small coffeepot and the simple wooden tray that held their evening meal in his hands. The only utensils they were allowed were forks and spoons and one extremely dull table knife. It would be a relatively simple thing to overpower that guard, but the shadow crossing the lintel from outside reminded Daniel that, as usual, Marta's porter wasn't alone. One of his cronies was just outside the door with a shotgun.

When Daniel stood up from his seat on the bunk against the wall, the guard stopped moving and gave him a hard stare. "You just stay right there, mister, or

114

else..." the guard began harshly. His obedience to the preacher's wife didn't extend to the preacher himself.

"Or else what?" Marta demanded as she turned on the guard with her hands on her hips. "You'll shoot him? Or have your cohort shoot him, since you don't have a gun? I don't think that would endear you to your employer. And besides, your hands are full." She strode haughtily over to Daniel's side, then turned and pointed at the table. "You may put our dinner down and go. And you might want to remember this, my uncouth friend: if you lay a hand on my husband, I will take my leave of the kitchen and you men will be left to fend for yourselves once again. Now, be gone with you!" She gestured imperiously at the door. The grumbling guard set the tray on the table, hurried from the room and slammed the door. The key rattled in the lock again and two sets of footsteps faded from earshot.

"The female of the species is obviously the more dangerous," Daniel chuckled. Marta gave him a bright smile.

"I do believe you may be right," she answered confidently. "Or at least that fellow thinks so. Why don't we eat before the food gets cold?" Daniel seated Marta, asked the Lord's blessing on the meal and picked up his fork.

"Tonight is the night," Daniel told Marta when they had finished eating. "We're leaving as soon as someone comes and picks up the tray. That way, we'll have until they come to get you to cook breakfast to get ahead of them." She nodded wordlessly. Practical sort that she was, she knew that if their captivity went on for much longer, her condition wouldn't allow them to escape, and under no circumstances would she even consider allowing her baby to be born in a dirty, drafty cave without any sort of medical care available. Such a thing didn't merit consideration. In addition, she had lately been having trouble with her balance, and her back ached constantly. Moreover, she was fairly convinced that she was carrying twins who occasionally had vehement disagreements with one another.

Their guard took away the supper tray and locked their door. Daniel waited thirty nervous minutes, as indicated by the slowly moving hands of his gold-cased hunter watch, before he lifted up the thin mattress on their bunk and removed the rope he had painstakingly pieced together from shorter sections that Marta had managed to smuggle in. Marta went to the door to keep watch. She listened at the barred window for several minutes, then looked over at Daniel and nodded. There was no sound outside the door except the chirping of the last few birds of the waning evening.

Daniel strode quickly across the narrow expanse of floor to the table, turned it on edge and put all his weight on one of the upper legs. The leg, made from a pine pole four inches through, had been clumsily tapered and pegged into a hole bored into the underside of the tabletop. The table leg broke with a sharp crack and Daniel flinched, waiting for a shout from outside, but none came. Step one of their escape plan was the loudest and therefore the most likely to be detected. He and Marta smiled nervously at one another as he moved on to step two.

Daniel went to the door of the improvised privy, pulled it open, and wedged it in place with a chip of rock from the edge of the shaft. The door was hinged such that it would for all practical purposes fold back

116

against the wall. He lifted the seating platform out of its chipped-out shelf and set that aside. Tying their rope to the center of the former table leg, Daniel laid the leg across the door opening.

Marta hurried to their bunk and pulled a pack she had smuggled from the kitchen building from its hiding place against the rock wall. The pack held several small candles, a container of matches, a small canteen of water and a packet of what she thought of as "only if we get desperate" rations; hardtack and jerked beef did not a banquet make, in her opinion. She went to where Daniel waited; it was only when she stood at the opening in the rock that her resolve momentarily wavered.

"Are you sure that we have to go down there?" she asked uncertainly.

"Only if we want to leave this place. I don't see any other way past the guards," Daniel answered soberly. She looked up at him and he gave her what he hoped was an encouraging smile. She sighed as she returned his smile with a rueful one of her own.

"I suppose you're right," she said. "I shouldn't be so squeamish, I know..."

"You'll be fine," Daniel assured her. He leaned forward to kiss her on the forehead. "Just don't think about it." He bent and picked up the rope. He had tied a loop in the end of it big enough to encircle Marta under her arms and padded it with strips torn from one of their blankets. There were knots evenly spaced along the length of the rope for handholds.

The day before, Daniel had lowered the rope down toward the side tunnel they had seen earlier. The rope was just long enough to let them reach the dark opening. He would put the loop around Marta and lower her down to the tunnel; once she was securely in the crosscut, he would climb down to her. He desperately wished that they could put everything back in place and make their escape a mystery, but he realized that their guards were going to know how they had left anyway, because the outside door would still be locked. This would instantly be seen as the only possible exit they could have taken.

Daniel looped the rope around his wife and guided her to the edge of the opening. The air flowing down into the vertical shaft fluttered the skirt of her dress and teased fine wisps of her hair around her ashen cheeks. She looked down and shivered.

Daniel turned her to face him and gently lifted her chin until their eyes met. "Do you trust me?" he asked softly.

"Yes, my love," she answered softly, her resolve strengthening. He bent his head and kissed her soft lips.

"Then I do believe that all that's left is to go."

"I do believe you're right," she replied firmly. She locked her eyes on his and stepped cautiously back. Daniel belayed the rope across his back and braced himself. Her weight settled on the rope; he lowered her slowly down the shaft, only now realizing what a hindrance the knots he had tied in the rope were going to be.

Marta reached the level of the crosscut. She was relieved to see that there was no barricade across the opening. "That's far enough," she called. "But you'll have to swing me over to it." In response, Daniel carefully shifted his footing and used his legs to begin to swing the rope back and forth.

Daniel felt Marta's weight lift from the rope at

the same time that he heard her say, "I'm there." He breathed a heartfelt sigh of relief as he stood up straight and stretched. He had been more worried than he let on about lowering Marta down the shaft. She wasn't especially heavy, but his anxiety at sending his beloved wife and their unborn child into the unknown at the end of a pieced-together tether was taxing both physically and mentally.

Daniel picked up their pack of supplies and slung it around his neck. He tugged on the anchor across the door opening, judged it to be solidly in place, then took a firm grip on the rope and began to climb down the shaft. He leaned back on the rope and braced his feet against the rock, moving slowly and carefully, hand over hand, down to the tunnel where Marta waited.

When he came even with the crosscut he found that he was too far away to step from the wall of the shaft to the tunnel floor. He began to work his way sideways, pushing with his toes on small protrusions in the rock wall while keeping his weight back against the rope. He was nearly to the tunnel mouth when he heard a scraping sound from above and the rope suddenly shifted. Adrenaline flooded his system and he lunged for his only refuge just as the table leg that had been his anchor broke loose and plummeted down the vertical shaft toward him.

Daniel crashed to the rough stone of the tunnel floor on his chest with his legs dangling down the shaft behind him. The impact drove the breath from his lungs and he lay stunned until the sudden swat of the table leg across the seat of his trousers galvanized him into scrambling the rest of the way into the tunnel. "Was that part of your plan?" his wife asked, her smile bright in the dim tunnel.

"Not especially," he answered, rubbing his behind where the table leg had struck.

He kept a tight grip on the rope as he dropped down to sit against the wall, waiting for the table leg to come to the end of its tether. The rope jerked tight, nearly pulling out of his hand, and the pine pole clattered against the side of the shaft. Daniel pulled rope and table leg back up, hand over hand. They might need the rope, and the table leg could come in handy as well. At the exact moment that the chunk of pine reached the mouth of the tunnel, a loud bang from overhead echoed the length of the shaft, and their world went completely dark.

~16~

Bowie was up with the first rooster's crow the next morning. He went down the stairs, through the deserted hotel lobby and out into the street. The only thing moving was a fat gray tomcat that scampered across the alley in front of Bowie as the deputy turned toward Tarrington's place, anticipation quickening his step. At the corral yard he greeted Shep, who stood back and barked at him until his master came out of the house, carrying a cup of coffee. The smell of frying bacon drifting on the morning breeze made Bowie's stomach rumble. "Mornin', Bowie," Tarrington greeted him. "You weren't kidding about being here at daylight, were you?" He smiled and handed Bowie a halter. "Here you go, my friend. I reckon it's hero time." He took a seat on a nearby block of wood to watch the show he knew was coming.

"I reckon you're right," Bowie answered with a grin as he strolled into the corral and walked up to the sorrel horse. "Morning, fella," he greeted the gelding merrily. He slipped the halter over the animal's nose and tied it behind the upright ears, then turned to lead the cayuse out of the corral. He tied the sorrel to a post while he went to get his gear. The red horse stood stock still as Bowie cinched the saddle in place and slipped the bit into its mouth, then followed obediently when Bowie led it away from the fence.

"Are you sure you don't wanna' do this inside a corral?" Tarrington questioned.

"Yeah, I'm sure," Bowie answered confidently. He snugged up the cinch, gathered the reins and stepped into the saddle. The sorrel stood quietly, head drooping and ears flat like it was almost asleep. Bowie looked over at Tarrington and said, "This horse is..." Before he could finish whatever he was going to say, he felt the horse suck in a deep breath and its muscles bunch; like a shot, a thousand pounds of horseflesh went straight in the air to twist sideways and swap ends, coming down looking out across the creek.

Bowie's right boot blew out of the stirrup with that first great leap, and it was only by taking a death grip on the saddle horn with one hand while he tried to keep his reins gathered with the other that he managed to stay in the saddle long enough for his foot to catch the flailing stirrup and slide back into place. With both feet solidly in the stirrups, Bowie let out a hoop and sank his heels into the horse's flanks, at which point the party really began; the sorrel was just waiting for some encouragement.

With a squall, Red took the bit in his teeth and threw his nose toward the ground, looking to get some slack in the reins. He expected Bowie to try to yank his head back up like most of his riders did when he swallowed the bit that way. Red would let them pull his head up and would follow it up high, rearing up on his hind feet, which unseated the majority of his riders as they ducked away from the hard skull that was right in front of their faces. But Bowie fooled him; instead, the heavyset deputy fed the gelding more rein, then buried

122

his heels in the big horse's ribs with enough force to make it grunt. One long jump later Red's head came up, and Bowie collected the reins, then yanked Red's nose toward his left knee. But the sorrel knew that one: he threw his hindquarters around to the right, following his nose and nearly unseating Bowie and dropping him into the well. Bowie stood up in his right stirrup and shifted his considerable weight to the outside to counter the motion, in the process relaxing his grip on the reins enough for Red to get his head back. The sorrel immediately went to pitching, sun-fishing and belly-rolling until Bowie wasn't sure where he was or which way he was heading; it was all he could do to stay in the middle of the hurricane deck of the saddle. He could vaguely hear Red's owner whooping and hollering, but he didn't know if the man was cheering on the horse, or the man on his back.

With one last squall and twist, Red suddenly stopped bucking and stood still with his sides heaving and sweat dripping from all over. Bowie was breathing just as hard as the horse and his nose was bleeding a little, but he was smiling like a madman. "I hope he doesn't do that every morning, but damn, that was fun!" Bowie yelled.

Tarrington walked up to man and horse, grinning broadly. "I told you he'd be a handful! He more than likely won't do that every day, but he can damn sure wake you up in the morning. Do you still want him?"

"If he travels the way he bucks, I might even buy this brute if he's for sale!" Bowie answered emphatically. He reached down and patted the sweaty shoulder. "This is pretty much of a horse!"

"That he is!" Tarrington declared proudly. "And

he'll get you from here to there and back again more than once." He grinned again and said, "Oh, by the way, his name's Redondo. Don't ask me why, I just like the sound of it. I generally just call him Red." He grinned once more. "Kind of fits, don't it?"

Bowie swung down and led Red to the side of the saddle shed where he'd left his Greener. His legs were shaking from the residual adrenaline in his system, but he was still grinning as he reached up and shoved the shotgun down into the scabbard under the offside stirrup leather. He swung back aboard the sorrel. "I reckon I'll see you later. I may see about stabling him at the hotel, so don't worry if I don't bring him back tonight."

"That'll be fine, Bowie. Adios."

"Adios." Bowie turned Red and crossed the stream, turning him towards the east to follow the wagon road that ran beside the creek.

~ ~ ~

Tarrington was right on the money about Red, Bowie decided. The gelding could cover country, and was about as smooth to ride as any horse Bowie had ever been on. Few men in the west had the time to do more than just break a horse; even fewer had the time to train a horse like Red. Out here, most folks were so busy making a living that once a horse was broke to the point that it wouldn't kill its rider and could be steered more or less in the right direction, it was good enough. Any further polishing the animal got came while it was working. But Red had obviously been well trained by someone who cared about horses.

124

Over the previous two days of fruitless search- ing Bowie had pretty much convinced himself that the wagon he was looking for had left Baker City via the road he was following now. The problem he had was that houses -- and therefore possible witnesses -- thinned out rapidly in that direction. While this made it easier on the kidnappers, it was a lot harder on their pursuer. He had ridden several miles and was nearly to the shallow canyon where Sutton Creek came down from the mountains when he was suddenly struck by a thought which for some reason hadn't crossed his mind before.

"What about Valentine?" Bowie addressed the horse as he reined him in. The gelding didn't answer as it switched a fly from its flank with its long tail. Over the years, Bowie had gotten in the habit, like many western men, of talking to his horse. He'd found that it often helped him get his thoughts straight. "Would Valentine go where Daniel is? And if he did, how would he travel?" Bowie turned Red back toward Baker City, mentally kicking himself for not asking those questions sooner. He would find the gun shop which Rand had mentioned, and leave a message there for him. After leaving the message, Bowie would stay where he could keep an eye on Valentine and follow the lawyer if he left town. The lawyer had caused the Martins to be kid- napped in the first place, and Bowie was sure that Val- entine would want to gloat over their plight if he was able. Doing so in person was always better than from a distance, and that meant traveling to wherever he had arranged to have the Martins held.

Based on Bowie's newly acquired knowledge of the Baker City area, there were two means of transpor- tation Valentine would probably use, either horse or carriage. It was Bowie's opinion that as a lawyer, Valentine would be more inclined toward traveling by carriage. So the next order of business would be to find out if Valentine had a carriage at his disposal. He nudged Red into a trot.

~ ~ ~

Rand stepped out onto the boardwalk in front of the Antlers Hotel. He was dressed this morning in more refined style than the faded trail garb he had worn on the stage. Today his starched white shirt shone in the morning sun where his tailored canvas range jacket hung open. He had taken the time to brush the dust from his boots and hat, and his gray wool trousers covered his boot tops. A dark blue silk scarf was knotted loosely around his throat. He could easily have been mistaken for a prosperous cattle buyer; in spite of his reason for being in Baker City, he welcomed this new sense that he was worlds away from his seat on the bench of the territorial court. He breathed deeply of the crisp morning air, pushing his anxiety over his family to the back of his mind until such time as he was able to act.

The fingers of his right hand briefly touched the butt of his crossdraw Colt where it nestled unobtrusively under the tail of his jacket, making sure it was secure, but not so secure that he couldn't draw it easily if need be. He was under no illusions that he was even remotely fast on the draw after all the years that had passed since he carried a gun for a living, but then Baker City didn't seem to be an especially dangerous place. On the other hand, he knew he had enemies here, and he also knew that once it was in his hand, that Colt would hit what he wanted it to hit; while that wasn't particularly reassuring, it would have to do.

"Pardon me, sir." Rand touched the sleeve of a well-dressed fellow who had just exited Peter Barstow's hardware store on Main Street carrying a paper-wrapped parcel tucked under his left arm.

"Yes?"

"I'm very sorry to bother you, but could you please tell me where I might find a gun shop? I believe I've heard of one that's run by a woman?"

"Indeed there is, friend. She's quite talented, in fact. Quite good-looking as well," the gentleman replied with a sly smile. "You'll need to go to Church Street. Go three blocks that way," he indicated the direction with a lift of his chin, "turn left across Main Street and you'll find Missus Kinsella's shop on the left some six blocks along. You can't miss it." Ignoring the man's comment about Frannie's beauty with an effort Rand politely thanked his benefactor for his kindness, then began to stroll slowly in the appropriate direction.

Half a block ahead, a neatly painted sign advertising "Worst Food in Town" hung over the walk. He hadn't had breakfast, and was so intrigued by the sign that he stepped into the establishment when he got to the door. Inside, the long narrow room was packed with bodies, and the rattle of flatware and the mixture of voices and accents echoed loudly from the whitewashed plank walls. Several ladies wearing food-stained white aprons dashed between two rows of tables, picking up dirty dishes and empty food platters and replacing them with full platters of bacon or biscuits, and bowls of gravy. Blue enamelware coffeepots in the hands of the eaters splashed hot Arbuckle's into a motley collection of heavy mugs and occasionally onto the surfaces of the oilcloth-covered tables.

One of the serving women, a pretty blonde clad in blue gingham, checked her headlong pace long enough to tell Rand, "Four bits, all you can eat, seat yourself and leave the money on the table when you're done," before she was off again. Rand saw an opening at one of the tables and wound his way in that direction, dodging a coffeepot and a platter of bacon along the way. He sat down as a plate and fork appeared over his shoulder to land with a thump and clatter on the table, followed by a chipped ceramic mug. The food smelled delicious and his stomach rumbled to let him know that it was way past time to snag a passing biscuit and to get down to business, which he immediately did.

Afterward, in the relative silence of the morning street, Rand took an ivory toothpick from his pocket and stood for a moment cleaning his teeth under the "Worst Food in Town" sign. *That is quite an interesting advertising gimmick,* he thought with a smile. It certainly seemed to have brought in the customers who, once seated, soon found to their delight that the sign had lied. Or at least it had lied as far as Rand was concerned. He stifled a belch as he stepped out to find Church Street and Frannie Kinsella's gun shop.

~ ~ ~

At the same time that Rand was sitting down

to breakfast, Bowie tied Red to the ring embedded in the granite post standing sentinel at the edge of the street in front of Frannie's shop on Church Street, then strode to the door. A small, elegantly painted sign on the barred door instructed all and sundry to *"Come on in. Push hard, the door sticks"*. He grinned and shoved his way inside. A small bell tinkled overhead, catching the attention of the lovely red-haired woman behind the glass-fronted counter that divided her work area from the rest of the room. She lifted her eyes from the dismantled rifle on her work table to look questioningly at the new arrival.

"Hello. Can I help you with something?"

"I hope so, ma'am," Bowie answered. "A friend of mine said he'd be by here sometime today or tomorrow, and that I could leave a message here for him. Maybe you know him?"

"Am I supposed to guess his name, or are you going to tell me?" she asked, a tiny smile tugging at her lips.

"Sorry, ma'am," Bowie replied with a sheepish grin. "His name's Rand. Rand Martin."

"As a matter of fact, I do expect a man by that name to come by." *Now I know his last name,* she thought with satisfaction. "What's the message?"

Bowie handed her a small envelope with Rand's name written on the outside. The envelope's flap was tucked in. The lady 'smith eyed the envelope. "Don't you trust me?" she asked tartly.

"Begging your pardon, ma'am," Bowie answered politely, "but I don't believe I know you that well yet." He gave her a bright smile to take some of the sting from his words and got an approving smile in return. He felt like he'd just passed a test of some sort.

"I do believe I could learn to like you, Mister..."

"Tyler, ma'am. Bowie Tyler."

"And I am Missus Frannie Kinsella."

"Pleased to make your acquaintance, ma'am."

"Say, you wouldn't be the 'unnamed gentleman' who 'foiled the daring daylight robbery of the North-west Stage Company coach' recently, would you?" Frannie suddenly asked, her green eyes twinkling mischievously. "You fit the description I got from the stage driver perfectly."

"If you mean the one those girls tried to rob, yes, ma'am, that was me." Bowie's ears turned red. "It didn't amount to anything, really, except for the hostler getting a knot on his noggin," he went on.

"But it could have ended quite badly, if not for you," Frannie replied.

"Shucks, ma'am, they really didn't have a clue what they were doing. That newspaper fella got a little carried away."

Frannie considered his words for moment. "Now I'm sure I like you!" she declared. She tucked Bowie's note to Rand away in a pocket of the protective leather apron she wore. "I'll see that Rand gets this. Is there anything else I can do for you?"

"I don't believe so..." When he paused Frannie gave him a quizzical look. "On second thought, maybe there is something," he said after a moment. "I wonder if I could ask you a few questions, about the town and all?"

"Go right ahead, Mister Tyler."

"I guess the first thing to ask is, who's the power in town?" She looked at him thoughtfully while she considered her answer.

"I'm going to assume that you're not talking

about the mayor and the town council," Frannie said, musing. Her voice rose slightly. "In that case, it would have to be Willie Morgan, Nolan Cashman, and Zeno Wilson. They own most of the saloons around town, plus a number of other businesses. Wilson also owns several gold claims out in Auburn Gulch." It was obvious to Bowie from her expression that she didn't approve of Zeno Wilson. It was equally obvious to her that those weren't the names Bowie expected to hear.

"What about lawyers?" he asked.

"Morgan's a lawyer," she answered. She studied his expression for several seconds, watching the play of his thoughts across his features. She suddenly felt that she knew what his questions were about. "But he's not the one you're thinking of, is he?" Bowie shook his head.

"Has anyone come to town recently?"

Frannie snorted in a decidedly unladylike fashion. "This was a new gold camp not too long ago, relatively speaking," she retorted. "It still is, after a fashion. The population around here can change more often than most of the residents change their socks. Would you care to narrow that down a bit?"

"Have any new lawyers hung out their shingle lately?"

"What do you mean by lately?"

"Say, the last month or so, maybe two months?"

"Why don't we stop beating around the bush?" Frannie demanded sharply. "I believe you have someone particular in mind, so why don't you just come out with it? I have a business to run, you know."

"Does the name Cyrus Valentine ring a bell?" Bowie asked, chagrined that she had seen through him so easily. *Some detective you are, Tyler*, he thought

131

ruefully.

Again, the disgusted snort: "That scoundrel! He's been in Baker City for roughly six months, and I assure you, he's no one's favorite shyster. He's free with his money, which gets him invited to the occasional society soiree, where he makes a big deal out of being crippled and tries to make everyone think he's the epitome of honesty, but the man's a snake. I do my best to ignore him."

She didn't mention that when he first came to town, Valentine had made some unwelcome advances to her and been rebuffed; or that he had afterward done his best to have her evicted from her shop. Because she owned, free-and-clear, the property the shop sat on, his efforts had been unsuccessful. "What is your interest in Cyrus Valentine?"

"I'd rather not say at the moment, if you don't mind," Bowie answered reticently. "Suffice it to say I need to find out as much about the man as I can, as quickly as I can."

"As a matter of fact, I do mind, and I would very much appreciate it if you would be honest with me, Mister Tyler!" Frannie snapped, her quick Irish temper beginning to flare. "I believe I have a right to know why you're asking so many questions." Green fire flashed in her eyes.

Reluctantly, Bowie reached into his vest and brought his Deputy Marshal's badge briefly into view. "I'm a U.S. Marshal working on a case," he answered stiffly. "I'd prefer that nobody else knows what I'm about."

Now that Bowie had admitted what she'd already heard from the stage driver, Frannie visibly forced her temper to cool. "Why didn't you say so to start with?"

132

she queried. "It would have made things easier for both of us, don't you think?"

"Yes, ma'am, in this case it probably would have done exactly that," he answered ruefully. "I'm just not in the habit of letting folks know I'm a lawdog," he went on by way of apology.

"I can see your point," Frannie replied. "Please accept my apology for taking your head off a moment ago."

"No apology necessary, ma'am. Now if we could maybe start over?"

"Certainly, Deputy. What else can I help you with?"

"I'm assuming that Mister Valentine has an office somewhere here in town?"

"I'd say so. It's right on Main Street. You can't miss it. You do know where Main Street is, right?" She grinned at him archly.

"Hey, I've been busy outside of town," Bowie protested with a grin. "But yes, I think I can find Main Street. It's that big expanse of dirt with the ruts in it that runs through the middle of town, right?"

"Go on with you, Deputy," Frannie chuckled. "I've got work to do. If I see your friend, I'll give him your message."

~17~

Having taken his time with breakfast, Rand now strolled along Church Street, enjoying the chance to stretch his legs and get some fresh air after spending the previous five days sitting on his backside in train cars and stagecoaches. The sign on Frannie's door brought a smile to his lips-- as it had Bowie's-- as he pushed his way inside. "I thought you might be here this morning," Frannie greeted him with a warm smile.

Startled, Rand asked, "What gave you that idea?"

"Oh, I don't know," the red-haired gunsmith replied with a saucy grin. "Maybe it was the 'calf eyes'."

Rand blushed mightily. "Madam, I assure you that I've outgrown making 'calf eyes' at anyone, let alone someone I just met a few days ago!" He sounded so stuffy that after her initial flash of stunned surprise, Frannie burst out laughing. Rand stood stoically indignant for a moment, then suddenly joined her, his face turning redder still.

When their laughter subsided Rand commented sheepishly, "That did sound a bit pompous, didn't it?"

"It certainly did," Frannie answered with a chuckle, "but I forgive you. Besides, I've never said that I don't want you to make 'calf eyes' at me." She reached

134

into the pocket of her apron and brought out Bowie's message. "That fellow who stopped the farm girls from robbing the stage was here earlier," she laughed lightly as she handed it across the counter. "He left you this."

Rand broke the seal on the folded paper and flattened it on the glass-topped counter. Frannie discreetly turned back to her workbench to give him some privacy.

Am looking into Valentine's affairs. Hoping he will lead me to Daniel and Marta.
BT

Rand folded the note and slipped it into his pocket. Bowie's idea had merit, and would probably bring matters to a swifter conclusion than would attempting to trace a wagon that may or may not have had anything to do with Daniel and Marta's disappearance. He lifted his eyes to Frannie's as she turned back toward him. "Thank you for holding that for me." She nodded her welcome silently, waiting to see if he was in her shop for another reason than the note. "I've been considering picking out a new gun," he went on. "Something of a bit larger caliber than my current one, perhaps?"

"There's nothing wrong with that .38 caliber you have there, and you shoot it well," Frannie replied reassuringly. "The only downside that I see is the weaker frame of that '51 compared to the newer guns. It won't make a very good club if the need arises."

"I don't plan to club anyone in the foreseeable future," he replied with a smile. She answered him with a smile of her own then she looked into the top of the display case she was leaning against.

"Let me see... Ah, here we go." She reached down, slid open the door of the case and picked up what at first looked like a run-of-the-mill Colt Model P, but then the grip caught Rand's eye. He'd never seen a grip profile such as this one wore on any other pistol he had ever examined. Out of habit, Frannie checked the gun to make sure that it wasn't loaded before she held it out to him. "Try that on for size."

Rand took the gun from her hand, checked for himself that it was empty, then wrapped his fingers around the walnut grip and pointed the pistol at the far wall. Whatever she had done to it, the handle felt natural in his hand, and when he closed his eyes, pointed the gun then opened his eyes, the sights were perfectly aligned. In fact, the reconfigured pistol felt better in his hand than his '51. "That's definitely an unusual style grip, but I like it," Rand said admiringly. "Your work?"

"Yes sir, it is," Frannie answered proudly. "I cut and re-contoured the grip frame so it's a lot like your Navy grip, but with a little more bulk so it sits a little better in the hand. I've got a friend who makes the grips for me. That shooter's chambered in .38-40 instead of your .38 rimfire, so it's got more power and shoots a bigger bullet, and if necessary the cases are easily re-loadable. Would you like to try shooting it?"

Rand found that he was intrigued with the gun and definitely wanted to shoot it to see how it handled under recoil. "I would. But I don't see a pistol range anywhere."

"Oh, ye of little faith!" Frannie quipped. "Things are not always as they seem, you know. Come with me!" She turned the 'Open' sign in the front window to 'Closed' before leading the way to the rear of the shop. As she passed by the counter she picked a box of cartridges from a shelf, then opened the back door.

Behind Frannie's shop was a large building which Rand had taken for a stable when he first arrived. "It used to be a stable," Frannie commented as if reading his mind. "Now it's my test range. Come on." Frannie lifted the bolt from the hasp on the small door to the side of the larger wagon gates and swung it open, gesturing for Rand to precede her. Inside the former horse barn, two rows of sandbags had been piled to form a shooting lane leading to a set of target stands. The height of the piled sandbags made it essentially impossible for any but the most inept shooter to send a bullet anywhere other than into burlap and sand. A loading table stood across the opening to the lane, with just enough room at one end to let a person squeeze by to walk down to the stands and put up targets. Skylights cut into the roof overhead provided adequate lighting for safety.

Frannie chuckled at the expression on Rand's face. "Never seen an indoor shooting range?"

"Not for anything bigger than .22's," he answered incredulously.

"That back wall," Frannie pointed behind the target stands, "will take anything short of a Sharps .50-90, and I'm not so sure it wouldn't stop that as well. Care to do some shooting?" She laid the modified Colt on the table with the loading gate open and the barrel pointed at the sandbag wall to the right of the table. She picked a target and a small hammer out of a box on the table and walked to the target stands; Rand found himself admiring her figure as she moved gracefully along the sandbagged alley. A few raps of the hammer fastened the target to the stand, then she was turning back. Rand quickly shifted his attention to the setup of the shooting range, in a vain attempt to keep Frannie from knowing that he had been watching her, but the savvy redhead knew. He saw it in the playful expression she wore and the twinkle in her green eyes, and his ears reddened again.

"It's nice to know that you're not a total iceberg," Frannie quipped with a smile.

"What do you mean, 'iceberg'?" Rand asked weakly. "I'm as warm as the next man."

"It looks to me like your ears are at least." At the sight of Frannie's mischievous grin Rand blushed deeper. She relented: "I'm sorry, I can't help myself; a woman in my business has to deal with all sorts, and I tend to be a bit forward."

Rand mumbled something unintelligible as Frannie hurriedly picked up the Colt in an effort to put things back on the right track. "As you can see, I lowered the hammer spur a little bit, which I think makes it easier to cock, and I widened the trigger. I also widened the rear sight notch. Some people don't care for the way the grip is shaped, but the ones who like it, really like it." She opened the box of cartridges and loaded five rounds in the cylinder, then lowered the hammer on the empty chamber and put the pistol back on the table. She reached into her apron pocket and brought out several irregularly shaped balls of what looked like wax with strings embedded in them. She held two of them out to Rand.

"I decided I wanted to keep my hearing, at least for a little while," she said. "If you stuff these in your ears, it deadens the sound quite a bit." She showed him how to insert the crude earplugs, then spoke loudly enough for him to hear. "See what I mean?"

Rand nodded. "I do. You're quite the inventor."

He picked up the gun. "May I?"

"Be my guest," Frannie called. Rand assumed a target stance: his right side was turned toward the target, right arm outstretched and left hand on his hip. He fired the first shot: a hole appeared in the center of the target. He let the recoil bring the hammer to his thumb, cocking the pistol as the Colt pivoted back to the horizontal. As soon as the sights returned to the target he fired again. He continued until all five shots had been fired. By then, the thick white haze of powder smoke was dimming the view of the target. He shucked the empties from the Colt, laid it on the table the way it had been before, then accompanied Frannie downrange to examine his target.

Five holes were clover-leafed in the center of the paper and Rand whistled in admiration. "That's excellent accuracy!" he exclaimed.

"You'll do better once you get used to it," Frannie replied matter-of-factly. Rand couldn't imagine shooting a better group with a revolver than the one in front of him, but he'd learned, even after their relatively short acquaintance, that arguing with the lady gunsmith was a fruitless endeavor and a waste of energy. She tacked up another target and the two returned to the loading table. "Why don't you try drawing it from the holster and shooting?" Frannie asked. "You might be surprised at how well you can do that way, as well."

"I don't think it will fit my holster," Rand answered. Frannie reached under the table to bring out a matching holster and belt.

"Why am I not surprised?" Rand asked with a smile. He unbuckled his gun belt, rolled it around the holstered '51 and laid the bundle on a nearby workbench. He strapped the belt Frannie handed him around his waist and settled the cross-draw holster in front of his left hip where his hand would fall the most naturally on it. He loaded and holstered the Colt, then stepped in front of the table. He closed his eyes for a moment and took a breath.

Rand's hand streaked to the grip of the Colt and slid it from the holster. He felt as slow as molasses in January, but Frannie was impressed with the speed of his draw. He kept his gaze locked on the target as his right thumb drew back the hammer; the pistol seemed to fire of its own accord. A .40 caliber hole appeared in the center of the target. Rand grinned back over his shoulder at the red-haired woman, then holstered the Colt.

By the time the pistol was empty the second time, Rand was grinning from ear to ear like a kid with a whole handful of penny candy. He walked back to the loading table. "I'll take it!"

Frannie pulled the wax plugs from her ears. "Excellent! I will personally guarantee it will do a good job for you. But what are you going to do with that one? Won't it get jealous?" She pointed at the rolled gun belt lying abandoned on the bench.

"I suppose it will just have to get used to sharing my affection," Rand answered cheerily. "I don't plan to sell that old gun, in case that's what you're getting at," he continued. "I've had it for too many years. It may not be worth much to anybody but me, but it has a lot of sentimental value. And you never know, it might come in handy some day." He shucked the empty cases from the Colt, reloaded it from the cartridge box on the table, and slid it into the holster. "Shall we go settle up?"

"By all means," Frannie answered. They stepped

out of the barn and she latched the door, then they walked side by side back to the shop. Back in her work area, she asked, "I suppose you plan to keep the leather, too, eh?"

"Add it to my bill, if you please. And another box of cartridges."

Frannie wrote an amount on a pad and pushed it across the counter to Rand. He raised an eyebrow, then reached into an inside pocket of his jacket for his wallet and counted out the bills onto the counter. "Are you sure about that price? It seems a trifle low for a custom gun like that one," he remarked.

"Consider it a 'friends' discount'," Frannie answered lightly.

"Then I insist on buying you dinner tonight!" Rand stated firmly. "We can celebrate my purchase over steaks and a bottle of wine."

"You're on! Be here at seven and bring the steaks. I've already got the wine."

Rand gave her a startled look. "I meant that I would take you to a restaurant," he protested.

"I know what you meant," Frannie commented dryly. "But I'm a better cook than the majority of the so-called chefs in town, and I keep a whole lot cleaner kitchen than some of them."

"But what will your neighbors think?"

"Why should I care what a bunch of self-righteous old biddies think about what I do? They already disapprove of my choice of occupation." She laughed lightheartedly. "You just bring the steaks; I'll worry about the neighbors. Like I said, be here at seven." As she talked she expertly wrapped his old pistol and the boxes of cartridges with brown paper, tied the parcel solidly with string and handed it to him.

A little dazed by the sudden turn of events he found himself caught up in, Rand mumbled, "Seven," then tipped his hat and strode out the door with the package securely under his arm, wondering wryly what he had gotten himself into; whatever it was, he also found himself hoping it would last.

~18~

Bowie stabled Red at the hotel, taking care to make sure that the hostler scooped the horse a generous helping of grain to go with the manger full of sweet-smelling meadow hay and the bucket of fresh water that stood in the corner of the stall. Bowie rubbed his hand along Red's neck, then dodged a halfhearted kick from the gelding as he left the stall. He slapped the sorrel on the hip as he slid the poles that did duty for a stall gate into place. "You don't give up, do you, pardner?" Bowie good-naturedly asked the horse, which promptly ignored him in favor of the oats in the pan.

Staying to the shady side of the street, Bowie strolled down the boardwalk, taking his time. After leaving Frannie's gunshop, he had ridden the length of Main Street and located Valentine's office, which was within easy walking distance of his hotel. Bowie didn't mind walking, and it would offer him a chance to get a better feel for what the town was like.

Gold had been discovered in the Baker City area in 1861, and it showed. After nearly twenty years of relative affluence, the city - for city indeed it was - had lost some of the rawness Bowie had seen in other gold towns. Hotels with crystal chandeliers stood cheek-by-jowl with saloons whose swampers still dumped their slop buckets in the gutters alongside mercantiles selling everything from candles to caviar. Baker City was now the county seat, thanks to a "midnight requisition" of the county records in 1868, roughly twelve years ago, from the original seat in Auburn Gulch, a few miles up the Powder River from the city.

But with growth had also come problems. In the raw uncivilized West of a few years before, it had often been hard for anyone to hide his dealings; a man could be as rough as he was big and tough enough to be, and many a "badman" found out the hard way that he wasn't nearly as big and tough as he thought he was. The population was scattered; gossip, often disguised as news, spread rapidly, and justice - as it was called - was often swift and violent. Prosperity, however, had provided many nooks and crannies that made it easier to hide, and easier for those whose forte` was not strength and swagger but cunning and deceit to bring their nefarious plans to fruition...and to take revenge for imagined slights, no matter how ancient.

Cyrus Valentine was one such villain who lived by cunning rather than intelligence, all the while believing he was smarter than those around him. While he was an intelligent man with a good mind, he had let emotion and laudanum rule his thinking for so long that the breath of reason no longer blew in his brain quite the way it once had. It wasn't that Valentine was insane in the accepted sense of the word; it was more that his thirst for vengeance, along with the drug, had clouded his perception.

Bowie found Valentine's office and settled down on a bench across the street to watch. He could see shadowy movement behind the sun-glazed windows, but the office door stayed closed throughout the morning and into the warm afternoon as he sat patiently and watched the life of the city move past him.

The rotund deputy was half asleep and thinking seriously about finding something to still the grumbling of his stomach, when a man on a well-lathered horse drew to a halt in front of Valentine's office, dropped the reins over the hitch rail and stepped up on the board-walk. As the brawny, bearded fellow dressed in rough miner's clothing reached for the handle on Valentine's door, he glanced furtively around the street before quickly slipping inside the office. Bowie pushed himself stiffly to his feet and strode across the thoroughfare.

As Digger Hartley slipped into his employer's of-fice, Valentine looked up from behind his paper-strewn desk. "What in the name of all that is holy do you think you're doing, coming here in the daylight?!" the attor-ney demanded of his henchman.

Digger yanked off his hat and stood crumpling it in his hands while he looked at his employer with something akin to panic in his eyes. His mouth worked silently for a moment until he suddenly blurted out, "Them two got away!", then stood waiting for the storm he knew would come; he was not disappointed.

"WHAT?" Valentine roared. "When did this happen? And how in thunder did you let such a thing occur?!"

"It was last night, and I didn't have n-n-nothin' to do with it," Digger stammered. "They made their-selves a rope and got into the mine tunnels."

Valentine was on his feet now, leaning both hands on his cluttered desk. His good eye was blazing. "Why wasn't the door locked?" he demanded.

"It was!" Digger answered plaintively. "They

went through the...the...privy!"

The attorney's angry shouts went unnoticed in the general hubbub of the street, but to Bowie's heightened awareness the burst of sound was equivalent to a gunshot. He grinned, thinking about the man who had just gone inside, and figuring rightly that that same man was bearing the brunt of the outburst from in yonder. Bowie leaned idly against the wall of the building housing Valentine's office and began to trim his fingernails with his pocketknife. He kept his head down and his face hidden, but every fiber of his being was concentrating on the words that came through the half-open window beside him.

"The privy? Are you serious?!" Valentine snarled. "How did that happen?!" The answer was too soft for Bowie to make out the words, but it took no effort to hear Valentine's response.

"Kill them!" Valentine ordered harshly.

Inside the office, Digger stared at his boss in disbelief. "K-k-kill 'em? Are you sure?"

"What part of what I said are you having trouble understanding?" Valentine demanded. "I said I want them dead!"

"But boss, if we kill a woman..." the ex-miner began.

"How will anyone know, unless you tell them?" his boss hissed. "Kill them and drop their bodies into the mine. No one will ever know what happened."

"I'm not sure I can do that, boss," Digger answered carefully. "I ain't got a problem with the preacher, but the woman? I ain't too much worried about bein' struck by lightning, but I damn sure don't wanna get hung..."

"Oh for pity's sake," Valentine snapped in dis-

146

gust. "Go and hitch up my carriage. I can see now that if I want anything truly important done I'll have to do it myself." He reached for his hat; Digger didn't move. "Well, what are you waiting for?" Valentine demanded. "Get my carriage!"

"We might best wait for morning, Mister Valentine," Digger answered diffidently. "It's gettin' late, and it's a long ways out there. The boys are lookin' for them two, and they'll lock 'em up when they find 'em."

"*If* they find them," Valentine answered disgustedly. "I don't have a great deal of confidence in your compatriots at the moment." He paused. "You're right, we will go in the morning. But I want my carriage ready at first light, do you hear me?"

"Yessir," Digger replied hurriedly. "It'll be here."

"Not here, you fool!" Valentine snarled. "Come to my house, and make sure you come to the back alley. I don't want you pulling up in front for all of my neighbors to see and comment on. Now, begone with you!" Valentine placed his hat back on its hook and sat down behind his desk, studiously ignoring his distraught employee. After a moment Hartley clumsily slapped his crumpled hat on his head and shuffled out the door. If he saw Bowie, he paid him no mind.

"Horse, we're in for it now," Digger said to his mount. "The boss has done gone crazy." He stood for a moment weighing his options, knowing all the while that he really had no realistic way to get out of the situation he now found himself in, except to follow orders. Valentine knew where all the skeletons were buried, so to speak, and his hold on Digger was total. His only other way out now was to shoot himself before a posse could hang him, and he wasn't ready to do that.

Digger led his tired horse down the street, Bowie following discreetly behind. It was just possible that Valentine's carriage was stored wherever this gent kept his horse. The miner was the best clue Bowie had; he would lead Bowie to the carriage, the deputy could then follow the carriage to Valentine's house and from there to wherever Daniel and Marta were being held.

~19~

The chill draft sliding steadily through the tunnel threatened the candle's flicker, throwing fantastic wavering shadows across the rough surface of the rock walls and floor. Daniel and Marta cautiously slipped through the darkness, their tiny globe of light barely bright enough to hint at whatever hazards there might be. The couple stumbled over chunks of loose rock that clattered, echoing, across the stone as they ducked past protrusions on the low, arching ceiling.

The darkness thinned appreciably some distance ahead; after a few halting steps Daniel was able to blow out the candle. They came to an intersection lit by a hurricane lamp hanging from a peg driven into a heavy pine support timber. The Martins waited for several long minutes, listening for any sound: the tunnel was tomb-silent except for the echoing, metronomic drip of water somewhere deeper in the mine.

The draft that had led them to this point tugged the lantern's flame toward the left-hand branch of the tunnel; the pair decided to follow, Daniel reasoning that there had to be an opening of some sort in that direction. He silently pointed to the left, and Marta nodded her agreement; they stepped out into the subdued pool of yellow light.

For a moment, Daniel considered taking the lantern. It would provide them with a better source of light than their stubby candles, but he was afraid that the theft might be noticed and would lead their captors to them before they had a chance to escape. Relighting the candle from the flame of the lantern, Daniel blew out the lantern, instantly plunging the tunnel into darkness except for the meager flicker of the candle flame. They began to move cautiously along this new passage, which showed signs of recent work. The floor was much smoother now and relatively litter-free, making for easier walking; the couple increased their pace until they were suddenly confronted with a blank wall of coarse gray stone, pocked with holes apparently made by drill steel in preparation for setting charges and blasting.

Picks, shovels, a single-jack and a heap of drill steel were scattered haphazardly at the foot of the blank rock face. "Oh, no!" Marta exclaimed in a whisper. "We're going to be trapped!"

"I don't think so," Daniel answered softly as he held the candle up toward the rough surface. "The draft is still pulling us ahead." He began to examine the rock, and soon discovered an area of greater darkness at one edge of the pick-scarred surface. "Look!" He beckoned to his wife, and together they peered into the twisted, forbidding mouth of a diagonal crack that seemed to lead upward into the native stone. Above them a thin line of gray light was fading rapidly. "That may be our way out!" Handing Marta the candle, Daniel began to climb carefully toward what he hoped was open air and freedom.

He worked his way gingerly up the steeply slanted chute, feeling for handholds that faded from view

150

as he climbed. At one point the fissure twisted back on itself in a writhing curve; Daniel worried that Marta might not be able to make it through. One more short climb brought him to the gap that they had seen from below. Like a gopher emerging from its burrow, Daniel cautiously stuck his sweat-drenched head just far enough above the surface to carefully scan the area around the opening, which was more vertical than horizontal and much larger than it had looked from the floor of the mineshaft. The aperture surfaced at the foot of a steeply-sloping face of granite which loomed over him in the dim starlight filtering down into the shallow gulley at the foot of the slope.

Listening intently for any sound of man, Daniel heard only the sleepy, end-of-the-day chirps of birds going to roost and the sighing of the tranquil evening breeze. He levered himself out into the gathering night and straightened up to stretch his tired muscles before his descent back into the mine to bring Marta out. He knew she would be worried about him.

"We can get out!"

Marta's answering smile was bright enough to light the Stygian blackness of the mine tunnel without any help from the candle. She threw her arms around Daniel's neck in delight as he stepped back into the shaft from the fissure, but quickly drew back when she felt the tension in his shoulders. She looked into his eyes. "What is it? What's wrong?"

"There's one place that's kind of tight..."

"And you're not sure that we," she patted her bulging waistline, "will fit. Am I right?" He nodded soberly. "I will not allow my children to be born here!" she

151

declared fiercely. "We will do whatever has to be done to remove ourselves from this place. And we will do so immediately! I will not countenance anything less!"

"I don't especially want to deliver a child under these circumstances either, my love," Daniel answered quietly. "I merely wanted you to know what the situation is." He picked up the knotted rope that had been their salvation already once this night. "I'll take the pack and the end of the rope. I believe that the rope is long enough to reach the surface. Once I'm there, loop the rope around yourself as you did before and I'll pull you up. You'll have to climb, but the slope isn't especially steep, and there are natural handholds along the way. It will be dark, so you'll have to take it easy and feel your way along."

Marta took his face in her hands and kissed him soundly. "Then I suppose that it would best be done as soon as possible, don't you?" she asked gently. She lowered her hands and stepped back. He looked at her for a long moment, worry for her evident in his eyes, before nodding curtly and turning to begin his climb back to the surface.

Having already made the trip once, Daniel found himself climbing much more rapidly than before, 'though he was somewhat hampered by the bulkiness of the pack. He felt sure that it was nearing midnight, and he was feeling the press of time passing when he again arrived at the bottom of the rocky draw that he hoped would lead them to safety.

"I'm here!" he called softly down the chute. He felt the rope stir in his hands; when it ceased moving, he took up the slack and waited for Marta to begin her climb. Almost immediately he felt the rope slacken and he stood to wrap it across his back diagonally from waist to shoulder, acting as her anchor as he began to pull.

When he judged that his wife should be entering the narrow, convoluted section of the passageway that had him worried, he ceased to pull, letting her find her own way through the twisted crevasse, careful to keep a tight grip on the rope in case she should slip.

Seconds crawled by like hours as he waited impatiently for her to move, until the suspense was nearly killing him. No sound came from below, and only the tiniest of movements of the rope gave any indication that Marta was even there. At last he knelt at the opening and whispered hoarsely, "Are you alright?"

"Give me a minute or two," the answer drifted back. "It's a tight fit, but I'm almost through. Just keep the rope tight." His fears only slightly relieved, Daniel stood up again to wait. The swooshing roar of a nighthawk's wings as it swooped down on its insect prey directly behind him nearly stopped his heart when at the same moment the rope suddenly went slack and he hurriedly drew it up tight again.

"I'm through," Marta called softly. She was now in the steepest part of the chute. "You'll have to help me from here." With renewed will, Daniel began to haul on the rope; a brief few moments later Marta appeared, sweat matting her wispy hair to her forehead. A smudge of black dust striped her left cheek and her dress was torn at the shoulder, but she had never looked lovelier to Daniel as he reached down to take her hand and draw her to her feet into the calm night air. They stood for a moment wrapped in each other's arms before Daniel stepped back.

"Are you alright to travel?" he asked, concern evident is his voice. "We need to get away from here before daylight."

"I'm fine," she answered. "Which way?"

"I believe that upstream might be our best way out."

"But that's away from help," Marta said worriedly. "And we don't even know which stream this is."

"It's also a direction that they won't expect us to go," Daniel reassured her. "With the number of settlers who have been moving into the area, we're bound to find someone who can help us." He took her hand confidently in his own. "We have only to trust the Lord to guide us to safety."

~20~

Rand strode purposefully toward Church Street. It had taken him far longer than expected to track down just the right steaks for his dinner with Frannie, but the paper-wrapped package clasped beneath his left arm held a pair of slabs of some very fine beef that had come from a small, out of the way butcher shop a few blocks from his hotel. Surprisingly, the premises had not been surrounded by flies as a pair of other purported "meat markets" that he had visited had been. With a small bouquet of wildflowers in his left hand, he hurried up the flagstone walk and around the house to the door of Frannie's residence. Before he could knock, a smiling Frannie opened the door, still wearing her working clothes. "I know I'm late..." Rand began as he handed her the flowers.

"Yes, you are," Frannie interrupted with a coy grin, "but so am I. I got tied up in the shop." She lifted the flowers to her nose for a sniff, smiled a gracious "Thank you", then stepped aside so Rand could enter. He doffed his hat as he walked through the doorway. Frannie pointed at a set of deer antlers nicely mounted on a wooden plaque next to the door. "You can hang your hat right there. Now, if you'll excuse me, I'm going to freshen up. I'll just be a few minutes. Set the steaks on the counter in the kitchen by the stove, please, and open the wine. There's a corkscrew next to the bottle." With a quick flourish of skirts she vanished down the hall. Rand heard a door close, and turned toward the kitchen.

Frannie's gun shop and house were both part of the rambling, white-washed clapboard structure that slouched comfortably on a large lot at the corner of Church and Ash streets. The business occupied one end of the building and had its own entrance and exit. It was completely separated from the living quarters by an insulated wall. The only access between the two was through a narrow door that opened into the kitchen. The workroom was bare-bones, designed-for-work utilitarian; by contrast, the rest of the house was more than comfortable. Colorful, neatly-sewn rag rugs were scattered over well-tended hardwood floors. A pair of gleaming bentwood rockers, each wearing nicely padded, quilted cushions on seat and back, flanked a small Franklin stove in what appeared to be the main living area.

The kitchen was relatively small; much of what might have been available floor space was taken up by a Monarch range that dominated one end of the room. A pitcher pump and sink had been installed in the counter under the small window in the east wall. An oak claw-foot table, surrounded by four ladder back chairs, occupied the center of the room. A row of pegs driven into a short half-round section of log that was fastened to the wall near the door leading out to the back porch did duty as a hat and coat rack.

Rand set the package of beef on the counter near the sink as ordered by his hostess; he removed his

156

jacket and pistol belt, hanging them on one of the pegs before moving to the bottle of wine Frannie had left on the table. He made short work of the cork before setting the bottle aside to breathe for a moment while he waited for his hostess to return.

When Frannie reappeared, her work clothes had been replaced by a nicely-cut dress of light green linen which complemented her emerald eyes. A small spray of blossoms from the flowers Rand had given to her was nestled becomingly in her hair above her left ear. The light scent of her perfume mixed with the delicate fragrance of the flowers and drifted gently to Rand's nose. "My, my, my," he murmured softly.

"I'm going to assume from the look on your face that you approve of my change of wardrobe?" Frannie questioned with a saucy smile.

"Most heartily, madam, most heartily!" Rand declared. "Not that there was a blessed thing wrong with what you were wearing before, but this..." he gestured as she struck a pose in the doorway, "this is a vision of loveliness. Such beauty deserves tribute." He lifted her hand to his lips, finding that he meant every word he had said. Now it was Frannie whose face reddened in response to *his* words. She shyly pulled her hand from his as she reached for the apron that was draped over the back of one of the chairs.

"Oh, go on with you," she quipped as she slipped the apron over her head. "I've heard sweet words before. Like I told you on the stage, I've had men around making 'calf eyes' at me who..."

"'Calf eyes' or not, this man has no interest in your business," Rand interrupted with a smile. "If I may be so bold, I'm here because of the woman who runs that business."

Frannie stopped her dinner preparations to turn and stare speculatively at him for several long moments, her bright green eyes widening. "You may be so bold," she answered softly before she turned away to stoke up the fire in the range. Her tone was hoarse, charged with unaccustomed emotion, as she spoke back over her shoulder. "Pour the wine, if you please."

Dinner had been reduced to a few bones and a bit of smeared gravy on the plates, the dishes washed and put away and the last drops of wine finished. Light conversation had graced the cozy kitchen as the food was prepared and eaten, but as Frannie poured coffee for them both a companionable silence came over the small room. They sat, one to each side of the table corner, their chairs pulled close together. Rand soon found himself telling her who he was, and something of how he had become a frontier judge...

The new and different road that Randolph Martin's life took after the bitter recriminations from Cyrus Valentine over the tragic death of his family led to prosperous and fulfilling territory. Although his law practice was doing well, he had long entertained aspirations to be more than just an attorney. He wanted to somehow make a difference in the growing country around him. After a great deal of introspection, he decided that the bench of justice would be the instrument of that difference; after further thought, he came to the conclusion that if he was going to judge criminals he needed to know criminals. He sold his house, resigned from the fire company and took a job as a deputy U. S. Marshal in the western territories.

158

For a young man of privilege who had spent his formative years not in making a living but in learning to be a gentleman and a scholar, the next three years were truly an education. Although he had hunted all his life and was no stranger to firearms, he soon found that being a successful lawman required much more than simply knowing how to shoot. In the words of Heck Miller, Randolph's mentor and first boss, "Any idjit can shoot a man; all it takes is a gun and a fool's notion. A real lawman brings his man in settin' on top of his saddle, not layin' acrost it." During his tour of duty as a deputy marshal, Randolph only shot one man, but Heck Miller would have been proud; the lawbreaker still went to jail "settin' on top of his saddle".

When he judged that it was time for him to leave the marshal's service Randolph hung out his shingle in Laramie, where he quickly gained a reputation as a determined defender of innocence who was equally as determined to see that the guilty got their just desserts. One of his greatest assets was an almost uncanny ability to tell the difference between the two. When another three years had passed the position of territorial judge came open, and there was no question in the minds of the voters who should be selected...

Rand finished the tale of his past and gradually explained his reason for now being in Baker City. His left hand rested lightly on the smooth tabletop as he watched Frannie's face from the corner of his eye; she listened raptly, her features composed and still, her breathing soft.

When he had finished the story of his journey Rand looked at her, waiting for comment. "You're deputy seems to be quite competent," Frannie commented quietly. "I'm sure that he'll find your son and his wife. Until then..." Her right hand had come to rest near Rand's left; as he slowly slipped his fingers over hers, they seemed to twine together naturally. He squeezed her hand gently.

"Thank you," he breathed quietly as a clock in another room chimed the nine o'clock hour. He released her hand and pushed back his chair.

"I'd better be going," he said reluctantly, pushing himself to his feet; although leaving this house and this woman was the last thing in the world that he wanted to do, proprieties must be observed. He strapped his pistol belt around his waist and shrugged into his jacket. Taking both of her hands in his, he lifted them to his lips. "May I see you again?"

Frannie rose up onto her tiptoes and kissed his cheek gently, then stepped away. Her sparkling eyes caught his gaze and gave him the answer he had hoped for. As he stepped past her and picked his hat from the antler rack near the front door, he turned back to say goodnight. She was standing silhouetted in the doorway, hands clasped at her waist. Rand bowed from the waist for a moment, then latched the door softly behind him and stepped out into the night. He walked slowly, his thoughts on Frannie and the evening they had spent together. Back in his room at the Antlers Hotel Judge Randolph Martin, senior jurist of the Wyoming Territorial Court, shook his head in wonder and disbelief. "I never thought I would ever feel this way again..."

~21~

The Barred Rock rooster stood up to its full height on the peak of the chicken shed roof, beak pointing at the first pearly light in the eastern sky as it announced the arrival of a new day to the world. Satisfied with its performance, the noisy bird fluttered to the ground to strut and preen for the few of its wives who had ventured out into the early dawn to scratch for bugs or left-over grain from the day before.

In the deep shadows of the alley down the street, the red horse shifted its hooves in the dust, eager to be off and traveling. "Easy, boy," Bowie whispered, patting the gelding's shoulder. "We'll be going shortly. We've gotta' hold up just a little longer."

Their wait was relatively short. The clatter of hooves and jingle of harness sounded from just out of sight, and a shadow deeper than the rest resolved itself into a polished carriage, drawn by a matched pair of high-stepping bays, which turned off into a side street one block from where Bowie sat his saddle. Bowie nudged Red forward, holding the gelding on a tight rein as it pranced along the street toward the glow of lamplight laying a golden rectangle diagonally across the front steps of Valentine's house. Following the

161

miner to his stable had been nothing more than exercise; the carriage hadn't been there. Instead, Bowie had spent a productive hour in a tavern a few doors down the street from Valentine's office, where the price of a couple of mugs of beer had yielded Valentine's address and a description of the lawyer's house.

A few moments later the lamplight disappeared, followed by the sound of wheels rolling on crushed stone. As the carriage came back into the street and turned to the left, away from Bowie, he dropped back until it was only a shadow in the dim light, then sat back in his saddle to follow. He couldn't see who was driving, but the silhouette bore a striking resemblance to that of the miner from the day before.

The first golden rim of the sun was peering over the ridges to the east as the sparkling carriage rolled across the bridge spanning the Powder River and struck the east-bound road. The top-hatted figure in the passenger compartment of the carriage turned to look back several times, as if checking to see if anyone might be following the carriage; Bowie nonchalantly continued his casual pace, which just happened to match that of his quarry. He felt sure that he had been seen every time Valentine looked back but that his appearance had elicited no feelings of alarm in his quarry.

The road followed the banks of Sutton Creek, meandering toward the narrow defile that the small stream had cut through the sagebrush-covered hills from this valley to the next over the eons of its existence. To either side of the dusty track were small farms or ranches, the farms boasting waving stands of wheat, oats or barley that would be ready for harvest in a few months. Between the cultivated fields and occasionally in them, depending on the state of the fences, Bowie

162

saw small herds of beef cattle, and once, a dozen black and white Holstein dairy cows.

The sun fairly leapt above the hills, rapidly warming the morning air. The miner kept the carriage horses moving at a fast pace, the spinning wheels throwing a haze of dust into the air. The dust was easy for Bowie to follow; the carriage was the fastest-moving object on the road. Those few farm wagons that were out on the road all moved at a considerably slower pace. Bowie relaxed in his saddle, sure that Valentine was not going to get away from him, at least not in the wide-open spaces of the Baker Valley.

~ ~ ~

Rand strolled down the stairs to the hotel lobby, his hat in his hand, headed for some breakfast. As he reached the door he heard his name called and turned to see the day clerk hurrying toward him holding out an envelope. "Somebody left you a note, Mister Martin," the nattily-dressed fellow said. "I didn't see who it was. The night man gave it to me this morning."

Instantly Rand tensed and apprehension sent chill fingers sliding up his spine for the span of seconds that it took to recognize Bowie's handwriting on the paper. He relaxed visibly as he reached for the envelope. "Is something wrong, Mister Martin?" the clerk asked. "You looked mighty worried there for a minute."

"No, no, everything's fine," Rand answered quickly. "You just startled me." He reached into his pocket for a coin to give to the clerk. "Thank you." He tucked the envelope into his shirt pocket, set his hat on his head and stepped out onto the boardwalk.

Rand stopped at the corner of the building, out of the flow of pedestrian traffic, and slipped a finger under the flap of the envelope, removing the slip of paper inside. He blew out a silent whistle as he read the short message:

D & M escaped. Your friend will lead me to them. More later.
BT

~22~

Digger kept the bays in a constant rhythm of "walk, trot, walk, trot" throughout the morning, not pushing the horses hard, but keeping them moving steadily. Occasionally, when the road crossed the creek, he would check them up and let them drink for a moment, careful not to let the animals have enough water to make them sick, yet still allowing them enough to keep going.

Late morning found the carriage crossing the small green valley leading toward Alder Creek. Digger pulled the horses up in the shade of a stand of cottonwoods. Roused from a fitful sleep slumped on the carriage's leather-covered cushions, Valentine demanded, "Why are we stopping?"

"Gotta rest the horses," Digger answered. He stepped down from the carriage to unhitch the horses, and led them to the small stream beneath the cottonwoods. He let the animals drink for a moment, pushing them back so they wouldn't overfill too quickly. After a few minutes, he allowed the bays to drink some more, then led them to a patch of green grass to graze for a while. Ten minutes later by his Ingersol watch, Digger hitched them into place ahead of the carriage, then

165

climbed back to the driver's seat and picked up the lines, clucking the horses into motion. They splashed lightly across the stream and jogged on.

Bowie watered Red in the same shaded stream where the carriage had stopped. This far from town the traffic on the road had thinned considerably; consequently, Bowie had been forced to lay back further and further as the morning wore on in order to avoid being seen following Valentine's carriage. The terrain ahead looked to be on the confining side, with relatively few places for the carriage to turn off, so the deputy took a short break to dig into a saddlebag for the paper-wrapped package of beef and biscuits that he'd packed there the night before, unwrapping it and taking a big bite of the tender meat and flaky bread before tucking the rest of the parcel back in the saddlebag. The loud crack of a stick behind him in the brush along the creek stilled the happy motion of his jaws; the short-barreled Colt appeared in his right hand as he spun to face the sound, sandwich temporarily forgotten in his other hand.

"Kinda jumpy, aren't you, mister?" The merry voice drifted from behind the biggest cottonwood, followed by a slim figure dressed in brown muslin shirt and patched wool britches. Blond braids hung down under weather-beaten, flat-brimmed brown felt to cover the canvas suspenders holding up the pants. A long-barreled pistol was belted, cross-draw, around the slender waist, balanced by a skinning knife in a beaded sheath that rode behind the right hip. High laced moccasins with fringed tops covered small feet. The Winchester carbine in the sprightly girl's right hand swung up to rest in the crook of her left elbow as she leaned back against the tree, grinning mischievously at Bowie.

166

Bowie quickly swallowed the bite of food, nearly choking in the process, which made his assailant's grin spread wider. "Only when I've been injun'd," he grumbled. "What do you want, girl?"

"Not a thing, I was just out looking for a deer to shoot and decided to get myself a drink of water," was the jolly answer to the grumpy question as she stepped out into the morning sunlight. Her voice was deep for a girl; on further examination, she turned out to be some years past girlhood, both in eye-pleasing figure and erect carriage. Bowie judged her to be close to his own age and only a pair of inches taller.

"You could get yourself hurt sneaking up on a fella that way," Bowie scolded her. "Who are you, anyway?"

"I don't think that little bitty Colt is gonna' shoot through that big old tree," she grinned, her bright blue eyes sparkling with mischief. "I'm Hanna Dalby." She let go of the rifle and hooked a thumb over her shoulder toward the southeast. "'Got me a homestead down the country a ways." She stuck out her hand.

"Bowie Tyler." He holstered his Colt and shook the proffered hand. "You've got your own homestead?"

"Yep. Proved up and all. What's the matter, don't you think a woman can homestead?"

"Ma'am, I do believe you could pretty much do whatever you set your mind to do," Bowie answered. "Now if you'll excuse me..." He ticked his hat brim with a finger, picked up the reins and stepped up alongside of Red to mount and be on his way. He'd totally forgotten about the food in his left hand.

"You're following that Valentine fella, aren't you?" After a moment's pause to gather his thoughts Bowie swung into the saddle, nearly dropping his snack in the process, finally stuffing it between his teeth while he mounted. He took the biscuit out of his mouth and looked down at Hanna Dalby.

"What makes you say that?"

"Call it womanly intuition," she answered with a smile. Bowie snorted in a most ungentlemanly fashion.

"How do you know Valentine?" he asked.

"Everybody in these parts knows that shyster, or knows who he is," she answered. "He's a two-legged skunk, if you ask me. He came in here and started throwing his weight around, making out like he was better than everybody else. Except for the head honchos that run Baker City; he sucks up to them."

"So tell me how you really feel about him," Bowie said with a smile of his own. Hanna shook her head then smiled ruefully back at him.

"Sorry about that," she told him. "But that man gets my dander up."

"What'd he do to you?"

"He treats women like dirt!" the young woman declared, temper flaring. "And especially women who..." she sputtered, suddenly at a loss for words.

"Don't dress like women?" Bowie asked innocently.

"That's right!" Hanna glared at him. "He had the gall to tell me that if I cleaned myself up and put on a dress, then maybe I could find a man who'd marry me! I take a bath every week, sometimes twice, and I'll be damned if..."

"Such language is so unbecoming of a lady," Bowie intoned, interrupting her in mid-sputter, knowing full well that it could just possibly get him shot out of his saddle if she was mad enough. Instead, Hanna went silent and glared at him, eyes flashing, for several seconds while he did his best to look as innocent as possible. A grudging smile finally crossed her lips.

"Has anybody ever told you that you're annoying as hell?" she asked.

"Not today," Bowie assured her.

"Well, you are! So anyway, are you gonna tell me why you're following that weasel Valentine, or do I have to guess? You're burning daylight, ya know."

"Do you have any idea where he's headed? And can you get me there ahead of him?" Bowie questioned.

"I reckon he's headed for the mine he's got in Gold Cliffs," Hanna said. "And I know a shortcut. But I'm not moving an inch until you tell me why you want to know."

Bowie sighed. "You're a nosy varmint, aren't you?" he groused. Hanna just stood there grinning at him. "And a trifle annoying yourself, if I do say so. But if it'll make you happy, I'll tell you this much: some people are missing, and I think Valentine knows where they are. Now can we go?"

Without a word Hanna turned and slipped into the brush along the stream, reappearing a couple of minutes later leading a short-coupled buckskin. She flipped the hackamore rein over the horse's ears and stepped into the McClellan saddle. Annoyed as he was with her, Bowie couldn't help but admire the way Hanna Dalby filled out her britches when she swung her leg over the buckskin's rump.

"When you're done admiring my behind, we'll go," Hanna snapped. Bowie blushed.

"Ready when you are, ma'am." With a disgusted sniff Hanna heeled the buckskin across the little creek and pointed it toward the hills to the east of the wagon road.

~23~

Sisley Creek chuckled merrily over its bed of smooth rocks as the Martins rested deep in the shade of a clump of willows which hung out over the grassy bank. A narrow, two-track wagon road crossed the stream and meandered through sage and bunch-grass along the foot of the hill. Daniel had done his best to make sure that they were out of sight from anyone who might travel the road, 'though it appeared that the last traffic had been two wagons which had passed by a couple of days before. Marta had removed her shoes and stockings and was soaking her aching feet in the coolness of a shallow pool when something bumped the sole of her foot. With a quiet squeal of alarm totally uncharacteristic of her, she yanked her feet from the water to discover a small, green apple bobbing in the shallow eddy she had so hurriedly vacated.

Daniel spun around from his examination of the nearby hillsides. "What..." he began, but Marta interrupted his exclamation.

"Look!" Marta grinned as she held up the apple. "Someone has apple trees growing upstream! We're safe!"

"We're not safe yet, my dear," he answered, relieved that the source of her cry was not only harmless, but edible as well. "But that tells me that we're getting closer." Suddenly he tensed, listening intently. At Marta's questioning look, he laid a finger across his lips, then reached out to pull her deeper under the cover of the willows. "Don't move!" he mouthed silently. Across the creek a horse appeared, moving at a slow walk, its rider peering intently at the dust of the road as he searched for tracks or some other sign of their presence. Marta recognized him as the one called Jordan, the man who had driven the wagon that brought them to their recently vacated prison. As the rider heeled his mount into a canter and disappeared around a bend in the stream, Daniel blew out a soft sigh of relief; that had been a close call. It was only the fact that they had stopped to rest which had saved them from discovery. He realized then that they would have to be much more careful in the coming hours, especially if they were to continue to travel by daylight, which, given the roughness of the terrain, was really their only option.

Marta leaned over to whisper in Daniel's ear, "Shouldn't we keep moving?"

He shook his head. "Not until Jordan comes back," he answered softly.

"But what if takes him a long time?"

"Then we wait that long. We can't take a chance on being caught out in the open when he returns. Why don't you rest for a while? You can use the pack for a pillow. I'll keep watch."

"You need to rest, too," she protested half-heartedly; the thought of a nap was enticing. She lay down on the soft grass with her head on the pack, and Daniel spread their only blanket over her. The laughing of the stream soon lulled her into a deep sleep. Daniel smiled lovingly as her features relaxed, then turned his attention back to watching for anyone else who might be hunting for them.

~ ~ ~

Malechai Jordan was sometimes a miner, sometimes a shoulder-striker for mine owners who wanted to break up the strikes that were becoming common in some of the bigger mines. He was at all times a natural-born bully, a big man who was familiar with the pistol he wore on his hip -- but was much more comfortable with the side-lock ten-gauge Parker double gun tucked into the scabbard under his leg or the cut-down Greener he carried in his saddlebag. He wasn't especially choosy whether or not his victims were facing him, either. It had been his job to kidnap the Martins in the first place, and he wanted to be the one who brought them back. So when the road he followed suddenly rounded a shoulder of weather-eroded rock and he saw smoke rising from the chimneys of two small cabins, Jordan saw what he thought was his chance to throw his weight around.

The Beckman brothers had built their cabins on either side of Sisley Creek where the canyon narrowed in such a way that the only possible passage went directly between their houses. High, rough granite outcroppings topped with wind-twisted mountain mahogany trees sheltered the dwellings from the worst of the winds that on occasion howled down the canyon, tearing branches from the tops of the tall cottonwoods that grew along the creek. Rows of apple, apricot and cherry trees were planted along the feet of the canyon walls and into the triangular mouth of a side draw that led down into the creek bottom from the northwest. The apple trees, many approaching six feet in height, had green fruit hanging from the branches. It was an apple from one of these trees that Marta had found floating in the creek.

The brothers had filed their claim on the canyon bottom for the next mile upstream; consequently, a pole fence and gate blocked further access to the upper end of the canyon. The two men had weathered some vicious feuds between families back in the mountains of Tennessee, and they'd seen how the violence could spill over onto folks not related to the combatants; the Beckmans were cautious men who wanted to know who their neighbors were. Not that they'd deny passage to anyone who was passing through on legitimate business: Joshua and Jedidiah Beckman were mainly just careful.

Jordan slid the shotgun from the scabbard and braced the butt stock on his hip, muzzles pointing skyward, as he rode up to the cabins. Joshua stepped from his house, coffee cup in his left hand. "Howdy, stranger," he called. "We don't get many visitors up here. Can I help you with something?"

Jordan didn't return the cordial greeting. Instead he snapped roughly, "I'm lookin' for a man and woman that might be comin' this way on foot. You seen anybody like that?"

"You're the first thing we've seen since we got home from down yonder, except for a bear or two," Joshua answered coolly. "Why're you looking for those folks?"

"That's none of your business!" Jordan snarled. "You just make sure an' send somebody to Valentine's mine if they do show up!"

"And if I decide not to do that?" the farmer asked mildly.

The shotgun barrels lowered threateningly. "Then me an' some of the boys'll be back, and you ain't gonna like what happens here. You all've got families here, ain't ya?"

"Yessir we do, as a matter of fact."

"Then you'd best do as I tell ya!"

The clink of a Winchester's action was followed by the voice of Jedidiah Beckman. "No, you'd best do what *I* tell *you*, mister," the older Beckman brother drawled coldly from the behind Jordan. The big man stiffened, and the muzzles of the shotgun slowly tilted skyward again. "I don't know who you think you are, but this here Winchester throws a mighty big chunk of lead, and even as big as you are I don't think it'll slow down much goin' through you at this range. Now, you real careful-like dump the shells outta' that shotgun and your pistol, and if you so much as look like you're thinkin' of takin' a shot at my brother while you're doin' it, I'll empty your saddle. You're way too close for me to miss."

Jordan shot a tentative look over his shoulder toward the voice, and saw the Winchester solidly resting against the trunk of a big juniper tree, muzzle unwavering. "Do it!" Jedidiah barked. Jordan hurriedly thumbed the lever and dumped the loads from the shotgun, laid it across his lap, action open, and reached for his pistol. Seeing Joshua still standing peacefully drinking coffee there in front of him, Jordan, just for a fleeting second, contemplated making a grab for his Colt. He desperately wanted to do something to wipe that mild expression from the farmer's face, but he also wanted to live. Still...

"Two fingers, friend!" Jedidiah reminded him. Jordan visibly relaxed as he carefully lifted the pistol from the leather and equally as carefully turned the cylinder, dropping the cartridges into the dust at his horse's feet. "Now take out the cylinder and put it in your pocket," Jedidiah ordered, "then get your sorry carcass out of here, and don't come back. We don't take kindly to threats."

"You'll be sorry for this!" Jordan blustered.

"I don't think so," Joshua responded cheerfully to the bully's snarl. "You and your friends had best stay down-canyon. The climate's a lot healthier there." He threw the coffee grounds from his cup as Jordan yanked his horse cruelly around and spurred it back the way he had come.

When Jordan was out of both sight and earshot downstream, Jedidiah stepped out into the open. "Who do you reckon that gent's hunting for?" he asked.

"I don't know, but whoever it is, I hope we find them first," Joshua answered worriedly.

Hanna reined in the buckskin just below the crest of the ridge she and Bowie were climbing and swung down. "We walk from here." Her manner was curt as she dropped the hackamore lead rope from where it was tucked under her belt to drape loosely over a tall sage. Without waiting for Bowie, she slipped through the sage and rabbit brush to the top of the slope and bellied down behind a clump of grass. As Bowie slid up beside her he extended the brass spyglass he'd brought from his saddlebag.

Across the narrow canyon a small, unnamed stream meandering through an even more constricted coulee dropped into the creek bottom through a slim defile which was flanked by a tall spire of rock on one side and a steep bunchgrass hillside on the other. A narrow road that looked to have been cut with a Fresno scraper crossed the creek and went up canyon, following the trickle of water. Several hundred yards from the junction with Sisley Creek, the canyon widened out into a bench which footed a broad sage-covered basin. Tucked into a cove near the gently-sloping rear of the bench was the headgear and tailings dump of a working gold mine, the deeply-shadowed mouth of the tunnel yawning in the early afternoon sunlight. Nearby, a small cabin and a collection of weather-stained, once-white tents were scattered through the sagebrush.

Clattering hooves and rumbling wheels heralded the arrival of Valentine's carriage. Bowie shifted his gaze from the huddle of men and horses in front of the mine adit to the top-hatted figure in the rear seat of the carriage, just as Digger hauled the horses into the turn onto the mine road. Valentine sat glaring malevolently ahead. Dust stirred up by the churning wheels drifted over the mob of lackeys as Digger hauled the bays to a stop in front of them.

From their perch on the ridge top, the deputy and his guide couldn't hear the words, but it was easy to tell by the lawyer's gestures and the posture of the men standing beside the carriage that he was reading them the riot act for their failure to find the Martins. Bowie looked at Hanna. "Well, they haven't found them yet, er, I mean, uhm..."

Hannah looked thoughtful as she began to put the story together. "Those missing people you told me about earlier were being held prisoner here, weren't they? And now they've somehow managed to get away, right? Are you gonna tell me who they are, or not? And who are you, anyway?"

Bowie looked over at her, frustration written on his face. "I suppose that you do deserve an explanation, after you got me here ahead of Valentine. Yes, as near as I can figure, the missing people were being held prisoner here, they're my boss's son and daughter-in-law, my name really is Tyler, I'm a U.S. Marshal among other things, and my boss got me the badge when his family was kidnapped."

"And just how did he do that?" she questioned, not believing. "They don't give appointments like that out like pie at a church social, you know."

"He's the senior judge in the Wyoming Territorial Court in Laramie. I'm one of several special deputies who work for him. He sent me to find his kin and get them away from the kidnappers; he thought I might need the extra authority of the federal badge."

Hanna eyed Bowie cynically. "Sounds to me like he gave you a hunting license!" Bowie turned on her instantly.

"No, ma'am! He would never do something like that, and I wouldn't either!" he declared. "My job is to bring the Martins back and to arrest the men who kidnapped them."

Hanna snorted. "Ha! Fat chance of that. You know what a jury's gonna do to them if you do get 'em into court, don't you? For kidnapping a woman? That'll get 'em hung by any jury that's not been bought off ahead of time...and maybe even lynched."

177

"She's pregnant, too."

"In that case, you better be good with those guns, 'cause you're gonna need 'em!" Hanna declared. "Those men yonder won't go peaceable. You're gonna be taking a bunch of 'em in across their horses."

"I hope it doesn't come to that." Bowie put the spyglass to his eye again. The crowd at the mine was dispersing. Some of the men walked toward the mine opening, others toward the string of saddled horses that stood waiting. Six men mounted and trotted down the road toward the main canyon; at the creek they split up. Three of the riders turned their mounts upstream and three down. The riders who turned downstream walked their horses, taking their time, scouring the willows, sage and sumac on each side of the creek. The other three riders disappeared beyond the sage-covered knob to Bowie's left. Near the mine, Valentine climbed down from the carriage and limped to the shake-roofed log cabin standing near the mine head. When the mine owner vanished inside, Digger stripped the harness from the carriage horses and led them to water before picketing them on a patch of grass near the small stream.

Bowie slid backwards down the hill on his belly until he was sure he was out of sight of anyone across the canyon, then got to his feet, brushing the debris from his clothes. "Looks like it's time to cut the odds down a skosh," he told Hanna. "And I need a favor."

"What might that be?"

He nodded at her buckskin where it stood nipping at the blades of summer-dried grass at its feet. "Will that critter make it back to Baker City in some semblance of a reasonable amount of time? And can you find another horse to bring you back out here?"

"Of course he will, and of course I can. I can get one the same place where you got that red horse you're riding. But who says I'm going to Baker City?"

"I do," he answered flatly. "I need you to find the lady gunsmith that lives there and have her get a message to my boss."

Hanna chuckled sourly. "And just how is having my aunt send a message to your boss in Wyoming going to help you here in Oregon?" she wanted to know.

He stared at her. "Miz' Kinsella is your aunt? How in the world...? Never mind, that's not important at the moment. And my boss isn't in Laramie; he's here, or at least he's in Baker City, waiting for me to tell him where his son and daughter-in-law are." He stopped, his thoughts running pell-mell through his head.

After a moment he said, "Okay, it's what, three or four o'clock?"

"More like two. Don't you own a watch?"

"No, ma'am, I don't. Anyway, you should be able to get to town about dark or a little later. Here's what I want you to do: when you get to Baker City, have your aunt tell my boss – his name's Randolph Martin - that I've found where Valentine was holding Daniel and Marta, and that they're still free. Then I want you to bring him back, and I'll meet you right here sometime shortly after daylight tomorrow morning. That'll give you some time to rest the horses along the way, and we'll be able to see what we're doing when we go over yonder." He leveled an expectant gaze on her. "Well, what are you waiting for? Get going, would you? This is important!'"

"I'm waiting for you to say please," Hanna answered stubbornly. "And to tell me what you're going to be doing meanwhile."

"Please!" he snapped impatiently. "And I'm gonna' be trying to cut down the odds against me, and find the Martins at the same time. Now scat, would you?"

"Sounds like you're taking a lot on yourself, but I guess that's your doin's," Hanna swung her leg over the buckskin's back and settled into her saddle. "Just don't go and get yourself killed while I'm gone."

"I didn't know you cared," Bowie said, sarcasm heavy in his tone.

"I don't care about you particularly," she answered. "I just don't wanna have to take on all them boys down yonder by myself to save that pregnant lady."

"You would, too, wouldn't you?" he asked wonderingly as the shadow of a grin barely cracked one corner of his mouth.

"You're darned right I would!" Hanna reined the buckskin around and heeled him into a trot toward the distant town.

"I think you would at that," Bowie muttered as he watched her disappear into a draw, following the game trail they'd climbed to get to their observation point. He checked his cinch, then mounted Red and turned the gelding down the length of the ridge. "Come on, horse, I wanna get ahead of those gents." The sorrel stepped out into a trot, following the contour of the hill and gradually dropping toward the low pass that was barely visible beneath them and which should, if Bowie had guessed correctly, give man and horse relatively easy access to the road that meandered alongside the creek.

~24~

The sun was well past its zenith when the big man on the bay horse trotted angrily past the Martin's hiding place on his return down the creek. Daniel shook Marta gently. "I'm sorry to wake you, but we have to go now," he whispered softly. "Jordan just passed by, and I want to put as much distance between us and him as I possibly can." He gathered their few belongings into their make-shift pack, then took her hand and lifted her to her feet. "Are you ready?"

Marta stretched and sighed. "I'm as ready as I'm going to get; let's go." The couple pushed their way through the edge of the willow brush that had hidden them, and found themselves on a game trail which was for all practical purposes a low-ceilinged tunnel through willow, sumac and head-high sage winding its way upstream, sometimes next to the creek, sometimes falling away, but always trending toward the upper reaches of the canyon. The hard-packed surface of the trail made for easy going, except where the brush grew so low and thick that they had to drop to their knees and crawl to get through.

In this fashion they put a mile behind them, stopped for a brief rest and a drink of water, then continued at their snail's pace for another mile. After another short break they were about to start again, when they heard voices and the clank of a steel horseshoe on rock coming from the road. Peering through a gap in the brush they spied two riders. They were unaware of the third man on their side of the creek until the sudden cracking of branches warned them of the rapidly approaching danger.

"Go!" Daniel hissed as he handed Marta the pack. "I'll draw them off, then I'll catch up with you!"

"No! I'm not going without you!" she whispered fiercely. "You'll be killed!"

"I won't let myself be killed!" he urged. "Now take our children and go...if you love me, go!" He pulled her to him, kissed her on the forehead then turned her and gave her a gentle shove upstream. "Go, please!" Glancing over her shoulder, Marta stared into his eyes for a long moment, then snapped her head around and started up the trail without looking back.

Once Marta was out of both sight and hearing, Daniel stood for a brief moment recalling the lay of the trail and the brush downstream from where he stood. In his memory a wider- than- usual stand of tall sage, centered around a wide granite boulder, stood out as a possible observation point. He scrambled through the pale green brush to the boulder and squatted beside it, eyes locked on the bushy overgrowth below him for the first sign of the rider.

The black and white paint horse pushed through the wall of sage, striding alongside the stone outcrop, moving at a stilted walk. Across the creek the other riders had pulled ahead, their horses having found much easier going than the grumbling miner who's chore was following the stream-side game trail. As the man's right stirrup passed in front of Daniel's face, the young pastor yanked the rider's boot from its perch, and using the full strength of his legs, stood suddenly, unseating the manhunter who crashed to the ground in a tangled heap on the far side of his mount. As Daniel grabbed for the bridle, the horse danced sideways away from its fallen rider, where its hindquarters collided with the boulder. Blocked on that side, the horse swung its body the other way; one steel-shod rear hoof struck the man on the ground in the ribs and the other slammed into his head with a sickening thud, leaving white bone showing through the sudden shower of blood.

Daniel led the horse away from the fallen man and quieted the frightened animal briefly. Tying it to a heavy sagebrush, he returned to the side of the fallen man, kneeling down to hold two fingers to the artery in the miner's neck. Feeling no pulse, Daniel sighed a quick, remorseful prayer for forgiveness for causing the man's death, then untied the paint and threw himself into the saddle. With a yell, he sent the paint charging up out of the brush toward the ridgeline to the east of the creek, away from the other hunters.

The paint horse was a runner; its blood was up and it was eager to move, ready to escape the smell of blood behind it and the yelling man on its back. It burst from the brush and out into open ground already at full stride, barely following the directions sent to it by the bridle as it raced for a nearby draw. Behind man and horse, frantic yells and shots echoed in the confines of the canyon as the two hunters across the creek struggled to no avail to quiet their own dancing mounts enough to shoot accurately at their fleeing quarry.

"Damn it, it's that there preacher!" Turley yelled. "How'd he get Danny's horse?"

"Don't talk -- shoot!" Zuckerman shouted in answer, levering a round into the chamber of his Winchester and bringing the rifle to his shoulder. "Hold still, ya' jughead!" he hollered at his horse as his first shot flew wide of the target. Their aim disrupted by the movements of their mounts, the two riders' bullets kicked up dirt and rock fragments around the rump of the racing black and white horse as it rapidly disappeared into the mouth of the draw.

"Fergit shootin' -- he's outta sight!" Turley snarled as he jerked his horse's head around toward the creek. "We better git after him, or we're in deep trouble!" The two men spurred their mounts into the water and out the other side, jostling each other roughly in their eagerness to follow the spotted horse and its runaway preacher.

As the two riders swept by her, shouting and cursing, Marta held her position on the trail. When they had passed, she stood and took several tentative steps toward the draw where her husband and his pursuers had gone, wanting to follow, yet knowing in her mind it was the wrong thing to do. Daniel expected her to take their unborn children to safety; although the tug of her heart yearned to follow him, her no-nonsense practicality reminded her that he was right: she and the children had to come first. If he had only to worry about himself, he would be better able to survive the trial that was his now. "Go with God, Daniel!" she whispered desperately as she turned and began to trudge upstream. "And make sure that you come back to us!" she finished fiercely.

~ ~ ~

Bowie reached the shallow pass he'd been aiming for and stepped down from his saddle, trailing the reins on the ground. Red stood as if rooted, breathing easily, as the deputy slipped forward to inspect the terrain ahead of him. Upstream a mile or more he could see the approaching hunters slouched comfortably in their saddles as they made their leisurely way along the creek. A few more minutes would see them out of sight behind a fold in the hill; Bowie waited until they disappeared, then trotted back to the sorrel, mounted and made his way down to the road, where he waited patiently with the hammer-cocked Greener across his lap, muzzles pointed upstream.

"I still don't think that there preacher and his woman ever got outta' them tunnels," a voice declared, just out of sight but through a trick of the breeze, clearly audible over the sound of the creek.

"Yeah, they prob'ly done fell down that shaft in yonder," another agreed. "But we're gettin' paid to look for 'em out here, and this sure beats the hell outta' searchin' that there undergroun', ya know?"

"That it do," the third voice acknowledged. As the three riders turned around the bend, they pulled up short at the sight of the resolute red horse standing calmly crossways in the road. Of much greater importance, as far as they were concerned, was the cocked shotgun staring them in their faces, held by the fat little man atop the sorrel horse. All three quickly reined in and threw their hands in the air.

"Howdy, fellas," Bowie smirked with a humorless smile. "Going somewhere?"

"Nowhere's in particular, mister," the stocky redhead on the left answered. "Why ya' wantin' to

185

know?"

"Why? Because I just now heard you boys talking about looking for, oh what was it...uhm...oh yeah, 'that there preacher and his woman'. Hearing that made me curious to see what kind of men would be hunting for a preacher, let alone 'his woman', as one of you referred to her." His smile faded as he grimly shook his head. "Now I see that you boys are pretty much the scum I thought you might be."

The three began vehemently and colorfully protesting their innocence, but Bowie interrupted them. "I think you gents had best shed your guns, your boots and your britches, then unsaddle those horses," he growled. Nobody moved until he lifted the Greener in both hands. "I'll give you a count of five to get started, then this shotgun is gonna' do my talking for me," he went on, ice in his voice. "NOW MOVE IT! One! Two! Thr..."

The first gunbelt hit the ground before he finished the word "three", closely followed by the others. The riders scrambled from their saddles, and all three began the awkward dance of hopping on one foot while frantically yanking at the other boot in their hurry to do as they were ordered. Bowie looked on disgustedly as they stripped out of their pants and yanked the latigos loose on their saddles, dumping them unceremoniously in the dust of the road, then standing practically at attention side by side in front of the shotgun.

"Who are you anyway, mister?" the redhead - the boldest of the three - asked, voice quavering.

"I'm the boogeyman your momma warned you about," Bowie answered as he reached into his shirt pocket for his badge. He smiled grimly at them as their faces fell even further. "I'm only going to ask this one time, and the only thing I'd better hear from any of you is the truth: where's the preacher and his wife?"

"Honest, mister, we don't know!" the bold one declared. The others nodded eager agreement. "We been lookin' high and low for 'em, and ain't nobody found 'em. I think they done fell down that there deep shaft back yonder! We ain't seen hide nor hair of neither one of 'em!"

"Yeah," the tallest of the three agreed. "There was some old burnt matches in a side tunnel but that was all, and them matches looked pretty old to me. I think they're dead!"

Bowie paused as he considered their words, then nodded to himself and said, "Here's what's gonna happen, gents. You boys are gonna get up on those horses, and you're gonna leave the country. If I ever see any of you again, anywhere, I won't arrest you, I won't talk to you, I'll just shoot you. You got that?"

"Without no saddles?"

"GIT!" Bowie roared.

There was a mad scramble as the three clambered awkwardly onto their bareback mounts and kicked them into motion down-canyon. Bowie kneed Red around as they passed to keep them covered with the shotgun, watching them until they vanished around a bend in the road. When he could no longer hear the clatter of the horses' hooves, he turned to begin the next phase of his search.

Upstream, muted by distance, but resounding clearly across the canyon, a flurry of shots rang out; cursing, Bowie spurred Red into a gallop toward the sound. The grade wasn't especially steep, but the road was all uphill, and in the first quarter of a mile Bowie knew that he would lose the race up the canyon. Red was all heart, but the sorrel had traveled a lot of miles this day and was tiring rapidly. Killing a perfectly good horse wouldn't help anyone; Bowie reined Red to a walk, letting his breathing settle, then urged the big horse once more into the jog that he knew the gelding could maintain for hours.

The canyon walls had long since poured their deep shadows across the creek bottom when Bowie finally arrived at the boulder where Daniel had made his run. The two-track road was torn by steel-shod hooves and littered with brass cartridge cases. Deep hoof prints in the soft clay of the creek bank pointed the way. Crossing the stream bed, the deputy found the dead man by following the sound of the flock of magpies squawking in the sage tops as they scolded the coyote that scampered out of sight when Bowie approached.

As he was about to follow the tracks up the draw leading toward the top of the ridge, Bowie's attention was inexplicably drawn toward the game trail that he had just crossed. Turning back, he stepped to the ground and hunkered down to use the last of the daylight trickling into the canyon bottom in an attempt to see some contrast in the shadows which now covered the trail. He had just started to push himself back to his feet when he saw the incongruent footprint. What looked to be the heel of a small shoe had pressed a fragrant yarrow stem down into the softer soil at the edge of the game track. He felt the print with his fingers. The edges were still crisp; whoever had been here hadn't been gone for more than an hour or two. On his hands and knees now, he lowered his face toward the ground, looking in the direction the track appeared to point, and discovered another footprint; just above that one a brightly-colored thread was snagged on a willow twig. It would seem that Daniel Martin had successfully led his pursuers away from his wife, who was using the time he had given her to make her way up the creek and away from her pursuers.

The bottom of the canyon was nearly dark now; only a silver rim showed in the sky over the ridgeline to the west. Although the moon would be full this night, moonrise was still hours away. There was no way that Bowie would be able to follow the footprints from here, and he didn't want to frighten the young woman he was trying to find. He would have to wait for morning.

Bowie led the sorrel horse to water before mounting and reining the gelding toward the western ridge. Earlier in the evening he had noticed a slanting trail leading in the general direction of the spot on the back side of the ridge where he was to meet Hanna; at the foot of the trail he gave Red his head. They made their way slowly to the top of the ridge, stopping frequently to let the horse catch its breath before moving on. Just before moonrise they topped out on the rim of the canyon and dropped into the downward-slanting swale where he would wait for the slim, eye-catching girl with the buckskin horse. Using his hat as a bucket, Bowie watered Red from his canteen, then picketed the sorrel on a patch of grass and rolled up in his blankets. He planned to spend most of the night alternating between napping and watching the mine across the canyon, but instead found his thoughts returning to Hanna.

Bowie was often lonely, a condition he hid from the world under a veneer of sarcastic comment. He was an orphan whose family had been taken from him by cholera when he was only three years old. He had never known a real family, but had always wished for such; and for someone to share the life he hoped some day to build. Hanna was independent and resourceful, outspoken and blunt, much as Bowie was himself. It was not always true that opposites attract; Bowie found himself profoundly attracted to Hanna Dalby.

~25~

The paint made good time up the narrow draw, pushing hard, without Daniel's urging, to get away from the shooting behind it. But now it was laboring, fighting for every step, unwilling to surrender though its strength was nearly gone. Unknown to Turley and Zuckerman, one of their bullets, skipping crazily from a boulder, had struck the horse behind the left stirrup, boring deep. Daniel had felt the impact through muscle and bone, and heard the grunt of pain that the strike of the bullet had forced from the black and white horse's lungs. Still, the gelding plunged on, carrying its rider higher to where the ridge was cloaked with juniper and mountain mahogany.

Without warning, the paint's front legs suddenly folded under it, plunging its nose into the soft soil of the ridge. Daniel kicked his feet from the stirrups and pushed himself free as the horse tumbled back down the slope, coming to rest in the branches of a lightning-felled juniper where it lay unmoving. Daniel trotted down to the horse to see what he would be able to salvage. To his chagrin, the canteen that had been strapped to the saddlehorn was crushed, the last of the water trickling from a ragged tear in the side of the vessel. The saddlebags had torn open, scattering dirty shirts, a box of cartridges and various other items down the slope.

A cloth bag held what turned out to be jerky; another contained several pieces of lint-covered horehound candy. Daniel tore off a piece of the salty dried meat and put it in his mouth to soften as he untied the blanket roll from behind the cantle of the saddle. In addition, the rifle that had belonged to the ill-fated paint horse's late owner had somehow miraculously come through intact.

Daniel was no stranger to firearms; he had served with distinction during the late War Between the States. When that conflict had ended, he had vowed to never again take up arms against his fellow man, and at the time he had meant to keep that vow, even if it killed him. Unbidden, the thought came to him as he retrieved the weapon that now he had more to think of than just himself. Marta and their baby - or babies, as his wife was sure that she was carrying twins – had entrusted their lives to him, as well. In all things he placed his trust in the Lord, and it could be that the Lord had made sure that the gun would be there for him to find.

Voicing a brief prayer for the Lord's guidance, Daniel slid the rifle from the scabbard, then reached down for the box of cartridges. He made sure that the Winchester's magazine was full, then rolled the remaining cartridges up in the blankets. Carrying the blanket roll over his left shoulder and the rifle in his right hand, he headed out on foot across the juniper-clad slope in the last of the day's sunlight, stepping on rocks wherever possible in order to leave the least possible sign of his passage for his pursuers to find.

Twenty minutes later Turley and Zuckerman found the dead horse. "Looks like one of us got a bullet in the horse, anyway," Turley opined.

"Yeah, but where's the preacher? And where's that woman? I didn't see her with him on the horse, did you?" Zuckerman questioned.

"Come to think of it, I din't neither. I was so busy tryin' to kill *him* that I done forgot about *her*!"

"You reckon she's back down yonder?"

"I'll just bet ya she is. Hell, we don't need to run him down. All we gotta' do is get ahold of that there woman, and he'll hand himself over to us easy as you please."

"Then what're we waitin' for?" Zuckerman reined his horse around and started back down the slope toward the dark bottom of the canyon, Turley following closely on his heels.

Daniel watched from the cover of a juniper thicket atop the ridge as the two riders found the dead horse. He lay behind the trunk of an ancient, wind-whipped juniper, rifle across the bulging roots, waiting for the two men to turn in his direction. They conferred briefly before turning their horses back toward the creek and out of sight. Though he didn't know the reason why they'd left his trail, he was glad they were gone. With night coming, he needed to get back to Marta.

Full dark snared him before he was half way back to the creek. He sat down under a spreading juniper to wait for the moon to rise and light his way down the ridge. Waiting galled; his worry over Marta was a goad that rasped his nerves raw. By the time the first silver light spread across the ridge top and down into the canyon he was nearly frantic; it was only when the moon-washed sage across the canyon became visible that he suddenly realized what he was doing – or wasn't doing. He forced himself to drop to his knees, hands clasped before his face; fervently he asked God for strength to overcome his worry, and for guidance and protection for himself, and even more so for his wife. When he continued down into the canyon this time, he was at peace.

Water splashed and tinkled over rounded stone, droplets glittering in the silver light. Daniel knelt and dipped up the cold water in his hands and drank deep, slaking the thirst born from hours of tension, fear and worry. He stood, wiped his hands on his trousers, took up rifle and blanket roll and started upstream. Now he walked in the road, confident that the hunters would have ended the chase for the night. He strode rapidly up the wagon track closest to the creek, sure that if Marta were there, she would see him and call out. The sudden rattle of bit chains as a horse tossed its head saved his life.

Without conscious thought the former cavalryman threw himself in a rolling dive into the tall stand of bunchgrass and sumac beyond the edge of the road as shots boomed and muzzle flashes lit up the night. Bullets lanced through the space he had just vacated. He levered the Winchester and returned fire, spacing his shots from left to right, purposefully holding high, hoping only to discourage the shooters. He wanted, not to kill them, but to make them think of their own possible deaths and ride off. Instead, the deadly blooms of fire came faster, lead whining from the rocks and tearing bits from the sage along the edge of the wagon track, spattering him with splinters and rock fragments. Then came the loudest sound that any shooter can possibly hear: the click of the hammer falling on an

194

empty chamber, while being sure at the same time that his opponent's weapon is still loaded.

Over the ringing in his ears Daniel could hear two voices cursing as the shooters hurried to reload their rifles. Taking a chance that they wouldn't expect him to be so bold, he slipped to his right twenty feet, then suddenly stood up, his back to the shadow of a cottonwood stretching toward him from the far bank of the creek. The two shooters were fully illuminated by the moonlight flowing down the ridge. Daniel levered a shell into the rifle's chamber and barked over the sound of the water, "You gentlemen drop your weapons and raise your hands!"

Turley and Zuckerman went still, rifles half-loaded. They looked at each other and Daniel could almost see their thoughts. They had him outnumbered two to one, and he was a preacher, and a preacher wouldn't shoot, would he? In an attempt to forestall any precipitous action by the two men, Daniel snapped, "Drop the guns! Now! I've got the drop on you!"

"You cain't git us both!" Turley yelled, raising his rifle. Daniel's bullet slammed him back against the hillside behind him. Turley's own shot blasted off into space as Zuckerman threw himself to the side. His shoulder slammed into a nearby juniper, his rifle skittering across the rocky ground. The miner turned hunter heard the cycling of the action of Daniel's rifle and frantically threw his hands in the air.

"Don't shoot, preacher!" he yelled. "I ain't shootin' no more!" He quickly lifted his pistol from the holster and tossed it out into the road. "I ain't shootin' no more!"

~ ~ ~

Marta stumbled through the deep darkness of the canyon bottom, the sound of the creek on her left guiding her, and only the occasional glint of starlight on water letting her see anything of her surroundings. She had a stitch in her side, a blister on her heel and an abominable ache in her back; still she stumbled on, stubbornly determined to find the source of the small green apple she had found in the water so many hours before.

When the lights came into sight ahead of her she stopped and stared wonderingly, hoping against hope that the warm gold of their invitation was real and not merely the product of her exhausted mind and wishful thinking. The sudden barking of a dog, the soft lowing of cattle and the sleepy bleat of a goat urged her hopefully forward.

Marta staggered toward the homey sounds; abruptly, a sudden clamping pain burst in her belly. "No, please, not now!" she pleaded, face raised to the heavens as her arms wrapped protectively around herself. The pain subsided and she continued walking, aiming for the comfort of the lights ahead.

Young Michael Beckman was in his bed in the loft of the one-room cabin, but he wasn't asleep. Although his had been a busy day, what with fishing, turning over rocks in the creek to look for crayfish and just generally doing little boy things, he was far from sleepy. So when the Beckman's shepherd dog, Bo, began to bark, Michael eagerly popped out of his blankets. "Hey Pa, what's Bo doin'? Can I go see? Are you goin' outside? Maybe it's a bear. Do ya think it's a bear, Pa?"

"You keep yourself where you are, son," Joshua answered, laughing at the boy's stream of words. "I'll see what's got Bo stirred up. It's probably just coyotes." Looking up from where she was knitting socks for their rambunctious son, Lizzie Beckman smiled at her husband as he crossed their small cabin toward the door.

His hand was on the latch when a soft rap sounded. Joshua reached above the door for his rifle as he called out sharply, "Who's there?"

A weak, plaintive cry seeped through the thick wooden door. "Please, can someone help me?" Keeping the rifle in his hand, Joshua cautiously opened the plank door a few inches, enough to let him see the source of the words. He was shocked to find a very pregnant young woman standing, trembling, on his doorstep.

"Please sir, can you help me?" Marta asked, doing her best not to tumble at the man's feet. "I believe that my baby is coming."

Joshua threw the door open wide, put the rifle back on its pegs above the door and reached out to take her arm. "Lizzie!" he called over his shoulder. His wife was instantly at his side. "Come in, please! Where did you come from! How did you get here?" As he and Lizzie led Marta to Lizzie's rocker by the fire and lowered her into the soft cushions, they exchanged glances over Marta's head. The young woman was dirty, and her clothing was torn. This had to be the woman whom the bully who had come to their homestead earlier in the day had been hunting for. That she had escaped from her pursuers was nothing short of a miracle.

"Please forgive my coming to you like this,"

Marta said softly. "I've been walking for hours, and my husband...my husband may have been killed. I have nowhere else to turn." Tears welled up in her eyes and trickled slowly down her cheeks, streaking the dirt caked there. Another pain caused her to bend forward. When it subsided she added, "And now my baby is coming. Can you help me?"

Lizzie was a decisive and practical sort, much like Marta herself. She immediately began snapping orders to her husband even as she grabbed a damp cloth to wash the dirt from Marta's cheeks. "Joshua, stoke up the fire, then get me some more water. Get the oilcloth out of the chest and put it on the bed, then you can take Michael over to your brother's house and send Kathleen over here. You men stay over yonder out of the way. We'll let you know when you can come back."

"Yes, ma'am."

While Joshua was following his orders, Lizzie knelt and removed Marta's shoes. She clucked her tongue in dismay at the tattered state of the young woman's stockings and the blisters on her heels. When her husband and her son had left the cabin, she spread a blanket over the oilcloth-covered bed and helped Marta to stand and hobble painfully to the bed. She helped Marta off with her dress. "How long ago did your water break, dear?" Lizzie asked.

"I...I'm not sure," Marta answered. "I think it was just after I saw your lights."

"Not long then." Lizzie crooned gently as she helped Marta to stay calm. "Let me help you off with these underthings, then you can lie down and get yourself ready for the big event." When Marta was comfortably tucked under a second blanket, Lizzie sat down beside the bed to wait for the baby to come.

The Beckman women, Lizzie and Kathleen, sat on either side of Marta, each grasping one of the young woman's hands as the labor pains surged through her. In a few brief sentences, Marta had explained something of the events of their kidnapping and captivity, and of the couple's daring escape from the gold mine. When she recalled how her husband had led the hunters away so that she could make her escape, they could hear the worry in her voice. Both were sure that the stress of the past days and hours would take their toll on the impending birth. Lizzie had midwifed several difficult deliveries, but those had all been under much more regular circumstances; this one most definitely would not be regular. "What are you going to do?" Kathleen whispered to her sister-in-law. "She's not supposed to have this baby yet!"

"Shh!" Lizzie cautioned. "She'll hear you."

"You needn't whisper," Marta panted, her pain abating for the moment. "I know it's not my time yet."

"Babies come when they will," Lizzie answered calmly, "and it doesn't matter what the rest of us think. All we can do is put it in the hands of the Lord."

"I believe that *babies* is the proper word," Marta said. "I believe that I'm carrying twins."

"Lord!" Kathleen said under her breath.

"We will see," Lizzie said, shooting her sister-in-law a stern look. "We will see."

The pains were coming faster now, peaking and subsiding, growing steadily stronger, each peak more intense than the last. Marta was panting, wanting only for the pain to go away. "You're doing fine," Lizzie told her soothingly. "Not much more to go." Marta cried out, and the baby's head began to appear. "Now I want you to push!" Lizzie told her, voice loud, hands ready for the new arrival to come. Another cry, and the head was fully out, shoulders pushing through one at a time, then the the tiny, wet, wrinkled red bundle was in Lizzie's hands. She quickly tied and cut the cord, then upended the tiny girl child and swatted her briskly on the behind. This indignity was met with a squall of righteous anger the size of its owner. Lizzie smiled and handed the little one to Kathleen, who quickly wiped the baby dry, then wrapped her in a blanket that had been warming by the fire. Lizzie turned back to Marta.

The young woman had been correct in that she was indeed carrying twins; however, the birth of the second child was much more difficult than the birth of the baby girl.

The second baby was a boy, and he was coming breech, or backward. Suddenly afraid, Lizzie carefully worked to turn the child around in order for the birth to be correct. "You can't push now!" she told Marta. "Please don't push!" Marta only heard "push" as she strained against the pressure. Lizzie could feel no movement from the child she was trying so hard to save. At last, unable to turn the baby, she drew first one leg, then the other, out into the open, keeping gentle pressure on them, wanting to help, not injure. Slowly, ever so slowly, more of the baby slipped free, but Lizzie's worries grew. When the hips were free, she pulled harder, hoping to prevent what she was sure she was going to find. Her worst fears were realized when she drew the baby free of his mother. The cord was twisted tightly around his neck and his face was blue.

The boy baby was dead.

Lizzie's eyes filled with tears as she tied and cut the second cord. Kathleen's own tear-filled eyes met hers as she handed Lizzie a towel; she wrapped the tiny body in the soft cloth and set it aside while she finished her work. Now was the time to care for the living.

~26~

Hanna's buckskin horse was all in. The gelding had covered a lot of miles and was ready for a long rest. Full dark had found them still two miles out of Baker City. Heads low, horse and rider pulled up in front of Frannie Kinsella's house and Hanna swung stiffly to the ground, dropping the reins, knowing the horse would stay where she left it. Her hands went to the small of her back and she stretched, a groan escaping her lips as she shuffled tiredly up to the front door.

The brass knocker sent echoes dancing along the street as she banged it once, then twice more, impatient for her aunt to answer the door. Lamplight flickered behind the lace curtained entryway window, and she heard her aunt's voice ask cautiously, "Who's there?"

"Aunt Frannie? It's me, Hanna," the young woman answered. "I need to talk to you. It's really important."

Locks turned, then the door swung silently open. Frannie stood wide-eyed in her night gown and robe, a lamp in her left hand and a pistol in her right. "Come in, girl, come in." She caught sight of the tired horse standing in her yard. "You'd better have a good reason for your horse to be that exhausted," she scolded her niece sternly as she turned toward the kitchen. "I think the coffee might still be warm. You look like you could use some. Then you can tell me what's so important that you have to ride a good horse down that way."

As she stirred two lumps of sugar into her coffee, Hanna explained where she'd been and why she was in Baker City. Frannie listened without a word to the whole story. "I know Tyler, and I know Randolph Martin. Can you make the ride back tonight?" Hanna nodded. "Good. Take your horse to Tarrington's and leave him, then get three more. Tell Marcus where we're headed; he'll know which horses we'll need. Tell him that I said to saddle them, then you bring them back here. I'll go get Rand. Hurry! I'll have some food ready for you to eat on the move when you get back."

"Are you going, too?" Hanna asked in surprise.

"Of course!" Frannie declared. "What made you think otherwise?"

"Well, I just didn't figure you..."

"I what?"

"Never mind. I'll go get the horses," Hanna answered. The girl picked up her hat from the table, dipped her free hand into Frannie's cookie jar on the counter and returned to her horse, stuffing the sweet into her mouth on the way. Frannie headed for her bedroom to change into clothing more suitable for a long night in the saddle.

The night clerk at the Antlers Hotel stared at Frannie as if he'd never before seen a woman wearing canvas pants, mule ear boots and a pistol; perhaps he hadn't. "You want me to what?" he gaped, apparently nonplussed by the sudden interruption of his usual peaceful routine.

"I want you to go to Rand Martin's room and give him that note there in front of you," Frannie commanded him firmly. "And I want you to do it now, not later."

"But who's gonna watch the front desk?" the fellow asked. Frannie looked around the hotel lobby.

"I don't exactly see crowds of people clamoring to check into this establishment," she answered derisively. "It'll only take a minute, and I'll be here the whole time."

"But, but..."

Disgusted, Frannie said, "Never mind, I'll do it myself. What room is he in?"

"I can't let you do that!" the clerk declared.

"How are you planning to stop me?" she asked. "Now what room is he in?" Sensing that discretion might be the better part of valor, the clerk gave her the information she was after, then turned his back, refusing to watch her climb the stairs. She strode purposefully to Rand's room, slowing as she approached the door, and knocked cautiously. She heard footsteps end well short of the door.

"Who is it?"

"Frannie Kinsella, Rand. I've got a message from Bowie Tyler."

"Just a moment." Chair legs scraped on board, the lock rattled and the door swung open. Rand took in the sight of her in men's clothing without blinking. From the lateness of the hour and the way that she was dressed he knew that what she had to say was important.

"Come in, come in! Has Bowie found something?"

"He sent my niece to tell you that as far as he knows they're still free, he knows where they were being held, and that she's to bring you to him. Hanna's bringing fresh horses to my house, so we can leave as soon as you're ready. I've already put some food together."

"We?"

"That's right. I'm going with you."

"Are you sure..."

"Yes, I'm sure. I'll wait for you in the lobby."

Hanna arrived back at Frannie's house, horses in tow, to find that her aunt and Rand were already in the gun shop. "You don't have a rifle with you, do you?" Frannie asked Rand. Before he could answer, she lifted a '76 Winchester from the rack near her workbench, opened the action and handed it to him. "Take this one. It's a .40-65, and it shoots very well out to two hundred yards." She slid a box of cartridges across the glass top of the counter, then took down another rifle for herself. Rand quickly closed the action and thumbed shells into the loading gate of the '76.

They stepped through the narrow doorway from the shop into the kitchen, where they found Hanna hurriedly munching roast beef and biscuits while she waited. Frannie shot her an amused look. "What?" Hanna asked around a mouthful of food. She swallowed and said, "Sorry, I was hungry. Are we ready?"

"That we are," Rand answered. "You must be Hanna?"

"Oh, sorry," the young woman answered. She wiped her hand on her pants and stuck it out in Rand's direction. They shook hands and she headed for the door, Rand and her aunt close behind. Frannie carried a parcel wrapped in brown paper and tied with stout twine. Their three mounts - a dun, a sorrel and a bay - stood tethered to the hitching post in front of the house. Frannie closed the door behind them and strode to the dun, slipped her rifle into the scabbard under the off-side stirrup and stuffed the parcel into a saddlebag.

"The bay's yours," she told Rand. "I don't know whether you'll have to adjust the stirrups or not."

He slid the 76 into the scabbard, then lifted the stirrup to tuck it under his arm, which was outstretched along the leather fender. His fingertips touched the edge of the saddle's worn-smooth seat. "Close enough," he answered. He pulled loose the slipknot that secured the bay's reins to the post, led the horse away from the others, tightened the cinch and stepped into the saddle. He settled his pistol where it was comfortably at hand, then nodded to Frannie.

"Vamonos, amigos," the redhead called. "Hanna, lead us out. You know where we're headed."

"Yes, ma'am!" Hanna reined the sorrel toward the road out of town and heeled it into a trot. They would have to hurry, but the smiling face of the full moon gave plenty of light to travel by. It was only in the last hours before sunrise that they'd lose the light; Hanna intended to be most of the way to the meeting place by that time.

Bowie lay on his belly, telescope to his eye, at

the same point on the ridge from which he and Hanna had watched Valentine's arrival that afternoon. From his vantage point, he could just make out movement as men went about their business at the mine; there wasn't enough light to see detail. He lowered the spyglass to the grass in front of him and rubbed his eyes. There really wasn't much sense in watching the mine from here, but it gave him something to do to take his mind off of the Martins and what might be happening to them.

He picked up the spyglass for another round of watching-not-much-happen in the ravine across the way; again, muted shots echoed down the canyon as Turley and Zuckerman sprang their ambush on Daniel Martin. The sounds were muted, at least a half mile away, and Bowie cursed helplessly. He couldn't possibly get to the site in time to help; in addition, he knew that it was too dark in the canyon to even try to get there with any kind of speed. The Martins were on their own until morning.

$$\sim \sim \sim$$

Turley felt the blood seeping through his fingers from the hole in his belly, down low on the left side. Life-threatening or not, he neither knew nor cared; he just knew that it felt like his insides were on fire. He groaned as a spasm of pain tore through him.

Ten feet away, Zuckerman lay on his side, hands securely bound behind him with his own lariat, feet tied and doubled up as near his backside as Daniel could make them. From the miner's ankles a short tether led up and around his throat; he was forced to keep his legs bent or risk strangling himself. "Yer a preacher!" he gasped through the pressure on his windpipe. "You ain't s'posed to be doin' this!"

"I'm also the husband of the woman you're trying to kill!" Daniel grated as he tied the last knot. "And I don't take kindly to such behavior. Count your lucky stars that I am a man of God; if not for that you'd be dead." He got to his feet and stepped over to where Turley lay curled on his left side. Lifting the wounded man's pistol from its holster, he emptied the cylinder and tossed the gun into the bushes. He knelt beside his recent adversary and struck a match, wanting to see how badly the man was hurt.

"Move your hands," Daniel ordered. When Turley didn't move, he reached down and forced the hands away from the wound. He rolled the wounded miner onto his right side, eliciting another groan from him. Turley's belly was wet with blood, but the stain was spreading slowly; no arteries had been cut. Daniel untucked the man's shirt and lifted it free of the wound. The bullet had gone through the muscle and fat just above Turley's belt, and possibly two inches in from his side, exiting out his back without doing much more than punch a hole.

"You're not hurt that badly," Daniel told him. "Lie still and I'll find something to bandage those holes with." He went to the men's horses, rummaged through saddlebags by feel in the darkness and came up with a reasonably clean-smelling shirt. Still working by feel and what little starlight found its way into the canyon bottom, he ripped the shirt into two pads, the first of which he pressed against the bullet's entry hole. He ordered Turley to "hold that tight", then tore the longest strips that he could get from the rest of the garment.

"I'm going to pull you up so I can wrap these pads in place," Daniel prepared the miner. He hauled him to a sitting position, pressed the second pad against the exit hole and quickly wrapped the two folded cloths in place with the remaining pieces of the shirt. "You shouldn't bleed to death now, anyway," he informed Turley. "I'm going to tie you to that tree over there, and I don't want to see either of you on my backtrail from here on out." Dragging the wounded man to the tree, he quickly bound him to it using what remained of Zuckerman's rope.

"I'm taking your horses. I'm sure some of your friends will be along some time after daylight. Goodbye." Daniel led the two horses out onto the road, stepped into the saddle and disappeared from sight upstream.

Keeping his mount at the fastest walk that he felt was safe under the circumstances, Daniel rode with the rifle across his lap, eyes and ears straining for any sight or sound of his wife.

~ ~ ~

The baby girl was hungry. She'd been unceremoniously brought out into bright light and cool air long before she should have been. Lizzie picked the tiny squirming bundle up and carried her to her mother, who looked at the baby with wonder and love as she held out her hands for her child. "She needs to eat, but I don't know if I have anything for her," Marta said sadly. "And she's so tiny. Will she live?"

Lizzie laid her hand on the young woman's shoulder. "We have goat's milk in the springhouse; we'll feed her some of that if you can't feed her. But you should try; her mother's first milk is important." She helped Marta to get the baby situated then watched, smiling tenderly, as the little one did her best to get her tiny belly full. "She's strong for her size," Lizzie said softly. "If we can keep her warm and fed, I've no doubt that she will be just fine."

As if suddenly realizing the circumstances of her daughter's birth, Marta began, "What about..." Lizzie shook her head. Tears filled Marta's eyes and trickled down her cheeks. As a single salty drop fell from her chin to splash on her little girl's forehead, the cloth in Lizzie's hand swooped down to wipe it clear. Her own eyes were wet; she knew what it was like to lose a baby during the birthing; a tiny headstone behind their cabin marked that baby's resting place.

"There'll be time enough for that when your husband arrives," Lizzie soothed. "For now, you have your daughter to care for. What are you going to call her?"

Marta didn't hesitate as she looked gratefully into Lizzie's kind eyes. "Elizabeth Kathleen."

Bo was a good watch dog. The shepherd was smart; he knew that coyotes were low on the list of varmints that he needed to worry about here in the canyon, and consequently he rarely barked when they sang their songs to the moon and stars. His job was to warn his people of whatever bigger critters might happen by, so when the two horses appeared, dark silhouettes in the silvery moonlight at the lower end of the Beckman's orchard, Bo sounded the alarm.

At the first sound of the dog, Daniel halted the horse he was riding; the one he led bumped his mount, then both stood still. As he drew to a stop, the light in the furthest cabin suddenly blinked out. Daniel heard a door creak open, then an uneasy silence, broken only by the sound of the gurgling stream, enveloped the homestead. He raised his hands to shoulder height, leaving the rifle aslant across his lap. "I'm friendly, mister," he called.

"You'd better be, coming to a man's house this time of night," a low voice rumbled from somewhere to his right and behind him. "What's your business here?"

"I'm looking for my wife," Daniel answered carefully.

"She run off from you?" the question rose from the shadows to the preacher's left. Daniel quickly assessed his situation: two men, two guns, and he was out in the wide open, brightly lit by the full moon hanging straight overhead, while they were safely out of sight in the shadows of the canyon bottom.

"No sir, she did not. We were kidnapped, and we managed to escape. Men are hunting us; I don't know how many. Two of them are tied up down-canyon, one with a bullet hole in him. Earlier today I drew them off and sent her on, but they went back down into the canyon. They ambushed me after dark and I don't know if she made it this far or not. Daniel paused, uncertainty suddenly engulfing him. "She's pregnant, and I have to find her!" he finished, his voice ragged with fear and worry.

"You reckon he's telling us the truth, brother?" the voice from the right asked.

"If he isn't, we'll find out pretty quick," the other

voice answered. "Mister," the same voice ordered, "If two men bushwhacked you in the dark and they're the ones that're tied up, then you must be right handy. So here's what I want you to do: you get yourself down off of that horse, real careful, and you lay that there shooter down flat on the ground and keep your hands where we can see 'em. We've already been threatened once today, and we don't take kindly to such behavior."

Moving slowly and carefully, Daniel dismounted and just as slowly and carefully laid the Winchester on the grass at his horse's feet. "Now drop the reins and step ahead," the voice from his right ordered. Daniel did as he was told, keeping his hopeful gaze locked on the golden glow from the oilskin-covered windows of the other cabin. Footsteps approached him from behind, then quick hands checked him thoroughly for other weapons while he kept his own hands raised. "You can drop your hands now, mister. What's your name?"

"Martin. Daniel Martin," he answered quickly. "My wife's name is Marta. Have you seen her? Is she here?"

"She's up yonder in my cabin," the first brother answered as he stepped up beside Daniel. "I'm Joshua Beckman. That short gent coming up on your other side is my brother Jedidiah." Daniel looked up at Jedidiah, who towered over him by most of a foot.

"Don't pay him no nevermind," Jedidiah chuckled. "He's just upset 'cause his wife booted him out of his cabin for the birthing."

"Birthing? What birthing? It's not Marta's time! It's too early!" Daniel nearly yelled. He began to trot toward the lights ahead.

"Hold on a minute, mister," Joshua called, hurrying to catch up. "You bust in there without asking and

212

Lizzie's liable to belt you upside the head with something. She can get a tad bit abrupt sometimes. You'd best let me go on ahead and see if she's ready for callers."

Daniel stopped long enough for Joshua to go ahead of him. "Hurry, please! I want to see my wife!"

Joshua tapped on the cabin door. "Lizzie? That woman's husband is here, and he wants to see his wife!" he called.

"Send him in, but you stay out!" Lizzie answered. "She doesn't need any other visitors!"

"Go on in, mister," Joshua told him. The cabin door swung open and Daniel hurried to Marta's side. Lizzie gave her husband a smile before she shut the door.

"Daniel! Oh, Daniel! You're alive!" Marta exclaimed.

"I told you I'd come for you, didn't I?"

"Yes you did, but I was so worried." She lifted the bundle in her arms. "Daniel, this is our daughter."

Daniel hesitated, then wonderingly reached out a finger to lightly stroke the soft skin of the baby's forehead. "She's beautiful, my love," he said softly. "And so are you. I've been so worried, but I prayed for us both to be safe, and for us to be brought back together, and here we are. And we have a beautiful new baby!" He sat carefully beside her, slipped his free arm behind her shoulders and hugged her gently, tenderly. "Thank the Lord; He has brought us safely through the valley!"

"It's not over yet, Daniel," Marta reminded him gently. "That man has to be brought to justice for what he has done to us."

"He will be, my love, he will be," Daniel answered. "But for now, you should rest." He leaned

213

down and kissed her forehead. He sat beside her until her eyelids drooped and she faded into sleep. Lizzie carefully lifted the baby from where she slept on her mother's chest and laid her in the blanket-lined box that Kathleen had prepared for her.

"Mister Martin, we need to talk," Lizzie said quietly, her solemn tone catching Daniel's attention.

"Is there a problem with Marta or the baby?" Daniel dreaded the answer.

"Your wife and daughter are fine," she assured him. "Your daughter was early, but she's strong." She paused for a moment, trying to choose the best words for what she had to say. She decided to tell him straight out. "There were two babies." She paused as his face paled. "Would you like me to go on?"

He straightened, preparing himself for what he knew was coming. "Please. I have to know."

"Your son was born dead." A knowing sadness rose in Lizzie's eyes. "I don't know any other way to say it."

Daniel closed his eyes, and Lizzie watched as his lips moved in silent prayer. "Where..."

"We wrapped the body in a cloth and laid it aside, out of your wife's sight... we felt that she was stressed enough from the birth."

"Thank you for your consideration," he breathed softly.

"You're welcome. Would you like to bury him here?"

"I think that would be best." Tears brimmed in Daniel's eyes. "Tomorrow morning..."

"That will be fine. Now please, you need to rest also. Your wife will need you to be strong."

"Sometimes I think that all of my strength comes

214

from her," he replied tiredly. "She is so...so...able. I know that I can count on her support when necessary." He smiled ruefully. "And on her sharp tongue when she thinks I need that, too."

~27~

The eastern ridge was outlined with gold, first light beginning to spread across the cliff tops, when Hanna led Rand and Frannie into the swale where she was to meet Bowie on the west side of the canyon. Red's nickered greeting was answered by his stable-mates as the three riders dismounted and Bowie strode down to meet them.

"Have you seen Daniel and Marta?" Rand asked as soon as he saw his deputy.

"Not yet," Bowie answered. "But those hard-cases across the canyon haven't found them, either. They're still sending out search parties. On the other hand, I heard shooting in the dark last night, so I'm not sure exactly what's going on. It came from up-canyon, so I figured to start there. Not knowing the country, I decided it would be best to wait for daylight."

"That was probably a good idea. It will be light in the canyon bottom shortly, then we can go." Rand turned to mount the bay.

"We need to rest the horses," Frannie stated sternly. "We'd best wait for a while before we ride down there."

Rand lowered his boot back to earth, chagrin written on his face. "You're right, of course. And we should probably get some rest ourselves." He turned to look at Bowie. "Your message said that you could show me where they were being held. I want to see it. Is Valentine still there?"

"His carriage is still parked over yonder," Bowie hooked a thumb over his shoulder, "so I reckon he hasn't left yet. Come on up to the top of the ridge and I'll show you." The two men went to Bowie's observation point and Bowie handed his boss the spyglass.

"My horse is rested, so I'm going to head up the canyon and see if I can find where the shooting came from." He looked at Rand. The judge looked tired, worn from worry and the miles a-horseback. "Are you sure you..." he began.

"You needn't worry about me, Deputy Tyler," Rand answered firmly without taking his eye from the telescope. "I'll hold up my end."

Bowie cast a skeptical glance toward the judge's gunbelt and cocked one eyebrow. "Can you use that hogleg you're carrying?" he asked bluntly. "You're probably going to need it before this whole show's over."

"I might just surprise you," his boss answered flatly.

"I don't need any more surprises," Bowie mumbled. Rand chuckled grimly.

The gray light filtering into the bottom of the canyon washed out the last vestiges of the night's shadows, leaving the sumac and sage muted and without contrast. Bowie dismounted in the wagon road and led Red to the creek to drink. When the sorrel had drunk his fill, Bowie stepped into the saddle and reined the gelding upstream, then heeled it into a jog. His eyes cast back and forth, searching for some sign of the fight he'd heard last night, but it was the pained shouting of a man in distress that reached him first.

"Help! Is anybody there? Help!"

Bowie rode forward at a trot toward the sound of the voice. He found Turley and Zuckerman; one struggling to keep from choking himself to death, the other sitting slumped at the base of a slender juniper, bloodstained bandages wrapped around his middle. He reined up and leaned forward with his forearms crossed on his saddlehorn. Zuckerman looked up at the newcomer hopefully. "Hey mister, cut us loose, will ya'?" he gasped. Sometime during the night he had managed to roll onto his back and wedge his feet against a rock, thereby taking some of the pressure from the tether around his neck. Still, the coarse fibers of the lariat had rubbed the skin of his throat raw.

"What happened to you boys?" Bowie inquired, finding himself amused at the evident trouble that had fallen on the two thugs.

"We was ambushed!" Zuckerman declared.

"Oh, really? How terrible!" Bowie commiserated sarcastically. "How many of them were there? And why didn't they just shoot you instead of tying you up and leaving you here for me to find?"

"There musta' been half a dozen or so of 'em!" Zuckerman exclaimed. "We din't have a chance! They shot my partner and tied us up and took our horses!"

"So who bandaged up your partner?"

"Well, er, ya' see..."

"What I see is that you're a liar!" Bowie interrupted, frost suddenly riming his words. "You were the ones who did the bushwhacking, and it backfired on you! The preacher was faster than you boys thought he

218

was, and he got the drop on you. You were lucky." He sat up in his saddle and lifted the reins. "Which way did he go?"

Zuckerman became suddenly defiant as sullenness shrouded his countenance. "Why should we tell you that? If you're so smart, figure it out for yourself."

"I already did," Bowie answered. "You gents take care now, you hear?" He kneed Red around and tapped the sorrel with his spurs.

"Ain't you gonna' cut us loose?" Turley wanted to know. Up until then he'd let his partner do all of the talking.

"Nope!" Bowie called back over his shoulder as he rode on up-canyon.

Two sets of hoofprints pointed the way that Daniel had gone during the night. Bowie followed the tracks at a trot with his Greener across his lap, his right hand wrapped around the wrist of the stock and his thumb on the hammers. 'Though there were wagon-tracks in the road, he was still surprised to hear the barking of a dog and find the two cabins set astraddle the creek, fingers of smoke lifting from the stone chimneys into the still morning air. The aroma of boiling coffee and baking biscuits made his stomach growl.

He drew rein in the small open area in front of the nearest cabin and called out, "Hallo, the house!"

"Why Bowie Tyler, what're you doing here?" Joshua asked from the corner of the cabin. He stepped out into the open, rifle muzzle pointed at the ground.

"Beckman?"

"The very same," Joshua answered. "What can we do for you this time of the morning? Would you care for some grub?"

Bowie slid the Greener into the scabbard under his stirrup and swung down from his saddle. "I'm looking for a man and a woman who may have come this way..."

"You better not be one of them from down yonder!" Joshua declared, sudden hostility in his tone as his rifle muzzle began rising. Bowie hurriedly held up his hands.

"No, now hold on!" he told the tall farmer. "I'm a federal marshal! The people that I'm looking for are my boss's son and daughter-in-law! They were kidnapped, and I've been trying to get them back!"

"You don't look like no lawman. Could I trouble you to show me a badge?"

"I try *not* to look like a lawman," Bowie answered. "And my badge is in my pocket." He carefully reached into his pocket, brought out the bright silver star and pinned it to his shirt. "There!"

Joshua lowered the rifle to his side. "I guess you're telling the truth," he said grudgingly. "There was a gent come ridin' up here yesterday who threatened us and our families if we didn't come tell him if those folks you're looking for showed up here. Jed and I don't take kindly to such doin's." He turned toward the cabin door. "Come on, they're both inside." He led the way to the door and pushed it open. "Lizzie, that Tyler fella's here, and it turns out he's a lawman. He's looking for the Martins," he called inside.

Daniel appeared in the doorway. "Deputy Tyler? How did you get here?"

"It's a long story, Daniel," Bowie answered tiredly, relief that Daniel and Marta were apparently safe etched across his unshaven countenance. He

220

didn't know the young man well, but they had been introduced in Judge Martin's office just after Daniel's return from the war. "Are you and Marta all right? Your father's just a few miles back down the road, waiting for me to let him know that I've found you."

"We're fine," Daniel assured him, a touch of sadness in his expression. "And we have...a new baby girl." As the words caught in his throat, the sudden realization of Bowie's words hit him. "My father's here?! Where is he? Is he nearby?"

"I'll take you to him, but we'll have to be careful. There are search parties out looking for you. I'd just as soon not have to fight my way back to him if I don't have to. You two can come back here while I go after Valentine." Bowie turned to Joshua. "Will you folks be safe enough while I take Daniel to his father?"

"Don't worry about us; we'll take good care of Missus Martin and the baby," Joshua assured him confidently. "But before you go, you'd best have a bite of grub." As he stepped into the cabin, voices wafted through the open doorway and Bowie silently breathed in the quiet sense of calm that seemed to rest comfortably over Daniel and Marta's safe haven. The gracious farmer soon returned with two biscuits, split and stuffed with several thin slices of some kind of meat. He handed the food to Bowie. "Venison backstrap," he said simply.

"Thanks!" Bowie answered gratefully. "My belly's started thinking my throat's been cut!" He took a bite of the warm meat and bread, chewed appreciatively and swallowed. "That's good!" As he swallowed the last bite, Daniel appeared from behind the cabin, leading Zuckerman's horse. The butt of a Winchester protruded from the scabbard under the offside stirrup, ready to hand. Daniel noticed Bowie's uneasy glance at the rifle.

"I was a captain of cavalry in the war, Deputy Tyler," Daniel stated quietly as he thrust his foot into the stirrup and swung himself into the saddle. "I hope not to use it, but I do know how if it becomes necessary. Shall we go?"

Giving in to the inevitable and not wanting to start an argument, Bowie answered, "I reckon." He gathered his reins and mounted. "Please thank your wife for the grub, if you would, Beckman," he said as he heeled Red into motion.

"Please tell Marta that I will return as soon as possible, Joshua," Daniel said to his host as he turned his mount to follow the sorrel gelding. "And thank you for everything you've done for us."

"Y'er most welcome, Daniel," Beckman drawled in return. "You boys be careful now, hear?"

"Careful as a long-tailed cat in a room full of rockin' chairs!" Bowie called back over his shoulder, the smile on his face reflected in his tone. He nudged Red into a trot and the two men vanished around the juniper-clad bend downstream, the clash of steel horse-shoes on granite gravel echoing from the surrounding slopes.

~28~

Shadows were yet long in the gold mine basin when Valentine heard, and chose to ignore, the diffident knock on the door of the small cabin where he'd spent one of the most thoroughly uncomfortable nights of his entire life. The hard, narrow bed, coarse wool blankets and pitter pat of rodent paws on the rough-sawn pine floor all served to prevent him from getting more than occasional snatches of sleep. Consequently, he was in a foul mood -- more so than usual. To make matters worse, he had used the last of his laudanum supply in the early hours of the morning, and the chronic pains that were normally masked by the narcotic were now clamoring for his attention.

A second, louder knock followed the first, accompanied by Digger's hesitant voice. "I...I brought you some breakfast, boss."

With a grimace, Valentine snapped, "Come in, then. And I hope for that so-called cook's sake that what you've brought me to eat this morning is more edible than the swill I was offered last night." The cabin door creaked open, one corner dragging on the splintered floorboards as Digger shoved against it. He carried a cloth-covered tray, which he set down on the rickety table that stood against the wall opposite the bed where Valentine sat.

The lawyer pushed himself to his feet, leaning heavily on his cane, to limp to the table. He lifted the cloth from the tray; there in the middle of a heavy, edge-chipped porcelain plate he found a slab of some unidentifiable meat swimming in a pool of what he identified from the odor as rapidly cooling and congealing bacon fat. At the edge of the pool of grease three biscuits, hard as the granite that made up the backbone of the ridge which the mine tunnels delved into, sat soaking up the fat. A large porcelain mug of black coffee sat beside the plate, the oil from too much time spent on the back burner of the stove making rainbow highlights on the surface of the cooling brew.

"That's disgusting!" Valentine snarled. He swept the tray off onto the floor, smashing the plate and cup, sending flatware flying and spattering Digger's boots with bacon grease and coffee. "How do you men eat such garbage?" he raged.

"Well, that there woman was doin' the cookin' up 'til..."

"SHE WHAT?" Valentine roared. "You let her out into the camp? What were you thinking? No wonder she was able to escape! Why didn't you just open the door for her and let her walk away? It would have been simpler!" Digger stood patiently waiting as his employer sputtered off first into incoherence, then silence.

"I see now that we done wrong, but it seemed like a good idea at the time," he sniveled at the enraged lawyer. Valentine glared at him, his fists clenched as he worked to get his temper under control.

"Clean up that mess, then make sure the search parties know that I want those two found immediate-

224

ly," Valentine ordered in a tight voice. "In fact, tell them that I'm paying five hundred dollars a man to find them and bring them to me, and I don't care what condition they are in."

"Y-Yes sir!" Digger grabbed the straw broom standing in the corner of the room and began to vigorously sweep the floor. When food and dish fragments were in a pile in the corner, he hurried out of the still-open door, leaving Valentine to follow at his own pace.

$$\sim \sim \sim$$

Bowie and Daniel arrived at the foot of the trail that Bowie had used to climb to the top of the ridge the night before. Twice they had been forced to detour around groups of searching riders and it had taken the pair far longer to return to Bowie's starting point than he had anticipated. Reining up in the cover of a pair of close-standing junipers, Bowie carefully surveyed the surrounding terrain for any sight or sound of the enemy before he gave the signal to climb the slope. When they arrived at the rendezvous undiscovered, Bowie silently breathed a sigh of relief.

At the sight of his father, Daniel flung himself from his horse and ran to where Rand stood waiting, an expression of glad relief on his face. He stopped and reached out his hand. Rand clasped it tightly then, pulled the young man into a stout embrace. They stepped apart. "What about Marta? Is she safe?"

"She and the baby are fine, Father," Daniel answered.

"The baby? Surely she wasn't due..."

"Marta went into labor last night; I'm sure it was caused by stress. Fortunately she was able to get to help before the baby arrived. We have a daughter. She was born early and is very small, but she's strong. I'm sure that she will grow up to be fine." He stopped speaking as a shadow crossed his tired features.

"What's the matter, Daniel?" his father asked.

"There was a boy child. He didn't survive the birth..."

Rand's voice cracked as he forced words from his suddenly dry throat. "I'm...so sorry, son." He wrapped an arm about his Daniel's shoulders. "So sorry."

"It was the Lord's will, Father," Daniel said softly. "We buried him at the Beckman's." As he stepped back and turned to meet his father's sympathetic gaze, he became suddenly aware of the two women who were trying their best not to intrude. "Aren't you going to introduce me to your friends?"

"Yes, yes, of course. Daniel, this lovely lady is Mrs. Frannie Kinsella of Baker City. Frannie, my son Daniel." Without a word Frannie stepped up to Daniel and impulsively hugged him.

"I'm so sorry to hear about your child," she said quietly. Daniel whispered his thanks. She stepped back and reached her hand out to grasp Hanna's sleeve and drag the girl forward. "This is my niece, Hanna Dalby." Hanna stuck out her hand awkwardly.

"Howdy," was all she managed to muster before stepping back.

Daniel gazed intently at Rand. "What are we going to do about the man who had Marta and me kidnapped? He can't be allowed to go free."

"What's this 'we' stuff?" Bowie cut in. "You and

your father are going back to your wife and baby, and I'm going to go pay Valentine a visit."

"Just like that?! 'Go pay him a visit'?!" Hanna asked incredulously.

"Just like that," Bowie replied confidently. "How hard can it be?"

"Have you completely forgot what we talked about yesterday?"

"No, I haven't," he admitted. "But I did send three of 'em packing yesterday afternoon."

"Which only leaves what, twenty or so? Are you insane?"

"All I want is Valentine," Bowie persisted stubbornly.

"You are the most cocky, mule-stubborn excuse for a man I have ever met! What you're gonna get is dead!" Hanna exclaimed, turning away from him. She stood staring down the ridge with her back stiff and her arms folded across her chest. The set of her shoulders radiated anger, underscored with what he thought might be worry. Bowie stared after her, a dumbfounded expression on his face. Was it possible that maybe she did have some feeling for him after all?

"If I may interject something here..." Daniel quickly had everyone's attention. "I am not going back to my wife until I can be sure that this is ordeal is truly finished." Bowie began to protest, but Daniel cut him off. "Deputy Tyler, I appreciate what you are trying to do, but I wouldn't feel right leaving all of this on your shoulders. You are going to need some help."

"He's right, Bowie," Rand added. "You can object all you want, but we're going with you."

"As am I!" Frannie declared. "Hanna, get our horses."

"Now wait just a minute, ma'am," Bowie began. "There could be a battle coming up, and I can't in good conscience have you putting yourself and Hanna in danger like that!"

"Deputy Tyler, I am no stranger to a gunfight!" Frannie declared bluntly. "My late husband and I were both deputies in some rough mining towns for five years before we settled in Baker City. And need I remind you that you are not my overseer in this matter?" Behind her Hanna nodded her agreement with her aunt's words.

Bowie gazed helplessly from Rand and Daniel to the two women and back again. Rand chuckled drily. "I think you're beaten, Bowie. I personally make it a point never to argue with a woman with a gun; especially when there are two of them. I strongly suggest that you get your horse and get ready to ride down there; otherwise I'm pretty certain that they're going to go without you." He pointedly turned his back and began to tighten the bay's cinch. Uncertain as to how to evaluate this turn of events, Daniel wordlessly followed his father's example.

"I reckon you're right, boss," Bowie replied resignedly as he strode to where his own horse was standing.

~29~

Malechai Jordan turned his horse north onto the wagon road as he led the four men of his search party toward the homesteaders and their orchard. He was still seething from being forced to back down the day before, and he planned to get his revenge. He felt sure that they were hiding the preacher and his woman, and he planned to make the 'nesters' give them up. Just this morning, Jordan's employer had promised five hundred dollars per hunter in gold coin for the Martins' return, alive or dead. Jordan had no qualms either way; dead was easiest, and he wanted that money.

They were moving along the dirt track at a rapid trot when Jordan heard someone call his name. He held up a hand to signal his men as he reined in his mount and turned toward the source of the voice. "Well, well, what have we here?" he queried of the morning air as he looked down at Zuckerman and Turley. "You boys are in a bit of pickle, ain't you?" he sneered.

"Cut us loose, Jordan," Zuckerman pleaded. "I can't hardly feel my hands no more." Jordan jerked his head toward the two bound men. One of the riders, a French-Canadian named Lebel, dropped to the ground, pulling his knife from its sheath. The razor sharp steel made short work of the tether around Zuckerman's throat, as well as the knotted strands binding his hands and feet. Lebel stepped over to Turley and did the same for the wounded man.

"Thees one, he been shot," Lebel observed, pointing at Turley. He sheathed his knife and swung back into his saddle.

"You gotta' take us back to camp," Zuckerman cut in from where he sat trying to massage some feeling back into his hands. Turley was attempting to do the same, wincing from the additional pain of the bullet hole in his side.

"I don't gotta' do nothin' of the sort," Jordan replied roughly. "I'm bettin' that preacher done this to you boys, didn't he? Which way did he go?"

"If you won't take us back to camp, why should we tell you?" Turley asked sourly.

Jordan cocked the hammers of the shotgun that lay across his saddle pommel. "Because I asked you, that's why!" he snapped. "That man and his woman are worth a lot of money to me, and I ain't lettin' you nor anybody else get in my way. So you got a choice: you can tell me what I wanna' know, or you can die. It makes me no never mind. Which is it gonna' be?"

"You'd shoot us just like that?"

Jordan lifted the shotgun and aimed the barrels directly between Turley's eyes. "You're damn right I would. Now, which way did he go?"

"H-He went upstream," Zuckerman blurted abruptly, realizing suddenly that Jordan wouldn't think twice about shooting both him and Turley and riding away without a backward glance.

"Now, see how easy that was?" Jordan sneered. "You boys have a nice walk." He lowered the shotgun's hammers, reined his horse around and kicked it into a

230

trot again. One of his followers

"Where're we headed?"

"There's some nesters on up this canyon," Jordan answered. "That's where that preacher has to be, if he went upstream like they said." He was silent for another twenty yards, then seethed through clenched teeth, "They think they're tough, but they ain't seen tough yet."

$$\sim \sim \sim$$

When the Beckmans had first settled in the Sisley Creek canyon, they had painstakingly dug a series of ditches to get water to the orchard they had planted there. Joshua was out among the trees, making sure that the water was headed where he wanted it to go, when he heard the clatter of hooves from down-canyon. He pursed his lips and a shrill, three-note whistle pierced the morning air. Picking up his rifle from its resting place among the branches of a small apple tree, Joshua made a beeline for the rock outcropping next to his cabin.

Without pausing to see what the emergency might be, Jedidiah Beckman slammed his axe into a log near the barn where he was chopping wood, snatched up his own rifle from where it leaned against a corral post, ran to the open barn door and slipped inside, turning to press his back against the logs to the right of the opening.

Lizzie heard the whistle from the vegetable garden where she was hard at work chopping weeds. Michael was nearby, digging for worms to use for fish bait;

the boy hollered his protest when his mother snatched up her skirts with one hand and her son with the other as she ran for their cabin. Inside, she slammed the split-log door and slid the locking bar across it. She lifted the double-barreled shotgun from the pegs above the hearth, then turned to the loophole beside the door and slid the muzzles of the gun through the small opening in the wall. There was no need to check if the gun was loaded; it was always loaded.

"What's the matter?" Marta asked sleepily. The slamming of the door had awakened her from a nap.

"Somebody's coming, and Joshua thinks there might be danger," Lizzie answered. "It's probably nothing, but we need to be ready. You just stay there, you'll be fine."

"I don't want your family to be injured because of me," Marta protested.

Lizzie turned to look directly at Marta, speaking calmly and firmly. "You are a guest in this house. As such, your welfare is important to us." Her tone softened. "We believe that a guest once welcomed becomes a member of the family. And we take care of our own." With a reassuring smile, and a quick glance toward Kathleen, she returned her gaze and full attention to the window.

The five riders of Jordan's gang spread in a line across the width of the canyon floor, two to the west of the creek and three to the east, where the canyon widened at the lower end of the Beckmans' homesteads. They slowed their horses to a walk before pushing ahead toward the cabins. Jordan carried his shotgun in his hands; Garner's rifle was braced muzzle-up on his hip. All five horses trod roughshod over and through the tender young trees that the brothers had so painstakingly kept alive. As the hunters reached the corner of the corral, Jedidiah's commanding voice rang out. "That's far enough, you men! State your business!"

Jordan kicked his horse out in front of the group. "We want that preacher and his woman, and we want 'em now. We mean to have 'em if we have to burn this place to the ground to flush 'em out!"

"   You aren't taking anybody, and you're not burning anything," Joshua replied calmly from among the pile of tumbled granite boulders at the foot of the canyon wall. "Now you boys had best turn those horses around and ride out of here while you can."

"Who's gonna stop us?" Jordan snarled. "Get 'em, boys!" He spurred his horse toward the sound of Joshua's voice, raising the shotgun to his shoulder and pulling both triggers as the horse leapt ahead. Powder smoke bloomed in white clouds and lead spattered on the rocks that made up Joshua's fort, powdering small bits of rock from the face of the boulder he crouched behind. Jordan never heard the rifle shot that killed him.

Behind Jordan, Lebel and his saddle-partner Greenlee dropped from their horses and ran toward the corral, pistols flaming as they peppered the barn wall with bullets. Jedidiah's rifle blasted, the big slug slamming Greenlee to the ground well short of cover. Running on, Lebel threw himself to the ground behind a corner post. Wood chips stung his face as Joshua's hastily fired second shot whined off the stout juniper post just at the French-Canadian's eye level. Lebel scurried around the post, leaving himself wide open to Jedidiah's lethal second shot.

The last two hunters were in full, panicked flight. They spurred their horses down-canyon, bent forward over the animals' necks, reins whipping as they willed the horses to run faster. A full mile down the road, they at last were able to draw their racing mounts back to a walk. Garner looked at the lanky, dark-skinned Blake. "I'm for Texas. Ya' with me?" Blake nodded wordlessly, and the two sent their horses into motion down the road. Neither one even considered stopping at the mine to ask for their wages.

"You all right, Jed?" Joshua called as he stepped out from behind the rocks and walked cautiously toward where Jordan lay sprawled, wide-open eyes staring upward at nothing.

"Fine! You?"

"Got stung by a couple of rock chips, but that's it," Joshua answered. Seeing that Jordan was dead, he strode to the cabin and tapped on the door. The shotgun disappeared and he heard the bar sliding. Lizzie opened the door an inch. "It's over, Lizzie, but keep Michael inside until I say different. We've got a bit of a mess to clean up out here." She nodded, shut the door and slid the bar back across it. Jedidiah came from the barn, leading one of their big draft horses, already harnessed. He walked the gelding to their stoneboat, hooked up the tow chains and led the horse to where of Lebel and Greenlee had fallen. The brothers loaded the two dead men into the stoneboat, led the horse up alongside Jordan's body and piled him in with the others.

Jedidiah was matter-of-fact as he helped Joshua spread loose dirt over the blood on the ground. "What'll we do with them?"

"Let's take 'em to the foot of that rockslide up

the creek and roll rocks down on 'em," the older Beck-man brother replied. "That should keep the varmints off." He strode over to the gate that barred access to the upper reaches of the canyon and lowered the poles.

~*30*~

The last of Valentine's search parties had already left the mine when Bowie led his grim-faced troupe out into the wagon road and turned Red toward the shaft. They crossed the creek and rounded the turn to start the climb uphill. The road up this side canyon was narrow, barely wider than the freight wagons that traversed it almost daily. In the lead, Bowie rode stirrup to stirrup with Rand, Greener butt-braced on his right hip, reins in his left hand. A bandoleer of brass-cased buckshot rounds slanted from left shoulder to right hip. His expression was blank, his thoughts on what the coming minutes might bring, trying to visualize and prepare for any contingency.

Riding wordlessly beside Bowie, Rand stared deliberately up the dusty, rock-strewn track. His rapidly whirling thoughts spun back and forth between his jurist's "He'll do life in prison at the very least" to the vengeful father and grandfather's "I want him dead for what he's done to my family". He was unsure which held the most appeal at the moment.

Frannie and Hanna were several long paces behind the two men, talking softly. "You really like him, I can tell," Hanna stated matter-of-factly.

"It could never work," Frannie replied, a tinge of regret coloring her steady voice.

Genuinely curious, Hanna's voice was soft. "Why not?" Hanna had seen her aunt throw herself into her work as a way to overcome her grief after the loss of her husband, shunning any and all advances from would-be suitors...until now. Something in Rand Martin had touched a chord in Frannie Kinsella, and Hanna was sure that the feeling was mutual.

"His life is in Wyoming." Frannie's eyes gazed steadily ahead at the ramrod-straight figure astride the bay horse. "Mine is here."

"Is it?" Hanna asked, sudden insight coloring her tone. "You ain't been truly alive in years, Aunt Frannie. I've seen more laughter and more...I don't know... *life* in you in the past twelve hours than I've seen in the past twelve months. And I think it's all 'cause of that man yonder."

Frannie smiled. "You may be right," she answered softly. She tilted her chin toward Bowie for a brief second. "What about you?"

"Ha!" Hanna sniffed. "That deputy's about the most annoying character I've ever met."

"He got you to ride clear into town and back, didn't he?"

"Humph!"

Not meaning to eavesdrop, but unavoidably witnessing the conversation in front of him, Daniel smiled to himself from his position at the rear of the make-shift posse. He was accustomed to making quick character judgments, and he had seen the look in his father's eyes when he had introduced Frannie as "this lovely lady". His father had clearly found something that he himself didn't even know he was looking for, and Daniel felt an unexpected gladness in his heart. He knew that loneliness had been his father's constant companion since his mother's death; he had watched helplessly as the man who had been so full of love and life retreated into solitude, pouring his heart and soul into his work in a vain effort to forget his grief.

Daniel missed his mother as well, but he also knew that love can come from unexpected directions, as he himself had experienced when he had fallen in love with the feisty daughter of his hometown's mercantile owner. He suspected that the feelings between his father and the lovely redhead riding between them would grow. After the years of loneliness that his father had endured since the death of his beloved Clarissa, Daniel wholeheartedly believed that it was time for Rand to experience true happiness once again.

A hundred yards before they reached the bench occupied by the mine buildings, Bowie reined in and turned Red sideways across the road. "I don't know if this is legal or not, but I think you all need to be deputized. All of you raise your right hand." All four of his companions did as he asked; their expressions ranged from amusement to skepticism. "Do you hereby solemnly swear to uphold the laws of whatever state you happen to be in to the best of your ability?" All four of them nodded solemnly. "Good. Now you're deputies, or close enough, if anybody should ask. Let's go."

The five armed riders spread out in a line at the foot of the rocky, wheel-rutted bench. Bowie centered the group; Rand rode a few yards to his right and Hanna sat her sorrel the same distance to his left. Frannie and the dun flanked Rand; Daniel anchored the opposite end of the uneven line. Frannie had already drawn her pistol; she kept the Smith & Wesson in her lap, mostly out of sight from the cluster of men huddled at the mine opening. The miners stood together near the tunnel, facing the oncoming posse as they listened to the bluster and rage spewing from the lips of the tall figure of Cyrus Valentine.

One by one, the miners began to focus their gaze beyond Valentine's rantings, which halted abruptly when he realized that something behind him had captured his men's attention. The lawyer spun angrily to stare at the new arrivals. His one good eye widened in sudden recognition as he caught sight of Rand and Daniel. "YOU!" he suddenly shouted, pointing at Rand. "How did you get here?" He spun to stare at Daniel. "And I ordered YOU killed! Why are you not dead?"

"Cyrus Valentine!" Bowie barked as he nudged Red out ahead of the others. His gleaming, highly polished badge glittered on his shirtfront. "You are under arrest for kidnapping. Surrender yourself immediately!" Hearing Bowie's words, the miners began to stir; Bowie turned his cold gaze on the group of men, some of whom were armed with pistols. "You men stand fast! I'll deal with you in a few minutes!"

Bowie's momentary distraction was all that Valentine needed. He turned and burst through the group of miners and hurried toward the mine opening, his clumsy run carrying him faster than any of the miners had ever seen him move. With vehemence born out of years of fruitless anger, jealousy and simmering vengeance Valentine screamed as he fled, "Kill them! A thousand dollars to the man who kills the preacher!" He disappeared into the mine.

"No!" Bowie yelled at the miners as those who were armed went for their guns, the others scattering for cover. He threw himself from the saddle, triggering both barrels of the Greener as he miraculously lit on his feet; he staggered with the recoil, wrists smarting, and saw two men go down. Around him, the others dove from their horses to spread out and run for whatever cover they could find. He threw himself down beside Hanna, who had taken cover behind a pile of dirt and rock and was calmly firing her pistol around and over the pile whenever a target presented itself.

"Well, that worked pretty good, didn't it?" the young woman hollered over the boom and crack of the battle; she fired again, and one of the miners dropped his pistol and ran. "Now what?"

Bowie reared up and sent a swarm of buckshot sleeting toward a miner who had taken cover behind the rain barrel at the corner of the small cabin. The shooter's pistol tumbled from his hand as the shot tore into his fingers.

"I've gotta go after Valentine!" he answered. "Watch my back!"

Hanna turned to put her own back against the pile, shucking the empties from her gun and thumbing fresh cartridges into the Colt. "You're too late," she shouted. "Rand is already after him."

Bowie risked a glance around the pile just in time to see Rand, who had somehow managed to get behind the shooting miners, vanish into the mine entrance. "Oh crap!" he grunted. Then he shrugged. There was nothing to do now but clean up what he'd started out here, and hope that the judge knew what he was doing.

Rand slipped silently inside the mine opening; his eyes straining for any clue as to Valentine's whereabouts. He stepped behind a nearby support timber

240

to flatten himself against the rough rock wall while he waited for his eyes to adjust to the dimness of the shaft after the bright morning light outside. He slid his linen duster off of his shoulders and let it drop to the floor, kicking it away from his feet. As he paused to collect his thoughts and calm his breathing, he heard what sounded like a rock tumbling across the tunnel floor somewhere in front of him.

"Cyrus!" His voice echoed through the tunnel complex. "Give yourself up! You can't escape from here!" The words rattled and twanged from rock and timber.

"NEVER...never...never..." echoed in answer. "I'll see you in HELL FIRST... hell first... hell first..."

Rand peered cautiously around the timber. Before him, a line of bulls-eye lanterns shed dim yellow light in pools along the tunnel. Each pool was separated from the next by Stygian, inky blackness that grew darker as the shaft bored its way further into the depths of the ridge. He drew his pistol and stood considering his options for a moment. With a sigh of resignation, he seated it back in the holster and hooked the rawhide tie-down over the hammer; this would not be a matter for guns.

A haphazard pile of tools against the ragged wall yielded a pick; he banged its head against the wall until it slid down the handle to land with a clang on the floor. Hefting the seasoned hickory in his hand, he stepped into the tunnel to begin his search. As he eased himself into the dim bore, the firing outside reached a crescendo; suddenly an explosion boomed, shaking dust from the timbers of the tunnel. The blast gradually faded to a few lingering echoes which reverberated from the canyon walls outside.

~31~

The horses survived the opening volley of the battle unscathed, except for a long, oozing scratch on the dun's neck. When the first shots were fired and their riders left their saddles, the animals had scattered back down the canyon. As Rand's bay had spun to run, the '76 clattered from its scabbard to lay unnoticed in the dust of the track.

While Hanna reloaded her Colt, Bowie took quick stock of their situation. Daniel and the two women each had their rifles and their pistols; Bowie had his pistol and shotgun. He slipped his hat off and peered around the heap of rock he was tucked behind. The armed miners had taken cover on the far side of a pile of wooden crates; at that range, pistol bullets plugged into the heavy wood without penetrating.

At sight of the dusty glimmer of Rand's heavy caliber rifle, Bowie was struck by a sudden inspiration. Waiting for a lull in the firing, he called to Hanna, "I'll be right back!" then rolled to his feet and made a sudden dash for the Winchester. He snatched it from the dust and charged forward, his short legs churning as he raced madly for the door of the small cabin. Throwing himself into the one-room building, he immediately discovered that someone else was already there before him. The miner whose hand he'd caught with the shotgun blast minutes before was trying desperately to stop the blood dripping steadily from his torn flesh. When Bowie suddenly crashed through the door the man threw his hands in the air, flinging red droplets across the room.

"Don't shoot, mister! I'm out of it!"

"You'd better be!" Bowie snapped. "Get out of here!" He pointed toward the window; the miner hurriedly picked up the strips of wool blanket he'd been using to bandage his hand and beat a hasty retreat. The markings on the box he used as a step in facilitating his exit caught Bowie's eye. *"GIANT POWDER"* was stenciled on the end of the small rope-handled crate. The miner's foot had kicked the lid askew to reveal sticks of powder whose waxy covering glowed in the light from the window. A brief search of the cabin rewarded Bowie with a small box of detonators, a coil of fuse and a box of matches. A broad smile lit up the deputy's face while he thought out his next move.

Bowie had handled powder before, but it still made him nervous. He carefully cut one of the sticks in two and laid the two halves on the table. Cutting several varying lengths of fuse, he took them to the stone fireplace to light them; it was important to know how fast the fuses burned. This particular coil turned out to be fast-burning, as he had hoped. He returned to the table, inserted the caps, then carefully crimped the fuses in place. He tucked the sticks in separate vest pockets, picked up the '76 and headed for the cabin door. "Hanna!"

"What?"

"I'm coming back! You three open up on that pile of crates with your rifles!"

"Okay!"

Hanna, Frannie and Daniel began firing at the miners' hiding place as fast as they could work the levers of their Winchesters. When Bowie was as sure as he could be that the miners had their heads down and were occupied with something other than shooting him full of holes, he dashed across the space between himself and Hanna to dive headlong behind the rock pile. He leaned back heavily, panting to catch his breath. When he had mostly recovered from his run, he brought out the dynamite.

"It took you long enough... where in the world did you get that?!" Hanna exclaimed.

"The cabin," Bowie replied calmly. "Where else?"

"What are you gonna' do with it?"

"Make those boys yonder surrender," he grinned. Hanna stared at him for a moment, then shook her head.

"You really are crazy, you know that?"

"I prefer to think of it as resourceful."

She rolled her eyes and shook her head again. "What do you want us to do?"

He held up one of the sticks of powder. "I'm going to throw one of these out in front of that pile of crates," Bowie explained. "Your job is to make sure that I don't get shot in the process. As soon as I light this thing, you start shooting. Are you ready?"

"I reckon," she answered skeptically, taking a firm grip on her rifle. Bowie scratched a match alight and held it to the first fuse. Sparks immediately began cascading to the ground.

"GO!" Following Hanna's lead, Frannie and Daniel opened up, firing faster than before; Bowie rolled to his knees, cocked back his arm and threw the stick of powder as hard as he could, then ducked back behind the pile of dirt. He reached up, grabbed a big handful of Hanna's sleeve and yanked her down beside him to wrap his arm around her shoulders. "FIRE IN THE HOLE!"

One of the miners saw the thin trail of sparks and smoke coming their way through the thick clouds of white powder smoke that hung and eddied in the damp air. "RUN!" he screamed, throwing himself back away from the crate he'd been hiding behind. Bowie had thrown better than he knew; the stick of powder bounced once, then rolled into the open side of one of the crates. As men scrambled away from the barricade, the powder exploded with an earth-shaking roar, the force partially contained by the walls of the crate, thereby making the blast more intense than it might have otherwise been. The pile of crates disintegrated into a welter of broken boards, splinters and nails that scattered like cannon shrapnel.

Dirt clods, rocks and chunks of charred lumber rattled down around Valentine's stunned men. As the last of the debris fell and the dust cleared, the only sound to be heard was the cursing and groaning of the miners; they had suffered the brunt of the blast. Hanna pulled her hands away from her ears and squeaked, her voice scratchy from the effects of the blast, "Bowie?"

"Yeah?"

"Are we alive?"

"I...think so," he answered tentatively. He coughed, trying to clear the charred dust from his lungs. "Damn!"

"Then let go of me so I can sit up."

"I'm not sure I can move. That was a helluva

blast."

She thumped him on the chest with her fist, hard enough to get his attention. "Let go! I gotta check on Aunt Frannie." His arm loosened its grip on her shoulders and she pushed herself up to a sitting position. She kept her face turned away so that he couldn't see the tiny smile touching her lips.

"You don't do things halfway, do you, Deputy Tyler?" Frannie queried as she gazed around at the wreckage, her normally melodious voice sounding tinny as it echoed through the ringing in Bowie's ears. She stood looking down at the deputy and her niece with a bemused expression on her face.

He grinned up at her then rolled to his knees, pushed himself upright and began to beat the dust from his clothes. Beside him, Hanna did the same. "I try not to, ma'am," he answered. He picked up the Greener, broke it open and reloaded, closed the shotgun and said, "I'd best go see how many of those gents are left over there." He started toward what remained of the heap of crates. Hanna stepped up on his right side, Frannie on his left. Daniel was striding rapidly toward the mine tunnel. "Where do you think you're going?" Bowie called.

"To help my father," Daniel answered over his shoulder, his pace not slowing.

"Do you want to get him killed?"

Daniel halted and turned to face Bowie. "What do you mean?"

"Right now, he knows that it's just him and Valentine in there. He doesn't have to worry about anybody but himself. If you go in there, it'll distract him, and he doesn't need that, not now. You'd best stay out here."

Daniel stared at him miserably for several moments. "I suppose you're right," he conceded. He looked longingly at the dark mouth of the tunnel. "Be careful, Father," he whispered.

~ ~ ~

Rand slipped warily along the tunnel, keeping as close to the wall as possible. He stopped frequently to listen for some sign of Valentine's location, but the only sounds were the drip of water somewhere deeper in the mine and the occasional creak of settling timbers. He kept the pick handle in his right hand, his left shoulder brushing the coarse rock wall. Instead of running in a straight line, the tunnel twisted and turned to follow the ore vein, forcing Rand to walk slowly and check each bend for Valentine's presence.

The black mouth of a side tunnel opened ahead of him on his left. A lantern, its wick turned low, hung at the intersection of the two shafts. Rand pressed his back against the wall at the edge of the opening, forcing himself to breathe as slowly and quietly as possible as he listened intently. He was about to peer around the corner into the tunnel when he heard what was most certainly the sound of someone panting softly, somewhere deep in this new shaft.

"Cyrus!" Rand called. "Please, come out and surrender. There's no need for this."

"You killed my family, Randolph, as surely as if you had set the fire yourself," Valentine blustered, his voice ragged. "I want you to suffer as I have suffered for all these many years."

"I did nothing of the sort, Cyrus," Rand answered his former friend flatly. "None of what happened to you and your family was my fault."

"Oh, but you did kill them, Randolph, and you must pay!" Valentine snarled. "Come here to me if you dare!"

Rand peered into the opening beside him; the only light emanated from the solitary lantern nearby. He picked it from its peg in the tunnel wall and turned up the wick, sending yellow light beaming into the shadowed opening. Movement in the dim interior caught his gaze; hefting the pick handle in his right hand, the lantern in his left, he ventured into the tunnel.

A much disheveled Cyrus Valentine was waiting for him in the murky confines of the shaft. The lawyer's fine silk hat was gone, lost somewhere during his desperate flight through the mine. His tall riding boots were scuffed, the finely tailored britches torn and dirty, and the once stiffly-starched white shirt hung wrinkled and wilted. His sparse hair stood up wildly, and the lantern light reflecting eerily off the ugly scar crossing the lawyer's face gave his features a devilish appearance. The black eye patch had been lost as well, so that the folded tissue remaining where Valentine's left eye had been stood in stark contrast to the mad gleam in his good eye. He leaned heavily on the gold dragon's head which topped his cane, left hand resting over the right; venomous hatred was evident as he glared derisively at Rand. "So..."

The single word seemed to hang, unsupported, poised in the softly whispering air of the tunnel. As Rand set the lantern on the tunnel floor next to the wall, Valentine straightened; his left hand grasped the

248

ebony shaft of the cane as his right hand suspended the cane waist-high, parallel to the floor. The tormented man's rage had gone cold; an icy serenity fell over his ravaged features. With a twist of his wrist, three feet of razor-edged steel hissed into view as the shaft of the cane clattered to the rough stone of the tunnel floor. Valentine's teeth bared in a soundless snarl as he lunged at Rand, intent on driving the honed Sheffield steel of the sword-cane's triangular blade completely through the heart of his target.

Rand clumsily parried the thrust with the shaft of seasoned hickory in his hand, swinging the pick handle up and across his body to bat the blade aside. The tip of Valentine's sword neatly slit his shirt and scored his ribs as he turned his body. He barely blocked the backhand slash that followed.

"You've not kept up with your fencing, Randolph," Valentine taunted. The blade dipped and leaped, pricking a wrist here, leaving a shallow cut on a shoulder there. Rand doggedly kept the pick handle in motion; he could have drawn his pistol but, for some reason he was unable to fathom, this confrontation had become a matter of honor to him. He would defeat Cyrus Valentine by hand, or not at all.

Slowly, as he worked to preserve his life, Rand's muscles remembered the lessons that he'd learned so many years before. While the pick handle was much heavier and more cumbersome than a fencing foil, and Rand wasn't in nearly as fine condition as he had been when he had first taken up fencing as a teenager, the moves were still ingrained in every muscle and nerve fiber. Gradually, he began to parry Valentine's strokes more effectively, until he was finally able to go on the offensive.

The weight of the pick handle worked to his advantage now. He batted the blade aside again to clash against stone, scattering sparks across the floor. Valentine desperately backhanded the blade, only to have it forced away once more. Rand brought the wood down hard, intent on smashing the hand holding the sword; only by scrambling hastily backward was Valentine able to avoid the blow. The hard leather sole of his left boot came down on the discarded ebony shaft of the cane, which rolled forward under the contact, throwing the startled attorney off-balance. He stumbled backward, arms flailing, his damaged leg muscles unable to support his weight properly. As he took several off-balance steps back, his right foot came down on the edge of the vertical shaft that had been the avenue of Daniel and Marta's escape from their prison above.

The sword flew from Valentine's grasp and sailed down into the black maw of the shaft, striking once against the wall on its downward flight. He teetered on the edge, nearly regaining his balance as Rand dropped the pick handle and lunged forward, desperately reaching out for the hand of the man he couldn't help thinking of as his friend. Their fingertips touched, Valentine's single blue eye meeting the anguished gaze of Rand's two gray ones, and Valentine smiled cruelly. "Goodbye, my friend! *We shall meet again...in hell!*" Rand watched in helpless dismay as Cyrus Valentine fell silently to his death.

~*32*~

Peering sadly down into the darkness, Rand listened for the sound of impact. A sodden thud drifted up from below and Rand turned slowly away. "Goodbye, Cyrus," he whispered softly. Bending wearily to pick up the lantern, he found the shaft of the cane and kicked it over the edge of the vertical drop, then headed resignedly back through the mine shaft, feeling much older than his years. Relief and anguish coursed through him in equal measure: relief that his family was finally safe; anguish for the loss of the friendship that had once been so precious to him and which he'd hoped to somehow salvage. The tiny sword cuts stung where the salt of his sweat entered them; he ignored the pain, intent on returning to the surface, praying that his son was alright -- praying in additional measure for the safety of the woman who had come to mean so much to him.

Astonishingly, none of the miners had been killed in the dynamite blast; their friend's warning had come barely in time. Several broken bones, numerous cuts, bruises and punctures and some shattered eardrums were the extent of the injuries. Daniel and Frannie were tending the wounded while Bowie and Hanna rounded up their own frightened saddle horses and enough of the mine's draft animals to pull the wagons necessary to transport the miners to the jail in Baker City. They also found the matched pair of bays that had pulled Valentine's carriage to the mine from town. Bowie led the pair over to Daniel. "Why don't you hitch up Valentine's carriage? You can use it to take your wife and baby home."

"What about Valentine?"

Before the deputy could answer, Rand appeared in the mine opening, his dirty linen duster draped over his sagging shoulders. His halting steps showed the depths of his physical and emotional exhaustion.

"Father!" Daniel raced to his father's side, concern and relief written clearly in the unspoken questions reflected in his eyes.

"He's gone, son," Rand said wearily. The two men embraced. "Let's go home."

Daniel's exclamation had brought everyone's attention to Rand's appearance in the tunnel opening. When she heard the words "go home" Frannie's face fell, and she returned to bandaging a miner's arm where a flying splinter of wood had slashed it open. She was concentrating on her work when a man-shaped shadow fell across her shoulder; she tied off the bandage before she looked up. Rand stood beside her, his left hand held out to her, an uncertain look on his face. She extended her right hand and he pulled her to her feet, turning her to face him. "When this is all over, may I come to call?" he asked softly.

Her smile was all the answer that he needed. He smiled widely himself as he wrapped her in a warm embrace, holding her tightly to his chest.

Bowie watched the couple from a distance, thinking, *I wonder if I'll ever find a woman like that.* From the corner of his eye he saw a wistful expression on Hanna's face that he was sure matched his own; He made up his mind on the spot to do what he could to get closer to Hanna.

Bowie led Red alongside Hanna. "I don't happen to see anything wrong with a woman wearing pants, if that's what's needed," he said diffidently. She turned to look at him, one eyebrow arched questioningly.

"Bowie Tyler, what are you trying to say?" she asked quietly.

He blushed deep scarlet and cleared his throat awkwardly. "I'm saying that I'd like to call on you, if I may, once this is all wrapped up."

"I think I'd like that," she answered softly, her eyes turning once more to Rand and Frannie. "Once this is all wrapped up, that is." She grinned at him then, her face lighting up, and she quickly pecked him on the cheek. She turned to point at the beat-up crowd of miners. "In which case you'd best get busy. You've got a fair amount of wrapping up to do."

Epilogue

Judge *Randolph Martin tendered his resignation from the bench of the Wyoming Territorial Court on October 14, 1880, sold his extensive real estate holdings in Laramie and moved to the goldfield boomtown of Baker City, Oregon. He and Frannie Kinsella were married by Pastor Daniel Martin on June 24, 1881. Best man at the couple's wedding was Deputy US Marshal Bowie Tyler; their maid of honor was Miss Hanna Dalby. The small ceremony took place in the parlor of the house attached to Frannie Kinsella's place of business, with only the pastor, his wife and daughter, and the above-named principals present.*

Randolph Martin established a successful law practice in the recently vacated office that had belonged to attorney Cyrus Valentine, who vanished without a trace in the summer of 1880. Frannie continued to operate her gunsmithing business from the shop on Church Street. The couple retired in 1896, sold the law office and gunshop and spent their sunset years in travel.

Elizabeth Kathleen Martin, daughter of Daniel and Marta Martin and the couple's only child, grew up to become a lawyer like her grandfather, and was the second woman to be appointed to the U.S. District

Court of Oregon, modeling her career after that of Mary Leonard, who was appointed to the same office in March of 1885.

Daniel Martin went on to minister to the spiritual needs of the ever-growing population of Baker City until his retirement from the ministry in 1916. He and Marta lived in Baker City until their deaths.

Hanna Dalby returned to her homestead, where Marshal Bowie Tyler was a regular visitor whenever his duties allowed.

Turn the page for an exciting preview of

Kershaw

an upcoming novel by

Chuck Buchanan

The Old Man, as he was known to the trigger-quick gunnies and high-liners who rode the Hole-in-the-Wall trails from Canada to Mexico, sat at a shadowy corner table in the rear of the smoky cantina. The bottle of pure quill Kaintuck bourbon sitting on the knife-scarred tabletop in front of him was half empty; the glass wrapped in the slender fingers of his left hand half full. Beside the bottle of amber liquid lay a long-barreled Colt revolver...

The room was silent except for the gurgle and gulp of poured liquor and the occasional slithering of pasteboard drifting from the desultory game of stud going on at the round table beyond the bar. The normally festive atmosphere of a Sonoita Saturday night was muted by the menacing presence sitting stolidly in the shadows at the back of the room, waiting. Waiting for the man, any man, to step into the cantina who might, somehow, be fast enough to kill him...

The beaded curtain that did duty as a door swirled; the clattering of glass beads against adobe was sharp in the quiet as a young man of perhaps twenty strutted confidently into the cantina. His midnight blue velvet charro jacket was opulently decorated. The intricate braiding that scrolled the length of his sleeves and across the shoulders of the jacket sparkled dully in the smoky light oozing down from the fat tallow candles that sagged around the perimeter of the wagonwheel chandelier suspended overhead. The polished conchos laced to the side seams of his pantalón de montar twinkled gaily as he strode to the bar. His highly-polished, silver-studded

258

black pistol belt and matching holster carried an ivory handled Colt revolver low and tied-down to his right thigh. It was obvious that what had just entered the room was *un hombre muy macho,* in his own eyes at least...

"Tequíla, señor! *I am thirsty!*" he called to the paunchy, mustachioed *tabernero.* When his drink arrived, the newcomer casually tossed a handful of silver coins onto the plank bar top, lifted the boldly-painted ceramic cup to his lips and drank deep of the potent liquor. The Old Man rose stiffly to his feet, holstering the Colt. The scrape of chair legs on hard packed clay caught the youngster's attention for a moment before he dismissed the *viejo* in the corner as beneath his notice...

The Old Man stepped up alongside the young *charro.* His right elbow lanced out, striking the other's wrist and sloshing liquor on the velvet of his sleeve. Immediately The Old Man stepped away from the bar, turning so that his back was to the solid adobe wall; his gaze was cold, calculating, as the young Mexican reacted as expected. "Señor! You presume much!" He indignantly raised his *tequíla*-soaked sleeve into the light. "For this you must apologize!"

"Like hell." The softly-spoken words took the younger man totally by surprise; he drew back sharply, momentarily startled, as if his assailant had suddenly shouted them in his face. Swiftly regaining his composure, he studied the black clad figure before him for several ticks of the cobweb-crusted Teutonia clock above the bar...

"Then I fear, *viejo,* that I shall be forced to seek recompense through blood." Fingertips lovingly caressed the use-worn ivory handle of the holstered

259

pistol. He eased himself away from the bar, polished spurs tinkling softly in rhythm with his steps...

"You pull that pistol and you'll die, boy." The matter of fact tone of the words that drifted through the smoky haze froze the young man in his tracks. His back stiffened but he did not turn to face this new potential threat; his whole attention was on the man who had insulted him. A tall individual who appeared to be in his late forties stepped forward to place himself between the old man and the young one. Taking a calculated risk, the newcomer turned his back on the older in order to speak to the younger. "That gent yonder will kill you," he stated bluntly. "You're not fast enough. I'm not sure anybody is." He turned slowly to face the boy's opponent. "Howdy."

"Step out of the way, Kershaw."

"I can't do that."

"You know me, Kershaw. You know I can kill you."

"Yes, I do know that," Kershaw replied calmly. "But I'm not letting you kill that kid."

"Señor..."

"Shut up, kid!" Kershaw ordered harshly without turning his head.

"He might get lucky," The Old Man went on as if no other words had been spoken.

"Not hardly."

"Move!" the Old Man barked.

"I can't do that," Kershaw repeated. "I won't do it. It's gone far enough. It's time to stand down."

"Not until I'm dead, it ain't." The Old Man's hand flashed to his holstered Colt and flame lit the room...

~1~

"**Who** the hell're you?" The harsh, prairie rattler buzz of the words cut through the end-of-the-day hubbub, the venom in their tone more than enough to lift a man's hackles and accelerate his heartbeat. Alton Kershaw, sensing that he was the questioner's target, slowly lifted his gaze from the bubbles drifting up out of the bottom of the half glass of beer on the polished mahogany in front of him to the cracked back-bar mirror. His casual movements belied the sudden tension that coursed through his lanky frame as he sighed inwardly in resignation. He'd only been in Concho for an hour and already some punk, ignoring the man and seeing only the stranger, had jumped to the mistaken conclusion that he was an easy mark.

Ten feet of spur-scarred planking off Kershaw's right shoulder a slender gunhawk sporting a gray cutaway coat, ruffled riverboat gambler's white shirt and black silk four-in-hand stood poised on the balls of his feet, his trembling right hand hovering over the polished ebony grips of one of Colonel Colt's finest. Keeping his cool gaze locked on the gunny's reflection in the mirror, Kershaw slid his left hand down off the edge of the bar and shifted his feet to lean almost imperceptibly to his right and away from the bar. "I'm a fella who minds his own business," he answered softly without turning his head. "I'd appreciate being left alone to do just exactly that." His voice carried clearly in the sudden silence that followed hard on the heels of the younger man's words. Knowing while he spoke that he was wasting his breath, Kershaw's fingers curled around the polished burl topping the heavy blackthorn walking stick that leaned out of sight against his left leg as he watched his words sink in. Ugly sparks flared like summer lightning in the dandy's eyes.

"Turn around, mister!" The command crackled in the air for a heartbeat before the fancy-dressed gunhand strode impatiently forward to drop a long-fingered hand on Kershaw's shoulder, intent on yanking the taller man away from his position at the bar. Using the impetus of the pull on his shoulder to help his turn, Kershaw spun on his right heel; the shaft of the blackthorn slapped into the cup of his right hand then the blunt, heat-hardened tip lanced out and over the polished silver buckle of the gunny's hand-carved belt to drive the air from his lungs in a startled squawk. As he doubled over in surprise and pain with his chest heaving in a vain attempt to make his paralyzed diaphragm pull even a cupful of oxygen into his tortured belly, the dandy somehow managed to yank the Colt from the holster. The blackthorn burl snapped down and across the young man's wrist; the crack of breaking bone was loud in the room, louder even than the thud of the pistol clattering to the floor. A gassy scream of pure agony escaped the dandy's lips. Cradling his broken right wrist with his cupped left hand, he gasped out, "I'll kill you for this, you son of a..."

"Not today," Kershaw growled in answer as the blackthorn lashed out for the third time. The gunhand crashed to the floor, out cold, with blood trickling from his lacerated scalp. The older man's icy gray eyes swept across the unbelieving faces of the other patrons of the establishment, gauging their intent, or lack of such, to step into the affair. Seeing that no one was so inclined, Kershaw turned back to the bar and reached for his beer as the noise started back up in the room, the saloon's clientele excitedly discussing what had just taken place.

"You might want to fork whatever bronc you rode in here on and light a shuck, mister." The words were quiet, the speaker a neatly dressed, chunky brunette cowboy who leaned on his right elbow against the bar to Kershaw's right. The blunt fingers of his left hand were wrapped loosely around the handle of a nearly empty glass of beer. "That boy ain't gonna be none too happy when he wakes up." He tilted his head toward where two stunned-looking cowhands were lifting the dandy from the floor, their hands hooked beneath his arms, in preparation for taking him outside. "For that matter, neither will his daddy when he hears about it."

Kershaw leaned on the blackthorn, favoring his stiff left leg. "I reckon he won't," he commented drily, pointing with his chin at the unconscious gunhand, "but I fail to see why that boy's displeasure, or his father's either, should have any bearing on whether or not I leave town. I just got here and I think I like it." He chuckled sourly. "Folks are so welcoming and neighborly." He swallowed some beer then set the mug on the polished mahogany.

The chunky cowhand brought his own glass

over to where Kershaw stood. "That 'boy' is Donovan Yeakley's son, Bart," he said, as if the name should mean something to Kershaw.

"And?"

"And Donovan Yeakley owns pretty much the entirety of the range in this here valley. At least the part Kurt Gore don't claim." The cowboy held out his hand. "I'm Carl Rocklin."

"Alton Kershaw." The two men shook hands, looking each other over like two strange ranch dogs trying to decide who the boss dog of the pack was going to be. Rocklin was a stocky-built, well set up fellow who looked "old enough to know better and still too young to care" as the saying went. His dark blue, band-collared shirt was crossed by tan suspenders. Wash-softened canvas britches were tucked into the tops of his tall, Texas Star boots. His black hat was sweat-stained and battered from exposure to the elements. The broad, unadorned belt cinched comfortably around his trim horseman's waist carried a bone-handled sheath knife ready to hand at his right side that was balanced by the well-worn Richards-Mason .44 revolver nestled in the cross-draw holster in front of his left hip. He was clean-shaven except for a bushy mustache that drooped around the corners of his mouth.

For his part, Rocklin saw a man several inches taller than his own five foot eight who was starting to gray around the edges. Brown hair liberally frosted with silver hung to Kershaw's shirt collar and complemented his neatly trimmed salt and pepper mustache and goatee. The ends of Kershaw's loosely-knotted, sun-bleached blue neckerchief were tucked behind the lapels of his wool vest; a silver watch chain decorated with an elk tooth hung in a gentle arc between the pockets of the vest. The red shirt, faded nearly pink from exposure to the elements, was tucked into the waistband of a pair of nearly new brown whipcord britches that he wore down over the tops of his flat-heeled boots. Small-roweled, silver-mounted spurs twinkled in the last fleeting rays of sunlight that peeked through the dust motes swirling in the blue clouds of tobacco smoke that formed a fog in the room. Kershaw's left leg moved stiffly, explaining without words the blackthorn walking stick that had given Bart Yeakley his comeuppance. What Rocklin's first appraising glance missed was the Smith & Wesson model 3 revolver holstered butt-forward at Kershaw's left hip. The pistol was so much a part of the man as to go unnoticed.

"If you don't mind my asking, what brings you to Concho?" Rocklin queried in a mild tone.

"I'm lookin' for a place to light," Kershaw answered amiably. "I'm planning to raise horses."

Rocklin took a sip of the flat beer that remained in his mug while he considered his reply. He swallowed and remarked, "There's only been one place for sale around here that I know of, and that's Pat Caldwell's Lazy C."

The big man whose hunch-shouldered frame was holding down the bar some distance to Kershaw's left suddenly jerked himself upright as if he'd been bee-stung. "If you know what's good for you, you'll stay away from the Lazy C!" he snapped, taking a step toward the pair.

Kershaw turned to face the belligerent newcomer to what had been until the interruption a private conversation. "And this is your business because...?" he questioned mildly. His tone was soft; the ice in his gray eyes was anything but.

"Because you ain't gettin' that spread!" the fellow grated. "I am!"

"Gore, Pat Caldwell wouldn't sell to you if you had the last dollar on earth!" Rocklin retorted.

"You stay out of this, Rocklin!" Gore growled.

Rocklin carefully set his glass on the polished mahogany of the bar top then stepped away from the bar to face his challenger. His right thumb was hooked over his belt near his holstered pistol. "You don't run me, Kurt," he replied. "You found that out the hard way a long time ago, remember?" Gore stood glaring angrily at the stocky cowboy for nearly a minute with his fists clenched into hard, white-knuckled lumps before brushing roughly past the two men to stamp out of the saloon. The batwing doors slammed hard against the outside walls as he stormed from the room.

"What was that all about?" Kershaw asked. "And who's that human grizzly bear?"

Rocklin answered with a question of his own. "How much do you know about the Lazy C?"

"I know that it's been proved up, and that it's got good water and grass."

"Have you talked to Pat Caldwell about it?"

"A little, back about three years ago. I was passing through and stopped to water my horses. He invited me in for some grub, and over coffee and bear sign he mentioned that he was thinking of selling out at some time in the relatively near future. I liked what I saw of the home place, so I told him that when he was ready to sell, I'd be interested. Left him an address where I could be reached. I'd about decided that he'd changed his mind when out of the blue I got a letter a couple of weeks ago saying that he was ready to sell and asking me if I was still looking to buy. I wired him the down payment, and here I am. My plan was to spend the night here in town and ride out that way first thing in the morning. Why?"

"Because if you buy the Lazy C, you'll be buying your way into the middle of one helluva mess, and you've already got one side mad at you."The Yeakley kid?"

"Yep. Donovan Yeakley sets a lot of store by that boy. Too much, if you ask me. Damn kid gets pretty much his own way 'cause his daddy owns so much of the country hereabouts. He's got himself convinced that since his Daddy's one of the he-coons in the valley every stranger's fair game."

"It's gonna get him killed if he isn't careful," Kershaw commented drily.

"Probably," Rocklin answered. "And whoever does that little job had best have a fast horse handy if he don't want to get his neck stretched."

"And I take it that Gore's the other 'he-coon' you were talking about."

"Yessir, Kurt Gore's it," Rocklin replied. "What Yeakly don't own, Gore does, or at least he'd like to. Him and Yeakley have been drooling over Caldwell's grass ever since they come into the valley. Caldwell got here when there was nothing here but Indians, coyotes and deer, filed on the springs in Lobo Basin then put together the rest of the place. He dickered when he could and fought when he had to." Rocklin drained his mug and set it on the bar.

Before he could lift his hand to signal for a refill, Kershaw waved the mustachioed bartender over and pointed at his and Rocklin's mugs, which were quickly replaced with full ones. Rocklin took a long drink, wiped the foam from his mustache with the back of his left hand and went on. "Much obliged. Now where was I... Oh yeah, Caldwell. So anyway, that canyon of Caldwell's goes way to hell and gone back up yonder, it's sheltered from the worst of the storms in the winter and shaded in the summer, both of the big dogs want it and Caldwell's told 'em both that they can't have it. There ain't been any bloodshed yet, but..."

"What would it take to get you to keep my reason for being here a secret?" Kershaw asked.

"After your little confab with Gore, I think maybe that particular cat's done been let out of the bag," Rocklin answered with a grin. "But I would sure like to have a ringside seat when the festivities start. I don't like either one of them boys."

"Deal!" Kershaw stuck out his hand and the pair shook. "The job pays forty dollars a month and some of the best grub you've ever laid a tooth to."

Rocklin was startled. "Job? What job?"

"As my foreman."

"But you don't know me from Adam's off ox," the cowboy protested.

Kershaw turned to look over at the bartender, who was standing a polite distance away polishing glasses with a relatively clean towel. "Do you know this gent?" The barkeep nodded his answer without stopping what he was doing. "Is he at least middling honest?" After a moment's silent thought the fellow nodded again. Kershaw turned back to Rocklin. "See? You can't argue with a character reference like that. And besides, the best seat in the house is right in the middle of the play, isn't it?" He didn't wait for Rocklin to answer; instead he quickly swallowed the last of his beer, set the mug on the bar and began limping toward the door. "See you out front of the livery at daylight," he called back over his shoulder. Rocklin stared after him.

"Well, I'll be damned," the cowboy muttered softly."